BLACK

A street tale by Tracy Brown

Published by Triple Crown Publications
P.O. Box 7212
Columbus, OH 43205

Library of Congress Control Number: 2003110040
ISBN 0-9702472-8-1

Edited by Angela Reese (Angela812@msn.com)
Cover Models: Tamara McNair and Tito Paul
Cover Photographer: www.NicoleMariePhotography.com
Graphics Design: www.ApolloPixel.com
Consulting: Vickie Stringer and Shannon Holmes

Printed in the United States of America

Dedication

This novel is dedicated to my children, who made my survival imperative. I love you each individually, with all my heart and soul.

And to my mother.

To my father who has always been there for me no matter what, thank you. You've always been in my corner, cheering me on the loudest. I love you tremendously and words can't express my gratitude.

To my "surrogate mother" Mosezetta Overby (Ruth 1:14-16), and to my "brothers" Lance, Larry and Maurice, thank you for welcoming me into your family at a time when I had none to call my own.

To my sisters Sandra and Neilia, all my love.

To my sister Clara, for instilling in me a love of reading. Thank you for showing me that a book can take you away from the pain.

And to "Finesse" (Sprite, Slice, Pepsi, Sunkist & 7UP), I hope this makes you reminisce on the good ole days. I'll never forget y'all.

Acknowledgments

To Regina Clark, the literary genius who offered me encouragement, constructive criticism and superb advice. Much of this would not have been possible without you. Thank you's are not enough to show my appreciation. I look forward to working with you again.

To Fred Hickson and Tiffany Bland: Not only are the two of you dear friends of mine, but your generosity and encouragement has been invaluable. You unselfishly pointed me in the right direction over and over, giving me support as well as advice and I am very grateful to you for that.

To Hubert Kenny Toussaint, you were my biggest supporter and my ally in this project. Thank you for giving me different options to research and telling me how to ensure that I was happy with the end result. Thanks for being a good friend and colleague.

To Phaedra Tucker, Arthur Smith, Tanara Brown and Jamillah Brown for offering your "amateur" opinions, helping me to work out all the nooks and crannies and doing much of the preliminary editing. I owe you all – big time!

And to the staff at Triple Crown Publications, untold thanks. You took a chance on a new jack like me. My gratitude can not be expressed in words.

PART ONE   CATERPILLAR

PART TWO   COCOON

PART THREE   BUTTERFLY

Prologue

Looking at the bloody remains of what had been Maurice Wesley, Kaia froze in horror. Her heartbeat echoed through the room like thunder. She heard her own thoughts clearly, as if there were a megaphone in her mind. Thoughts no four-year-old child should conceive.

"What should I do? He's dead, he's dead...daddy's dead!" Kaia could hear her own voice vividly, though her lips spoke no words. *"She killed daddy."*

Kaia's mother turned to her with the knife still in her hand. Taking a step in Kaia's direction, Janice Wesley stared at her daughter icily. Janice said through clenched teeth, "Don't move."

Kaia stood silent letting the words blanket the air. She would never challenge her mother. She knew that it would be wrong to do that. At that moment, she was scared. Not just of her mother, but also of having a life without Daddy.

Janice methodically called 911...told them that her husband was bleeding and needed help. She then slowly placed the receiver on the cradle. Turning to Kaia she said, "When they get here, you tell them what I say, you understand?" Kaia nodded her head in agreement as she stared blankly into her mother's cold, evil eyes.

Janice Wesley sat her daughter, Kaia Wesley, down and rehearsed The Story. Kaia knew The Story so well by the time the ambulance arrived 20 minutes later, that she spoke it like it was the truth. *Daddy had beat Janice. Kaia ran to the kitchen and got the knife she had seen her mother cutting the onions with earlier. She ran back to her parent's room and gave the knife to her mother as she struggled with Maurice on their bedroom floor. While Maurice choked her, Janice had plunged the knife into his chest.*

Kaia was an innocent child. She told the police The Story Janice had concocted. Kaia believed her mother when she told her that she was trying to protect her from the police. Janice told Kaia that if she didn't say exactly what they had rehearsed, Kaia would be taken to live with strangers who would abuse her. Kaia's four-year-old mind couldn't perceive a web as silkily woven as the one spun within her family. She trusted her mother. But it would be the last time she ever did.

PART ONE

Caterpillar

Slowly I advance

Often overlooked, stepped upon, crushed

Looking for a shelter... a haven... protection

Under the gaze of those who see me

I feel unfairly judged

Looked upon as an ugly being

Frightful and aghast

No one ever stops to notice

That my movements are poetic

My stride is determined

My spirit is free

Those who claim to recognize beauty

For all it's worth

Look at me and see

Nothing to love

Chapter One

Silent War

Kaia's nightmares began the summer after Maurice's death. Almost every night she was plagued by dreams of snakes. Lots of them. Everywhere. They tried to swallow her. They tried to squeeze the life out of her. She would wake up in a sweat and relief would overwhelm her once she realized that she was safe. She would lay there and try to force her eyes to stay open for as long as she could. She fought the urge to close them when they were heavy with fatigue. Eventually, she would fall asleep and find herself fighting to stay alive all over again.

Kaia wondered why her sisters, Nubia and Asha, never had to fight the snakes at night. They were the lucky ones. The three girls were close in age, but different from one another in every possible way. Kaia was five years old and longed for the freedom her sisters enjoyed. Asha was ten years old and Nubia was 12. Being the youngest, Kaia was frustrated by the fact that she was not allowed the same privileges as her sisters. Asha and Nubia had always been able to escape the confines of their housing project apartment in Staten Island. They never had to stay at home, where the mood was always tense and the conversations were always forced. In Kaia's opinion, they had always been the lucky ones. As young as she was, Kaia knew that the reason her sisters never had to battle with the snakes at night like she did was because they had missed much of the war that had been waged daily between Maurice and Janice.

Every day after school, Nubia and Asha came home and dropped their book bags on their bedroom floor. Then they ran back out the door headed for the neighborhood playground known as The Big Park. On a few occasions, Kaia had begged them to take her, too. They always refused. "You're a kid! What you gonna look like coming with us?" Kaia couldn't imagine what they could be doing that was so special. But her sisters never explained it. Kaia was always left behind.

Now that Nubia was twenty-four and had an apartment of her own, and Asha was twenty two and living with her man, Kaia really felt deserted by her sisters. She was now alone with the one woman she could hardly stand. Her mother.

Kaia spent much of her adolescence caged in her bedroom.

2

That room became her sanctuary because Janice wouldn't allow her the freedom that so many of her peers were afforded. She recalled spending countless days looking out of her project window watching the other kids her age playing and socializing. Kaia wished she could trade places with them, but Janice was strict. Her rules were not to be questioned, and Kaia learned not rock the boat. Instead, she daydreamed and stared out of her bedroom window at the world going on outside. Kaia found herself envious of the butterflies that fluttered past her window every so often. She thought they were beautiful with their pretty colors and she envied their freedom. She sometimes imagined herself as a butterfly - a black butterfly with beautiful patterns on he wings. She longed for the day that she could fly away and escape the clutches of her mother.

Now that she was almost seventeen, Kaia realized that she never had much of a family. What Kaia had were relatives. There is a big difference between family and relatives. Kaia's *relatives* were Nubia, Asha and their mother, Janice. Her *family* was the girls she rolled with. Giselle, Symphany, and Talia were all residents of the Mariners Harbor Housing Project on the north shore of New York's fifth borough, Staten Island. They had known one another since kindergarten and the four of them were as tight as a fist.

Since Kaia was finally old enough to enjoy the freedom for which she had so envied her sisters, most often her free time was spent watching movies or music videos at the home of one of her friends. Kaia was rarely home with Janice. Nubia and Asha rarely came by to visit, unless it was a holiday. They had both moved out immediately after they graduated high school. Their mother had always been a difficult woman to live with. Barking orders. Cold glares. Insulting remarks. Years later, the girls would accept that this was abuse – both verbal and emotional. But for now, they just accepted the fact that this is how their mother was and she would never change.

Janice Wesley had always been a cold woman. Even her daughters feared her more than they loved her. Janice was a very private woman. She never socialized with the other tenants in the building and you could bet your last dollar that none of them had ever stepped inside of her apartment. But, she did provide her daughters with the physical things they needed to grow up. Food, clothing and shelter. Janice was a remarkable cook, which didn't surprise anyone since she was born and raised in Louisiana. New York women just didn't hold a torch to Southern women in the kitchen. Janice had a house so clean and neat that you could eat off the floor. The only pets she allowed were two goldfish, and even they had been confined to Kaia's bedroom. She ran a tight ship and always stayed on top of the laundry. There was never a dish in the sink. When Kaia reflected on her relationship with her mother, she was always confronted by the same ugly truth. Janice never loved Kaia. She never even *liked* Kaia. Nubia and Asha had not been the target of Janice's rage. But Kaia had always been the recipient of her mother's cruel remarks, low expectations, cold looks and hateful language. She often wondered how a mother could hate her own flesh and blood.

Then Daddy would come to mind...

Kaia liked to believe that there had been two versions of Daddy. Good Daddy and Bad Daddy. When Good Daddy came home, he would give his wife a big kiss and talk about what happened at work. But on payday, the guys would get together after work and drink themselves into a stupor. It was then that Bad Daddy usually surfaced.

On payday, after consuming enough liquor to drown a horse, Maurice Wesley would return to the fifth floor apartment he shared with his wife and children. He had a decent job as a postal employee, three lovely and intelligent daughters, and a faithful wife who worked part time at the hospital as a dietary aide. But he still found reasons to complain.

Maurice felt that Janice was lucky to have him for a husband. While he was usually content to keep this belief to himself, whenever he was drunk he felt the need to point this out to Janice. So on payday, when Bad Daddy walked into the house, with the smell of rum seeping through his pores, he was always in a bad mood and always determined to start a fight.

"Who the fuck ate my peanuts?" Maurice was in rare form on these evenings. As he stood on wobbly legs peering into the cabinet he glared at his wife. Janice decided she was not in the mood for his antics and walked out of the kitchen without answering his question.

"Dizzy bitch! Walking around here like you the fuckin' Queen of Sheba...you ain't shit. I'm the best-looking muthafucka in New York City! Your country ass should be glad somebody wants you. Ignorant country ass walking around here like somebody suppose' ta kiss your ass..fuck you..."

This would go on for most of the evening. Maurice would rant and rave to himself between sips of rum and sing along to the 45's that played on the record player. Janice would sit in her bedroom and pretend not to hear the insults being hurled at her from the living room. Nubia and Asha were safely out of harms way at the park or at the home of one of their friend's, having learned that they'd rather be anywhere but at home. Kaia was left to play by herself in her room and try to figure out the meaning of some of the words Bad Daddy was yelling out from the living room. She passed the time by pretending to be a princess who was locked in a dungeon. The dungeon would be unlocked once her sisters came home (to rescue her). It was never easy to pretend when all she could hear were Motown records and Bad Daddy's drunken voice.

Maurice would sometimes call Kaia to come and sit with him in the living room. He would pull her onto his lap and she, being only three years old, seemed not to notice the smell of alcohol on his breath. He would tell her about the good ole' days of doo-wop and processed hair. A time of afros and dashikis and Kaia would be mesmerized by her big, strong Daddy. He was like a teddy bear to her...big and cuddly able to protect her from all harm. His stories took her on imaginary journeys illustrated by Maurice's colorful descriptions of seeing music legends perform a New York's Apollo theater long before Kaia was born. She loved her father with every fiber of her being because no matter how angry and nasty he treated her mother, he was always sweet and gentle with Kaia.

And that is what fueled the hatred Janice felt toward her baby girl. Kaia was the recipient of all of Maurice's love and Janice was his doormat. Janice found herself hating Maurice and subconsciously loathing her own daughter. Kaia was oblivious to this fact until the day her father was killed in the midst of a thunderous argument with her mother.

It had been a rainy Sunday afternoon in March. Kaia had been perched on the living room sofa watching *Tarzan* on the black and white television. Janice was mopping the kitchen floor and Nubia and Asha were dressing to go outside to play. Maurice had left hours ago to have some drinks at a bar called the Meeting Place on Jersey Street. All was calm, until the peace was shattered by the sound of Maurice's keys jingling outside the apartment door. Nubia and Asha hurriedly grabbed their things and headed for the safety of the outdoors before Hurricane Maurice shattered the Wesley household. They knew their father would be drunk and ready for round one and they both wanted to be nowhere in sight. Nubia startled her father when she pulled the apartment door open before he had a chance to find the correct key to the lock.

"Hey," she said as she breezed past him into the hallway and disappeared down the stairs. Asha was right behind her.

"Hey, yourself," Maurice mumbled as he trudged into his home. He saw Kaia sitting on the couch and smiled a toothy grin.

"Hey, Daddy's girl!"

Kaia's heart leapt. "Daaaaaady!" She ran to him and planted a big kiss on his cheek as he scooped her up in his arms.

Maurice smiled. "Pretty, just like your daddy! Yes you are."

He put her down and headed toward his bedroom where Janice was putting newly washed and folded laundry into the dresser drawers.

"Hey, "Magilla Gorilla"!" Maurice erupted in laughter at his own humor as he addressed his wife.

"Don't come in here starting shit with me, Maurice. I ain't in the mood today." Janice's jaw clenched and twitched as the cruel insult Maurice had hurled at her made its mark.

"I don't give a fuck about your mood!" Maurice sat on the edge of the bed. "Who the fuck is you? You don't run a muthafuckin' thing around here."

Kaia covered her ears to block out the torrent of insults and curse words as her parents' arguing grew louder and louder. Finally unable to stand it anymore, she went into her parents' room and stood between them as they screamed at one another.

"STOP IT!!! STOP IT!!!! STOP IT!!! STOP..." Kaia's cries were cut short by the resounding **SMACK** Janice planted across her four-year-old face. Kaia fell to the floor holding her face and bellowing, tears streaming down her face. Maurice stormed at Janice in one quick motion but she sidestepped him just in time. Maurice swung around and grabbed Janice by the neck as she kicked, punched and scratched him. Kaia's cries were like sirens as her parents scuffled on their bedroom floor like animals. In his drunken stupor, Maurice couldn't prevent Janice from straddling him and she clawed at his eyes.

Holding his eyes and yelling in pain, Maurice loosened his grip on his wife. He lay on the floor rolling around in agony as blood trickled from his left eye and his right was swollen shut. Janice ran from the room and Kaia ran to her father's side.

"Are you alright, Daddy? Daddy, you want me to call..."

Kaia's words were cut short by the sight she beheld looming in her parent's doorway. Janice walked in holding a large knife and advanced toward her husband and child. Kaia backed away in horror and hid her face as Janice plunged the knife into Maurice's chest. Her father lay defenseless and bled to death right before her eyes. *What should I do? He's dead, he's dead...daddy's dead!"* Kaia could hear her own voice vividly though her lips spoke no words. *"She killed daddy."*

Kaia's mother turned to her with the knife still in her hand. Taking a step in Kaia's direction, Janice Wesley stared at her daughter icily.

Janice said through clenched teeth. "Don't move."

Kaia obeyed. She stood frozen in that spot and watched her mother methodically concoct a story to clear herself of any wrongdoing. Kaia didn't move or speak up when Janice told the police The Story. And neither Kaia, nor Janice, ever discussed the truth as it happened that Sunday in March when Kaia was four years old. But Kaia knew her father had died defending her from the mother who hated her, and Janice knew that Kaia knew the truth.

The reality of it was enough to draw a very large wedge between the two of them. In the days, weeks and months that followed, Kaia expected a secret apology from her mother. No one else knew their secret. Nubia and Asha had been told The Story and they never questioned it. Surely, Janice would come to Kaia eventually and explain why she'd gone for the knife. Surely, Janice would say she was sorry for hitting Kaia...that she was sorry for killing Maurice. But Janice never apologized. When they were alone, Janice did not speak to Kaia. Kaia was four years old and felt responsible somehow for all that had taken place in her family. Daddy shouldn't be dead. Janice shouldn't be ignoring her. Nubia and Asha shouldn't be running away every day. Kaia felt responsible for it all.

Nubia and Asha also seemed to withdraw from Kaia. After Maurice's death, Janice became very mean and verbally abusive towards Kaia. Even her sisters noticed that Janice seldom called Kaia by her name. Instead, she referred to her as "that bitch".

"Tell that bitch to come and eat." "Bring that bitch to catch the school bus." "Make sure that bitch puts on a coat today." "That bitch burned the damn toast!"

anting to be the targets of Janice' cruelty, Nubia and Asha
eir way to please her. To Kaia it seemed she never did
leased Janice. And when Kaia tried to interact with her
older sisters while watching television or playing in their room, they
usually taunted and teased her so badly that she would cry. Then they
would laugh at her and continue their activity with no regard for her
feelings. As she got older, she theorized that her sisters had labeled her
the "black sheep" as a way of winning their mother's approval. Kaia
wondered if she would have done the same thing if one of her sisters had
been the one that Janice hated instead of Kaia.

Kaia would lay in bed telling herself that *tomorrow* her mother
would talk to her. *Tomorrow* Janice would be nice to her. Eventually, she
would fall asleep on her bed only to be confronted by those miserable
snakes. Whenever she awoke in terror, she was relieved to see that
Nubia and Asha had come home. She'd crawl out of bed and maneuver
her way into Nubia's bed. Lying beside her, she felt safe and secure.
Secretly, she wished she could be Nubia instead of herself. She longed
for the day when she would be allowed to go outside by herself like her
sisters could. She just wanted to get away.

The funniest thing was that even as she grew up, she never lost
that desire to escape her reality. She wondered if she ever would.

June of 1991 began like a warm breath on the nape of Kaia's
neck. Summer was days away and Kaia anxiously awaited the upcoming
vacation. In September, she would be entering her senior year of high
school. Just one more year, and Kaia would be an adult with the freedom
to do as she pleased. She couldn't wait.

This didn't mean that life at home had improved. In fact, Kaia
felt that it had only worsened. It seemed that every time Janice looked at
her daughters, she was reminded of all the years of bullshit she'd suffered
with Maurice. Nubia usually stopped by once a month, bringing books for
her sister and money for her mother. Nubia was clearly Janice's favorite
for that very reason. Asha, at the age of twenty-two, had met and fell in
love with a man from a very prominent family. They had been together
for close to a year and were talking about marriage. Kaia thought the guy
was a little too proper and hated to hear him speak. He never used a

slang term and didn't even listen to hip-hop. But Asha was happy and Kaia was happy for her. Janice was proud of her two oldest daughters. Whenever she spoke about her children, it was Nubia and Asha that received all of her praise. Kaia was hardly ever mentioned.

Kaia may as well have been living in solitary confinement. She had grown accustomed to the lack of conversation in their apartment. Janice often ignored Kaia and Kaia had learned to do the same.

Part of Kaia was angry with Nubia and Asha for moving out and leaving her to deal with the situation on her own. It was bad enough that they had never been there when she was a scared and lonely little girl watching the horror movie that was their parents' marriage. But, now she was left to weather yet another family storm all by herself.

Janice, like her daughter, wished the situation were different. She longed for the day that Kaia would turn eighteen and get out. She was consumed with anger and hurt. In her eyes, she'd wasted her entire life away. Marriage, children and a career were supposed to provide a sense of joy in a person's life. But what do you do when the marriage you're in is choking the life out of you? What do you do when the children you created in the midst of love and euphoria, are now constant reminders of how naïve you once were. Reminders of a man you once loved. A man who tore your heart out and killed your spirit?

Not knowing how to express these feelings, Janice withdrew from the world and from her children. She never quite realized the impact it was having on them. Especially Kaia. Janice ate dinner in her bedroom with the door closed, leaving Kaia to eat alone at the kitchen table. She sat in her bedroom to watch television, leaving Kaia to watch television alone in the living room. Janice raised her child in a house filled with deafening silence, leaving Kaia yearning for attention. Thirsty for it.

So Kaia occupied her time in the company of her girlfriends. Giselle Murphy lived in the building next to Kaia. She had a very witty and outgoing personality. She became a friend of Kaia's almost immediately after the first day of school and the two often talked their lunch hour away about all sorts of things. Like Kaia, she had seen and experienced many things and had grown up long before the age of 18. Giselle was dark-skinned with the body of a model. She was confident but not conceited and she was the one who was the recipient of most of the male attention.

Symphony James was always the "round the way girl". She somehow always managed to remain dressed to impress. Even the casual jeans and sweats she wore were designer labels. Symphony was small in stature, standing only 5 feet 2 inches tall. She was slim and petite with "chinky" eyes and a caramel complexion. She always had the latest hairstyle and it seemed she knew people everywhere she went. Despite the fact that she was just seventeen years old, Symphony was always in attendance at the biggest events in town. She would fight anyone who fucked with her whether she was alone or with a crew of ten, and she was fiercely loyal to her clique.

Talia Hampton was the quiet storm. Brown skinned with eyes like a cat, she spoke only when she had something profound to say. Talia was the type to attend the biggest party of the summer with her girls just so that she could stand back and observe certain people. From time to time, some people misconstrued her quietness for weakness, and that's when the storm would come. Talia, like a cat, didn't like to be cornered. When she was, she'd strike back with a thunderous fury. Her style of dress was best defined as sporty. She was always the first to rock the latest sneakers and she was always the only one who had an interest in sports. Talia would hold lengthy conversations with the boys on the basketball team about who averaged the most points, who played better defense and who sucked at the free throw line. She had the utmost respect of the boys in school for that reason. They thought nothing was better than a girl who loved sports.

At the age of sixteen, all of the girls were involved in "relationships". Unlike her peers, Kaia hadn't concerned herself with the thought of a potential boyfriend.

Aaron Banks, however, had already decided that Kaia would be his girl. From the moment she sat next to him in English class their freshman year, he had plans for her.

Aaron hung out with some of the boys from Kaia's neighborhood. He was a handsome boy with smooth dark skin and words as sweet as cotton candy. He set his sights on Kaia almost immediately. There was something about her that made her stand out among the rest of the girls their age. She was pretty and smart. Not too shy and not too loud. She was just right. Aaron decided that this would be his first order of business. He had to win Kaia over.

Aaron got on her nerves. He was constantly giving her compliments, which was flattering at first. However, after several months of unrelenting compliments, Kaia just wished Aaron would shut up. He was as persistent as ever. Kaia, however, wanted nothing to do with him.

On this particular day, as Kaia contemplated the beginning of summer, she decided to skip her 7th period Global Studies class. It was the end of the school year and she had excelled in that class all semester. One day wouldn't hurt. She sat on the bench in the park adjacent to the school and read a book she had borrowed from her sister. It was called *Assata* and it chronicled the life of Assata Shakur, a black activist from the 60's.

As she read the book, someone approached and cast a shadow over her as the sun beat down. She looked up expecting one of her girls and instead saw the unwelcomed image of Aaron standing in front of her. She had managed to tolerate him as the years went by, but today she was not in the mood.

Aaron was a cutie. He stood about six feet tall with a dark chocolate complexion. He sported a neat fade haircut and a muscular build. He was, by any definition, a very handsome young man with eyes that lit up when he smiled.

"Can I help you?" Kaia asked.

Aaron smiled and sat beside her. "You already have," he answered in his deep baritone voice.

"What's that mean?" Kaia was confused.

"Just the sight of you sitting here has made my day," Aaron said as he smiled slyly. He had become accustomed to Kaia's cold shoulder and her constant barrage of mean-spirited remarks.

Kaia, on the other hand, was tired of Aaron's non-stop flirting. "Why do you always have to say some corny shit like that?"

Aaron laughed. "Wow, that was corny to you?"

"I'm just saying that you can speak to me like a regular person," Kaia closed her book and placed it on her lap.

"Well, you're not a regular person. You're unique."

Despite the question lingering in her mind (*Why am I even talking to him?*), Kaia was curious. "What's so 'unique' about me?" she asked.

"You're not like the other girls you run with," Aaron explained. "You're very pretty but you're also smart and you're not afraid to show it. Look at what you're doing right now?" Aaron nodded toward the book in Kaia's lap. "What other girl do you know cuts class to sit in the park and read?"

11

"Well, you're not very different from other guys." Kaia pulled no punches, as she looked Aaron squarely in the eyes.

"Why do you say that?"

Kaia continued, "You smoke weed like all the other guys. You steal cars. You get in trouble. So you're no different."

Aaron chuckled. "First of all, I smoke weed because it relaxes me and not because I'm like the other guys. As far as stealing cars and all that, I don't do that shit anymore."

"Why not?" Kaia asked, surprising herself at the sudden interest she was taking in the pest.

Aaron's face looked serious. Kaia had never seen him look serious before. "Can I be honest with you?"

"No," Kaia answered sarcastically. "I want you to lie to me."

Aaron didn't laugh. Instead he answered her earnestly. " I got in some trouble recently. I was arrested because of something I didn't do."

"Yeah, right." Kaia was unconvinced.

"I wouldn't lie about nothing like that. I was with my boy and he asked me if I knew how to break into cars. I told him I did. So we went and took a car from around the way and drove around. He asked me to stop at this spot on Targee Street...a store. I waited in the car while he went inside. He never told me he was gonna rob the store." Kaia noticed, once again, how sincere Aaron seemed as he told his story. He continued, "Well, the cops came and we both got locked up. That was the end of my life of crime."

"So who's the guy you were with?" Kaia asked.

"Wayne from the Park Hill Projects."

Kaia recalled hearing about that incident but hadn't known that Aaron was involved. "But Wayne is still locked up," she pointed out. "Why are you walking around free?"

Aaron's facial expression betrayed his emotions. He was uncomfortable with the next part of the story. "I told the cops that I didn't do it. I took responsibility for stealing the car but I told them that he robbed the store by himself."

Again, Kaia was blunt. "So you snitched on him?"

"Nah. I ain't no snitch. Like I said, I admitted what I did. I'm not going down for something somebody else did."

Kaia gave this some thought for a moment. She wondered what she would have done in the same situation. The code on the street was that you never ratted anybody out. But would she be able to go to jail for something she hadn't done just to have street credibility?

Aaron took out a blunt and lit it. He looked at Kaia and noticed the disapproving look on her face. "Do you ever break any rules, Kaia?"

"I'm cutting class. That's breaking a rule."

Aaron laughed. "That's not what I mean. Have you ever done something no one thought you would do or are you always predictable?"

Kaia thought about how angry Janice's strict rules made her feel. She had always wanted to rebel in some way, but was always too afraid of the punishment to go through with anything.

Aaron took a drag and passed the blunt to Kaia.

Surprisingly, she accepted it.

Kaia held the brown leaf-textured object in her hand and reflected on the lectures, movies and literature from her school's drug awareness classes. She asked, "I'm not going to act like a fool, right? Am I gonna get addicted?"

Aaron reassured her with a smile. "You can trust me, sweetheart."

She liked the sound of it when he called her 'sweetheart' but Kaia was still hesitant. "I never smoked before," she confessed. "Is it going to make me sick?"

"This ain't crack or no shit like that," Aaron answered with a laugh. "It's like having a drink or two. Just inhale and swallow. Then blow it out easy."

Kaia still had few questions before she went through with it. "Okay, but let me know how it's supposed to feel. Am I going to see little people in the trees or spots in the sky or..."

"Nah," Aaron smiled again. "It will make you feel relaxed. It'll make everything seem funny and you might get the munchies."

Kaia felt surprisingly reassured by Aaron's words. As she considered his statement she realized that Aaron was one of the few guys she knew who had never seemed like a complete asshole. Aaron joked around and flirted, but he was never one of the cutthroat cats.

Kaia placed the blunt to her lips and inhaled. Resisting the urge to cough, she followed Aaron's instructions and gently swallowed the contents. She slowly exhaled, the weed causing her chest to heave repeatedly. Finally, she coughed as Aaron reached over and firmly patted and rubbed her back.

"You okay?" he asked. He offered a sip of his orange *Slice*.

Kaia accepted it and sipped the soda as she caught her breath. To Aaron's surprise, she took another pull and passed it back to him. Kaia's body tingled. Her head felt as if it were floating. *'Now I know what Cloud Nine feels like,'* she thought. Kaia grinned at her own mental joke. The grin turned into a chuckle. Kaia peeked at Aaron and he, too, was laughing. They sat there and laughed harder than either of them had laughed in a long time. Kaia laughing at her private joke and the lightheaded feeling she was experiencing for the first time. Aaron laughing at the effect the weed was having on her.

They composed themselves and sat on the bench passing the blunt and talking about school. Kaia told him about the book she was reading and Aaron was genuinely interested. They discussed their plans for the future. Aaron wanted to be an architect and Kaia wanted to become a teacher.

Before they knew it, an hour had passed. Already late for class, and now high as a kite, they decided to head back to school. As they stood up, Aaron took Kaia's hand in his.

"Thank you for talking to me today," he said. "I've been trying to get you to give me the time of day for two whole years – almost three!"

Kaia smiled. "All you had to do was talk to me like a regular person."

"I already told you, you're not a regular person." Aaron kissed her hand like the gentleman that he was.

Kaia noticed for the first time how beautiful Aaron's eyes were. When he smiled they lit up like lights on a Christmas tree. She thought to herself *'This must be some good weed.'*

Aaron looked at Kaia and wondered how it was possible that he had never gotten over the crush he'd had on her since he was 14. He took her hand and smiled in a way that seemed to melt her heart.

"Can I kiss you?"

Kaia had never been asked anything like that before. Most guys just did it. Maybe Aaron was different after all.

She nodded.

Aaron leaned in and kissed her softly. Then again. And again.

He looked shyly at their clasped hands. "Can I spend some time with you this summer?"

Kaia was speechless. She had never felt a gentler kiss and was left feeling like silk. She finally found her voice. "Yeah. I guess so. My mother is kind of strict," Kaia felt embarrassed by the truth of her words.

She figured Aaron would think she was a big baby. Once he knew she couldn't date like the other kids their age, she was sure Aaron wouldn't want to be bothered.

"Well," Aaron answered with a smile. "I guess I'll have to teach you how to break some more rules, then."

"Sounds good to me," Kaia said, returning the smile.

Together, they headed back toward the school.

For the remaining two weeks of school, Kaia and Aaron were inseparable. Aaron would meet her at the Staten Island ferry terminal each morning and together, they rode the bus to school. He met her in the park each day for lunch on what they now referred to as 'their' bench. Kaia tried unsuccessfully to convince Aaron to read some of the books that she was reading.

"That looks boring," Aaron would say as she showed him the latest book her sister had given her.

"Don't you know that you can't judge a book by its cover?" she would remind him with a smile.

On the weekends, Kaia would call him whenever Janice wasn't around. She had made the mistake of asking her mother for permission to allow Aaron to call. Janice had responded with a barrage of curse words and insults. Kaia had been called a nasty bitch, a slut, and a piece of shit so many times that evening that she found herself recollecting the evenings when, as a child, she'd sat in her room and listened to Maurice's tirades. She and Janice hadn't spoken a word to each other since and Kaia was more determined to occupy her time with what truly made her happy. Aaron.

On the last day of school, Aaron approached Kaia in the hall as she stood talking to Darlene.

"Can I talk to you for a minute?" he asked.

They walked to a nearby stairwell for privacy.

Kaia looked at Aaron's beautiful eyes and wondered what was obviously troubling him.

"I can't stop thinking about not seeing you in school everyday for a whole summer," Aaron said.

Kaia was touched. He seemed genuinely upset that his time with her would now be limited.

"That is so sweet, Aaron," she said. "We'll still see each other. My mother will be at work so it won't be too hard for me to get away from time to time."

"I know but I don't want to just sneak around all the time. I want to take you to the movies or the zoo or..."

"The zoo? What would you know about the zoo?" Kaia laughed. "You don't seem like the type to..."

Aaron cut her off, "I thought you said not to judge a book by its cover, sweetheart."

Kaia smiled. At least now she knew he listened to her.

Aaron continued, "I want to do a lot of things with you."

Kaia's smile broadened and she took his hand. She leaned forward and kissed him. Her tongue gently parted his lips and mingled with his tongue. They kissed with an intensity they never had before. Pulling away, Aaron's face was flushed.

"Why you trying to get me all excited?" Aaron smiled, embarrassed.

Kaia noticed the bulge in his pants and laughed. She kissed him gently on the lips.

"That's better," Aaron said.

Kaia smiled.

"I have a surprise for you," Aaron announced.

"And what might that be?" Kaia asked.

"I'll show you after school, Aaron said. "Meet me on our bench in the park."

Kaia agreed and they went their separate ways to class.

For the rest of the day, Kaia anticipated what Aaron had in store for her. As soon as the bell rang signaling the end of eighth period, Kaia darted out of the school and headed toward their bench in the park. Aaron was waiting for her with a playful smile.

"Look at you," he said. "Just like a woman. As soon as you tell them you have a surprise for them, they can't even hide their excitement."

"Just tell me what it is!" Kaia responded. She sat down next to him and waited.

Aaron grabbed his backpack and removed a small package, which he'd wrapped in a brown paper bag. He handed it to Kaia. Kaia couldn't hide the smile that graced her lips. She tore through the paper and held a copy of the new book she was reading, *The Autobiography of Malcolm X.* She had just received this book from her sister after finishing *Assata.* Kaia was confused.

"I already have this book, Aaron. I showed it to you yesterday, remember?

Aaron smiled. "I know that, sweetheart. This isn't for you." He took the book back as Kaia sat, bewildered. "It's for me. I'm going to read it with you."

Kaia was breathless. This thugged-out, weed-smoking, criminal record-having boy was going to read a book with her. "Oh my God, Aaron, that is so sweet!!!"

"Don't get all mushy or anything. I just want to try something you enjoy since you already tried something I enjoy."

"What?" Again, Kaia was confused.

Instead of answering, Aaron held up another blunt. Kaia smiled.

"Well, light it up, nigga, what you waiting for?"

The two of them sat hand in hand and blazed their second L together.

They were both thinking the same thing: *'It's going to be a good summer.*

Chapter Two

Seasons Change

Summers in New York feel like hot candle wax dripping onto naked skin. Heat and humidity mesh into a thick blanket for sweaty lovers. It was in this mist that Kaia and Aaron discovered each other. Piecing a puzzle that was new and exciting. '91 was the year of Terminator II and Boyz 'N The Hood. It was the summer of Color Me Badd and Boyz II Men. Bo Jackson and Michael Jordan had the world captivated. There was a revolt underway in Russia, Operation Dessert Storm was coming to an end and a racial war between Blacks and Jews was growing in Brooklyn. George Bush's racist ass was the President, while New York City had its first Black Mayor, David Dinkins. And in the midst of one of New York's hottest summers, Kaia and Aaron would meet each day at noon in the park on Grandview Avenue and watch the season emerge. They discussed books, held hands, played and ate ice cream cones. Sometimes, Aaron's friends would come and Kaia proudly watched her man do his thing on the basketball court. She never told Aaron that he was her man. But she knew that's just what he was, and she couldn't believe it. A few months ago, she would have dreaded sitting near him in class. But now, she knew she would cut a bitch if they tried to get with Aaron.

Today, Aaron's friends had joined him on the court and so had his older brother Keith. Kaia had heard a lot about him from Aaron, but he had not introduced them yet. The guys began a game of '21'. She watched them start their game as she sat on the nearby benches with Giselle, Talia and Symphany.

Aaron was nice on the court, too. The muscles in his lean legs flexed whenever he made a jump shot. Kaia noticed every ripple, as her womanhood throbbed with every muscle he flexed. His dark chocolate skin glistened with salty nectar. His long lean fingers palmed the ball and Kaia reflected on how it felt when he palmed her ass. Aaron was making her weak.

18

"So, Kaia he got you over there ready to cum on yourself, huh?" Giselle laughed at Kaia's involuntary facial expressions. Symphany and Talia laughed, too.

"Shut up," Kaia turned her head, embarrassed.

"I told you all you need is some sex, Kaia," Symphany knew how horny Kaia must feel. Kaia was the only one who hadn't lost her virginity. Kaia changed the subject. "Well let's talk about how much you've been doing it lately."

Symphany smiled. "Don't be jealous."

The girls laughed. Giselle said, "I met this guy named Paulie. He got *dough*. He's 25. He drives a ..."

"25? What'chu mean he's 25?" Talia was amazed.

"And I thought you was messing with Ron," Kaia chimed in.

"Well damn, when did you rehearse for this press conference?" Giselle got defensive.

"You can't just say something like that and not expect us to say nothing," Symphany fired back.

"I said he's 25. He's older but age is not important if you're on the same level." Giselle pointed to her head. Symphany shook her head and Kaia rolled her eyes. Giselle continued, "And I like Ron but he's not ready for the type of commitment Paulie is, so I have to do what's best for me."

"Well, don't let your mama find out." Kaia said.

Giselle smiled. "She ain't sober long enough to know nothing about me." They sat in silence for a few tense moments. Giselle's mother had been an alcoholic for as long as they could remember.

Symphany shook her head compassionately. Kaia laughed. "Well I wish somebody would give Janice a goddamn drink and knock her the fuck out."

The girls laughed heartily and Giselle was grateful that Kaia had broken the ice.

After the game, Aaron introduced Kaia to his brother Keith. Keith was 26 and he was the only family Aaron had. Their parents had not been in their lives for over ten years. Their mother died of cancer when Aaron and Keith were only seven and sixteen years old. Their father left the boys in the care of their aging grandmother. When she died, their father didn't even come to the funeral. At the age of 21, Keith had put his college education on hold and taken the responsibility of caring for his younger brother. He worked two jobs to make ends meet and, for that, he had Aaron's utmost respect.

Keith was fine. He was tall like his brother but sported a neatly trimmed goatee. He had dark features, which were accentuated by his coffee brown skin. He had an air about him that made any woman's heart skip a beat.

Later, Keith welcomed Kaia into what he and Aaron referred to as their 'bachelor pad'. Their small two-bedroom apartment was located on Westervelt Avenue in the New Brighton section of Staten Island. The two-family house in which they lived was on a quiet street, just one block over from the New Brighton projects. There was a man who rented the apartment upstairs and Aaron and Keith shared the first floor apartment. The owner of the house lived elsewhere and only came by to collect the rent money.

To her surprise, the place was very neat, considering the fact that there was no woman living there. The sound of *Shut 'em Down* by Public Enemy drifted from the speakers of the big stereo system in the living room. She accepted when Aaron offered to pour her some juice and made herself comfortable on the couch while he went to get it. Keith sat in the chair across from her and smiled.

Kaia smiled back. "What?" she asked.

Keith whispered, "My brother really likes you."

Kaia was so happy to hear that. "I like him, too."

Aaron returned with the juice and sat on the couch with his arm around Kaia. Keith looked at the young couple and got right to the point.

"I was your age once, so I know you two are young and horny. So, all I have to say is be careful."

Kaia was embarrassed. Aaron laughed. "Mind your business, man," Aaron said, smiling.

Keith was laughing, too, and now Kaia felt a little more at ease.

Keith continued, "Yeah, nigga, you know what I'm saying." Looking at Kaia he said, "No disrespect, love, but I was the same age as you are once upon a time. I just don't want no beef with nobody's moms."

Kaia laughed. "Trust me, I don't want no beef with her either."

Keith got up and headed toward the door. "I'll be back at 7:00," he said.

Kaia noticed Aaron glance at the clock, which read 5:43. Keith closed the door and Kaia and Aaron were alone.

They sat watching television. Video Music Box showed the latest videos from Jodeci, Bell Biv DeVoe, and Guy. After a few minutes, Aaron took Kaia to see his room.

They entered Aaron's private space filled with posters of Leaders of da New School, De La Soul, EPMD and Public Enemy. There were sneaker boxes lined up against the wall and a stereo and television on the dresser. After Aaron turned on the radio and the sound of Pete Rock and C.L. Smooth's *Reminisce* filled the room, Kaia sat on his twin-sized bed and patted for him to sit next to her. Aaron did, and he leaned over and kissed her. They tongued and stroked each other for minutes that lingered like decades. Their hands intertwined and they were suspended in time.

Kaia whispered his name.

"Aaron..."

Aaron kissed her lips gently and said, "Close your eyes."

She did.

Aaron kissed each eyelid gently. He lightly licked her nose and chin. Kaia smiled as he traced his tongue down her neck, stopping at her collarbone.

Kaia's breath slipped quietly away. She felt chills run down her spine as he slowly unbuttoned her blouse. Butterflies fluttered in her stomach as Aaron's hands caressed her breasts through her bra. She anxiously awaited the feel of his hands against her bare skin as he gently kissed her lips.

He fought with the clasp on her bra, and after numerous frustrating attempts, opted instead to lift it over her full breasts. She whispered his name as Aaron slowly glided his tongue back and forth across her nipple. He repeated the same on her other breast and tried to contain the hot fluid that bubbled within his own organ. Taking one nipple in each hand, he straddled her and inserted his tongue between her parted lips. He toyed with her breasts gently and kissed her erotically. Kaia shuddered in ecstasy and felt that, at any minute, she was likely to go insane with pleasure.

She blindly reached for his belt and fought to undo the buckle. Aaron continued to tongue her as they both discarded their pants and underwear. Finally pulling away, Kaia unhooked her bra and lay back in the middle of the bed.

Aaron stood amazed at the beautiful creature that lay before him and felt like the luckiest guy alive. He pulled his T-shirt over his head and

21

lay beside her. Lying on his side, he kissed her and gently stroked her vagina. He began to trace her lips with his fingers and softly stroked her clit. Kaia could no longer hold back the throaty moan that escaped her lips. Her moans encouraged Aaron, who was trying desperately to be patient and gentle. His body was crying out to ravage her but he maintained control.

"Kaia," he whispered. "Can I please put it in?"

"Yes!" Kaia had never wanted anything so badly in her whole life.

Aaron climbed on top of her and rubbed the head of his hardened dick across Kaia's puss. Finding her entrance, he gently pushed. Kaia cringed at the pain and gripped Aaron's back. Aaron paused.

"I don't want to hurt you. Tell me if I hurt you, okay?" Aaron's voice trembled as the heat of the moment surged through him.

Kaia nodded and bit her lip, determined to finish what they'd started.

Aaron thrust his hips upward, deeper, until he penetrated her virgin walls. The pain she initially felt was slowly replaced by an erotic sensation. She loosened the grip she had on his back and allowed herself to relax and enjoy the wonderful feeling he was giving her.

"Damn, sweetheart," Aaron whispered. "You feel good, Kaia."

Too breathless to speak, Kaia again called his name and his momentum began to build. Kaia assumed that he was about to bust.

"Pull out, Aaron. Make sure you pull out," Kaia whispered as he climaxed.

"I can't," Aaron replied as his penis erupted in volcanic bursts of semen.

They lay together. Aaron feeling exhausted and Kaia feeling liberated. She was finally a woman.

Lying across her bed at home that night, Kaia held Aaron's chain. He had given it to her to wear as a symbol of their relationship. She had never been so proud to possess anything for as long as she could remember. She wanted to share this moment with someone, so she called Talia. Kaia told her about the events of that day and Talia shared the moment with her as only a good friend could.

"Welcome to womanhood," Talia had said.

Kaia pressed her lips to the chain entangled in her fingers and floated.

In the weeks that followed, Kaia and Aaron made love twice more at his house. Aaron would lay with her afterwards in his bed and they talked. About anything. About everything. Aaron made her think about things she never had before. On one occasion, he asked her a question that Kaia would never forget.

"What is your biggest fear?" he asked.

Kaia thought for a moment and answered, "I'm afraid of snakes. When I was a little girl, I used to have nightmares about them all the time."

"Why do you think you had those nightmares?' Aaron asked.

Kaia shrugged. "I don't know," she said. "All I know is I had them all the time. I still do every once in awhile."

"What did the snakes do in your dream?"

"They were just everywhere," Kaia said, shuddering at the memory. "Sometimes they hissed at me. Sometimes they tried to wrap around me and squeeze me to death."

Aaron hung on her every word and after a few moments he asked, "What was going on in your life back then?"

Kaia recalled the years of her childhood. "My parents used to fight all the time," she said. "My father used to drink a lot and when he got drunk he would yell at my mother and call her names." Kaia told Aaron the story about the drama in her parents' marriage. She conveniently left out the truth about the abrupt end to the mayhem and inserted The Story instead.

"Where were you when all of this bullshit was going on?" Aaron asked.

"Usually in my room by myself. My sisters were never home and I just remember being by myself a lot."

Aaron paused before asking, "Do you want me to tell you why I think you have those nightmares?"

"Uh oh, Matlock. Did you crack the case?" Kaia asked, being her usual sarcastic self.

"Do you want to know or not?" Aaron asked as he playfully mushed her in the head.

"Tell me," she said.

Aaron propped himself on his elbow and looked her in the eyes. "I think the snakes represent all the things in your life that prevent you from growing...from breathing."

Kaia hadn't thought of it like that before, and she felt refreshed by Aaron's conversation. She had never met a guy who spoke so openly about what was on his mind. "Well," she said, "I haven't had those dreams since I found you." She sat up and kissed his thick lips.

Aaron smiled. "Well, hopefully I can make sure that you never have those dreams again. As long as you're with me, I won't let nothing happen to you."

Kaia felt the love in her heart drip through her veins and pulsate through her body. She kissed him again long and full.

She asked him, "What is your biggest fear?"

"Death."

His answer caught Kaia off guard and she said, "Wow! I wasn't expecting that."

Aaron explained, "When my mother and my grandmother died, they both suffered so much. I remember my grandmother praying that God would forgive her for all the bad things she'd done in her life and begging him to end her suffering. I know we all have to go sometime, but I just don't want to suffer."

Kaia nodded. She laid her head on his chest and caressed his skin. They sat cloaked in silence for awhile. She leaned over and kissed his lips gently. "I understand."

That was what Aaron loved about Kaia. She didn't criticize him. She didn't make him feel silly or corny. She understood.

Kaia turned to face Aaron. "What was your mother like?" she asked.

Aaron smiled at the memory. "She was funny. She was small just like you, and she could cook better than any professional chef in the world could. She was the best."

Kaia smiled. She recalled Symphany telling her once that you can tell a good man by the way that he treats his mother. Aaron definitely scored major points for his glowing tribute to his mom. "Introduce me to her," she said.

Aaron looked at Kaia like she had lost her mind. "She's dead, Kaia."

"I know that, Aaron," Kaia said. "Introduce me to her like she was still alive."

Aaron felt silly, but he gave in. "Ma, this is Kaia. She's a sweet girl and I know you would like her. She's very special to me and I care about her a lot."

Aaron smiled at the thought of his mother "meeting" Kaia, and he meant what he said. Kaia was becoming more and more special to him with each moment they spent together.

On the morning of July 4th, Kaia boarded the bus to Aaron's house.

When she arrived, he greeted her at the door wearing boxer shorts and a T-shirt and gave her a big bear hug.

"Where's Keith?" she asked.

"He went to his shorty's house last night and never came back."

"I didn't know he had a girlfriend," Kaia said.

"Yeah, they been together for a minute now."

Aaron held her hand and led her to his room. "Sit down," he told her as he rifled through his dresser drawer.

Kaia obeyed and kicked off her sneakers. She reclined across his bed and leaned on his pillow.

Aaron approached her holding a piece of paper. He handed it to her as he sat beside her.

"What's this?" Kaia asked as she looked at the sketch of the Tudor-style house.

"That's the design of the house I'm going to build for you someday," Aaron said. "See, there's a fountain in the yard just like the one you fell in love with on Clove Road. You liked it so much I thought you should have one of your own."

Kaia sat speechless for what seemed like eternity. Aaron frowned and asked, "What's the matter?"

Kaia, deeply touched, asked, "Why are you so good to me?"

"Huh? You don't like it when I'm good to you?"

Kaia shook her head. "It's not that. I just wonder if I deserve it."

"Why wouldn't you deserve it?"

Kaia searched for the words to explain but came up empty. She wanted to tell him that no one had ever made her feel so special. She wanted to say that she had never thought much of herself. But not knowing how to say these things she said, "It's just that no one has ever been this nice to me."

Aaron smiled. "It's about time that someone treated you like a diamond. That's what you are. You're my diamond in the rough."

Kaia liked the sound of that. She smiled and held Aaron's hand in hers. "I wish I could design a house for you or analyze your dreams, but I can't. I want to show you how much you mean to me, too."

Aaron responded with a barrage of tickles. He tickled her feet, her belly, her armpits, sending Kaia into a fit of giggles. When she begged for mercy, he kissed her in every place he had tickled her and finally kissed her lips.

"Come on," he said. "You can start by making me breakfast."

After making pancakes and scrambled eggs while listening to the newest Cypress Hill tape, Kaia joined Aaron on the sofa. "So what are we going to do today?" she asked.

Aaron grinned. "I'm going to take you exactly where I promised to take you." Noticing the blank expression on her face he said, "I'm taking you to the zoo."

Like a kid on Christmas morning, Kaia jumped off the couch and pulled Aaron to his feet. "Let's go! Let's go!"

Aaron laughed and went to get dressed.

They arrived at the Staten Island Zoo and immediately headed toward the reptile exhibit. Hand in hand they gazed at crocodiles, alligators, Gila monsters and other lizards. They moved on to the petting

26

zoo and Aaron convinced a hesitant Kaia to touch the llamas. Later in the afternoon, he treated her to lunch in the food court and they sat feasting on hot dogs and fries on a bench. A few times, people stopped and smiled at the young couple so obviously in love. But Aaron and Kaia only half-noticed the attention they were receiving. They were so wrapped up in one another. Kaia never remembered a time when she felt so liberated, so unconstrained and free.

Before leaving the zoo, Aaron had one more exhibit he insisted on visiting. Kaia held tightly to his hand as they entered the snake exhibit. She begged him to spare her this torture but he was adamant. He dragged her into the room where dozens of snakes sat behind thick glass. In a calm and soothing voice he said, "Trust me, Kaia. They're not gonna hurt you. Just look at them." Kaia peeked at the slithering demons and quickly shut her eyes again. Aaron decided to use drastic measures to achieve his goal. He pulled her over to a man who was holding a long snake in his hands so that a little boy could feel its scaly skin. "Can she pet it, mister?" Aaron asked. The zookeeper smiled and nodded. "He's been defanged so he's harmless," the man said noticing Kaia's tight grip on Aaron.

Aaron turned to Kaia and said, "The best way to get over any fear is to face it. Trust me. Just touch the snake." He held Kaia's hand in his and slowly pet the snake. Kaia squirmed.

"It feels funny," she said. She felt a little more relaxed and she continued to stroke the cold, scaly exterior of the animal that had haunted her for so long.

"See," Aaron said, "It's not that bad, right?"

Kaia nodded and thought to herself that she must have been a fool to have never noticed that the guy of her dreams had been right under her nose for so long. It was as if the sun had begun to shine on that day in the park in June when Aaron had opened the door to her heart. Kaia was grateful that her own Ghetto Prince Charming had galloped into her life. Aaron was helping her face her fears and teaching her to dream. She had never had the courage to do either of these things until now.

As the sun began to set, the two of them headed to St. George and boarded the Staten Island Ferry bound for Manhattan. They sat amidst the tourists gawking at the Statue of Liberty and they kissed like they were the only two on board. When the twenty-minute ride was over and the boat docked in the city, they strolled hand in hand to Battery Park.

Joining the throngs of onlookers on that warm summer evening, they became a stitch in the patchwork of New York City. They pointed toward the sky as the fireworks erupted above. Aaron lifted Kaia in his arms and kissed her amidst the explosions both overhead and within their hearts.

And if they could have read each other's minds, there would have been one common thought.

I wish this night would never end.

The sad lesson, which they would soon learn, is that all good things come to an end.

Chapter Three

Shedding Innocence

In the final month of summer vacation, the good things came to an end as far as Kaia was concerned. Gone were the days when her biggest problem was finding an excuse to leave the prison of her project apartment and sneaking off to spend time with Aaron. She had much bigger problems now.

Kaia had not had her period in two months. She knew she was pregnant and she had no idea what she was going to do.

She had ignored the absence of her period in July, dismissing it as "no big deal". But today was August 21st, and her usually precise monthly visit had failed to arrive in the first week of the month like it always had. And it still had not come.

Kaia stared at her reflection in her bathroom mirror as if looking for a way out. Her mother would kill her. She had to figure out a way to deal with this and fast.

She still had not told Aaron and wasn't sure when she would muster the courage to do it. Kaia had only told one person, Giselle, and she had suggested that Kaia have an abortion.

"What the hell are you going to do with a baby?" Giselle had asked her. "How will you go to college? You're going to throw all of that away to become a statistic?"

Kaia didn't want to become a statistic. She never thought something like this would happen to her. Never, in her wildest dreams, did she think she would find herself facing this situation.

She spoke to her reflection in the mirror. "Think, Kaia," she told the girl in the mirror. "What can you do? You can kill *it* or you can let Janice kill *you*."

The tears that fell from the eyes of the girl in the mirror cascaded down her cheeks and rested on her chin. "How did you let this happen?" she asked her reflection. "How could you be so stupid?"

She thought about Aaron and wondered how she was going to break it to him.

"What if he leaves me? What if he doesn't talk to me anymore? He's not ready to be a parent and neither am I? He'll wish he never met me. I never should have sexed him." The thoughts came one after the other. She contemplated suicide. *"Might as well kill myself. If I don't do it, Janice will."* But she was too afraid of pain to do anything so drastic.

The phone rang and Kaia grabbed a towel to dry her tears. She walked into the kitchen and picked up the wall-mounted phone.

"Hello."

"Hey, girl." It was Symphany.

"Hey."

"What's the matter with you?" Symphany could hear the sadness in her friend's voice.

"Nothing."

"Something *is* wrong. Just tell me."

"It's nothing, Symphany, I'm just tired," Kaia lied.

"Well I have some good news, so wake up!"

"What good news?"

"I got my own apartment!" Kaia could hear the excitement in her friend's voice and was genuinely happy for her. She knew how much Symphany hated living with her mother. Symphany's mother was not thrilled about her daughter's life in the fast line. Symphany had a way of defying her mother and often stayed out for days at a time at her boyfriend, Sean's, house. Her mother had finally stood up to her, telling her that if she was grown enough to spend the night with her boyfriend, she was grown enough to get her own place. It seemed Symphany had done just that.

"Wow, Symphany, how did you get an apartment so fast?"

"Well you know that I've been saving my money, girl."

"Yeah."

"Well I saved enough so that I could move out of this concentration camp."

Kaia frowned. "How did you save that much money? And how much is the rent, anyway?"

"See, Kaia, every time I tell you some good news, you go looking for a reason to lecture me. Stop being so negative."

Kaia sighed.

"And for your information," Symphany continued, "the apartment is on Bement Avenue. It's a nice little one-bedroom and Sean is going to help me pay the rent."

"So when are you moving in?"

"I'm starting now so that, by this weekend, I'll be all set up. Why don't you come by on Saturday and chill with me for a while?"

"Yeah, I'll come. Where is it?"

Kaia copied the address and congratulated her friend before hanging up. Symphany was only seventeen and living on her own already. Some girls had all the luck. Her thoughts drifted right back to where they were before the phone rang.

What am I going to do?

She went to her room and closed the door. Kaia gazed out of her bedroom window. She felt the wind whistling through the leaves and watched the clouds caress the sky. She closed her eyes and took a deep breath.

"What am I going to do?"

Her mind was resounding with questions.

"What now? What the hell am I going to do now? If I run away, where will I go? Who should I tell? What about school? What about everything?"

"What the fuck am I going to do?"

Kaia wanted to cry...longed to cry. The tears wouldn't come. She trembled and shook from the overwhelming emotions that surged through her being. She had to scream. Scanning the room, she felt desperate. She grabbed her pillows and rammed her face into the fluffiness. She screamed. Screamed from the pit of her stomach. Screamed until her life seemed to slip through her fingers.

"What will I do with a baby?"

She longed for the ability to go back in time. Oh, how she would do things differently! Contemplating the thought of telling Aaron, Kaia felt herself on the verge of a tearful outpour. She fought back the tears and imagined Aaron's face. His smile made her heart stand still. Even in the midst of impending chaos, Kaia felt a twinge of joy at the thought of a part of Aaron growing inside of her. Was it a girl or a boy? Who would the child look like?

Disgusted with herself for even contemplating such frivolous things, Kaia started to cry. She cried until she no longer had the energy for the sobs that lingered in her heart. She cried until the tears would no longer stream down her face. She cried until her body, despite the echoes in her mind, could no longer stand it. Kaia fell asleep, clutching the pillow as if letting go would send her plummeting to her death.

Saturday arrived before she knew it, and as Kaia stepped off the bus on Bement Avenue, she looked around at the neighborhood her friend now called home. Every house was beautiful. Just like the sketch Aaron had drawn her of her dream house.

She smiled at a little girl across the street who waved at her and wondered what her own child would look like. That is, if she ever got to see her child. She still was unsure of what she was going to do. But today she would tell Symphany that she was pregnant. She figured that if anyone would stand by her side no matter what, Symphany would.

As she approached the door of the house's side entrance where Symphany's apartment was located, Kaia was nervous. How do you tell someone that you're pregnant at the age of seventeen? What would be her friend's reaction?

Realizing that she had nothing to lose, Kaia rang the bell and prayed silently for guidance. She wished the ground would swallow her up and spare her the embarrassment of this inevitable moment.

Symphany answered the door smiling from ear to ear. "Come in, girl. I can't wait to show you around."

Symphany offered Kaia a seat on the bamboo futon and went into the kitchen. Kaia looked around at the walls, which were graced with authentic African masks. Kente cloth throws draped the chairs and the smooth sounds of Sade seeped through the speakers of the stereo system. Kaia found herself once again longing for the ability to trade lives with someone. Symphany was so lucky.

Symphany reentered the living room and sat Indian style on a pillow on the floor. She handed Kaia a Heineken. Lighting incense as she analyzed the worried expression on Kaia's face, Symphany spoke softly.

"What's up, girl?" Symphany asked. Kaia couldn't help wondering how Symphany always knew when something was on her mind.

Kaia took a deep breath and tried to summon the courage to level with her friend. Symphony sensed her friend's hesitation and wondered what was wrong. She decided to reassure her.

"Before you speak, let me say one thing. Kaia, anything you tell me will stay between the two of us. I don't want you to worry about me telling anyone else. Is it about Janice?" Symphony knew Kaia's mother could be a real bitch when she wanted to.

Kaia fought back the tears that welled up in her eyes and shook her head. "I'm pregnant, Symphony."

The silence that followed was so profound that Kaia was unsure that Symphony had heard her. But she had. Symphony had heard her loud and clear.

Slowly rising to her feet, Symphony walked over to where Kaia sat. She knelt before her and opened her arms for a hug. Kaia read the expression of sympathy on her friend's face and could no longer fight the tears. She held onto Symphony and cried. In her friend's embrace, Symphony felt the sense of utter despair that Kaia possessed. Together they cried and sat otherwise silent as the incense continued to perfume the air. Pulling back from the hug, Symphony looked at Kaia's tearstained face. "What are we going to do?" she asked.

Kaia noticed her use of the word 'we' and felt more genuine love for Symphony at that moment than she ever had before. "I don't know." Wiping her eyes she looked toward the ceiling in anguish. "I'm in some serious trouble now. I can't tell Janice or she will literally kill me. I can't quit school, but I don't want to kill my baby."

Symphony listened patiently as Kaia described the absence of her period for the past two months. She listened to all the details of the morning sickness. When Kaia paused to collect herself, Symphony broke her silence.

"Listen to me, Kaia. First of all, let me say that this is a very unfortunate and unwelcomed thing. But it is *not* the end of the world." Symphony continued, "I'm against the idea of abortion. But, again, that is *my* opinion and I will support you no matter what decision you make. There is always adoption or..."

"I want to raise my own baby." The words surprised even Kaia who, up to this point, had not realized that her mind was made up. "I want to keep my baby, Symphony. But how can I finish school with a baby? How can I go to college with a baby? How can I support a baby?"

"Have you told Aaron?"

"No. I don't know how."

"The same way you just sat here and told me. You have to know how he feels about this, Kaia. It is your decision as I said, but he should also be allowed to voice his opinion before you make your final decision."

Symphony stood and turned toward the kitchen. She paused and picked up the beer she had given Kaia. "Guess you won't be drinking this now," Symphony said, smiling.

Kaia laughed through her tears. Symphony headed for the kitchen and poured her friend some juice. When she returned, she decided to stop beating around the bush and cut to the chase.

"Kaia what are you going to tell your mother?"

Kaia cringed. That was the question she'd been struggling with for weeks. "I don't know what to tell her. Symphony, regardless of how much I try to break the ice with her, Janice doesn't even say 'good morning' to me. At this point, I know she's gon' throw me out. I don't care anymore."

Symphony sighed. "I think the first thing you should do is tell Aaron. I'll go with you if you want me to."

Kaia thought about it. "I would really appreciate it if you would go with me. I don't think I can do it by myself."

They talked some more and then pulled themselves together. Symphony gave her friend a tour of the apartment before they headed over to Aaron's place.

Kaia called Aaron and told him that she was bringing Symphony over and that she had something important to tell him.

Aaron and Keith sat on the porch and waited for the ladies to arrive. Kaia had said she'd be there in about ten minutes. Keith smoked a cigarette and sat in silence. Aaron wondered what Kaia had up her sleeve.

"What do you think they want?" Aaron asked his brother.

"We'll find out now 'cuz here they come."

Kaia and Symphony walked up to the house and climbed the stairs leading to the porch. They all exchanged pleasantries.

"Wow, you're just as pretty as your friend," Keith said to Symphany with a smile. Symphany had caught his eye on previous occasions but he had never had an opportunity to really get to know her.

Symphany returned the smile and looking at Kaia said, "I like him."

Kaia managed a weak smile and nudged Aaron. She whispered, "I need to talk to you."

Aaron was really worried now. "Um, you two can chill for a minute right?" he asked Symphany and Keith.

"Yeah. Y'all go ahead," Symphany said. She sat down next to Keith and struck up a conversation. Keith was more than happy to oblige.

Kaia and Aaron headed to his bedroom where they could talk in privacy. Kaia sat on the bed and Aaron turned on the radio. *"When Will I See You Smile Again"* by Bell Biv DeVoe filled the room and Aaron wasted no time getting to the point. "What's the matter?" he asked.

Kaia took a deep breath. "I have something to tell you and I don't think you're going to like it," she said.

Aaron could see the tears in her eyes and he kneeled down in front of her and lifted her chin in his hand. "Whatever it is you can tell me. You can tell me anything."

As the tears began to fall from her eyes, Aaron held her close and was genuinely worried. "Kaia, just tell me. Tell me what happened. Did your mother find out about us?"

Kaia shook her head. She couldn't find the courage to tell him. Her mouth wouldn't form the words.

Aaron was getting frustrated. "Girl, tell me what happened!"

Kaia looked in Aaron's eyes and saw the panic and worry they held. She loved him so much.

"Aaron," she said, "I'm pregnant."

Aaron sat for a few moments in silence and stared at her in disbelief. Then, to Kaia's amazement, a smile crept slowly across his lips. He gently stroked her cheek, wiping away each tear as they drifted down her face.

He kissed her. Then again. And again. Just as he'd done the first time he'd kissed her in the park. Kaia's heart was full and she threw her arms around his neck and cried. Aaron rocked her and stroked her hair. "Is that what you were having such a hard time telling me?"

Kaia nodded and wiped her eyes. Aaron held her tightly in his arms.

"I didn't know what you would do. But I didn't expect you to smile about it. Aaron, we're in big trouble."

"You don't think I know that, Kaia?" Aaron held her face in his hands. "When you came over here with your friend I thought you were coming to tell me that we couldn't see each other anymore or some shit. I know this is a big problem and we have a lot to talk about, but we're going to handle this together. I ain't leaving you, baby." He smiled again and rubbed her belly. "That's *my* baby in there, Kaia, and I'm going to make sure everything is alright, you hear me?"

Kaia threw her arms around Aaron's neck and held on for dear life. She loved him more at that moment then she had ever loved anyone in her life.

"I love you," he whispered.

Kaia held him tighter, willing every emotion she felt to be communicated in her grasp. She clung to him with an urgency that spoke volumes. "I love you, too," she said. "I'm scared, Aaron."

Aaron pulled away and held her tender face in his hands. "I won't let nothing happen to you, you hear me?"

Aaron's eyes told her he was sincere. She nodded.

"Nothing will ever hurt you as long as I'm around. You believe me, right?"

Kaia kissed him over and over. She did believe him. She trusted him and she believed him with all her heart.

Aaron smiled again. "Now what are we going to do about this?" he asked.

They were interrupted by a knock on the door. Keith and Symphany came in.

"Is everything okay in here?" Symphany asked.

"Yeah," Aaron answered. "Kaia just told me. I want you to know that I'm going to stand by her no matter what she decides to do."

Symphany nodded her head and smiled. "That's what your brother was just telling me."

Keith laughed. "Actually what I said was that you would take care of your responsibility or I would bust your ass."

Everybody laughed and the mood was a little lighter. Kaia still sat wiping the tears that had fallen earlier. Symphany asked, "Well what *have* the two of you decided to do?"

Aaron and Kaia looked at each other. Aaron said, "Honestly, I know about this women's rights stuff and all that. But I want this baby."

Keith shook his head in disapproval. "How are you going to support a baby, Aaron? You better think about what you're saying."

Aaron replied, "I'm a man. I'll handle it like a man. But I want Kaia to have my baby. Just because we didn't plan it doesn't mean it's not a blessing." He looked at Kaia. "But if you don't want to keep it, I understand and I'll go with you to get an abortion."

Kaia held Keith's hand and looked around the room at everyone. Symphany was on her side no matter what. She knew that Talia and Giselle would be, too. But she could tell Keith was against her having this baby. She thought about her mother and how she would react once she found out. But when Kaia looked at Aaron, she saw a man she could trust. She saw someone who loved her and who would do anything for her.

"I want the baby," she said. Aaron smiled, relieved. "I don't want to have an abortion. And I know it's going to be hard on both of us, but we'll get through it. It's not the end of the world."

Keith and Symphany exchanged glances. Keith shrugged his shoulders and said, "Well, if that's what y'all want to do, then I guess all I can say is congratulations." Aaron stood and shook his brother's hand, and with their clasped hands pressed between them, they hugged. Keith looked at Kaia and added, "And it better be a boy!"

Kaia smiled and the mood was definitely lighter.

Everyone went to the living room and Keith got everyone a glass of juice. Symphany again asked the inevitable question. " When are you going to tell Janice?"

Kaia and Aaron looked at each other. Aaron said, "I would like to be a man and go with you to tell your mother. You shouldn't have to face her alone."

Kaia nodded. "Aaron, that's very admirable of you. However, my mother isn't your typical mother. She'll beat you *down*."

Symphany agreed. "So maybe me and Keith should come with you just in case."

Keith agreed. "Yeah, you don't want to be in a room alone with a woman who just found out her 17-year-old daughter is pregnant. Not unless you have a death wish."

Aaron agreed and added, "Well, if she throws her out..."

"Which she will," Kaia interrupted.

"Well when she does, I want Kaia to come stay with me." Aaron looked defiantly at his brother.

Symphany shook her head. "No, Kaia can stay with me. I just got my own place and I'm a woman and I can help her through the pregnancy."

"But I'm the baby's father and it's my responsibility to take care of both of them from now on," Aaron countered.

"Why not let Kaia decide," Keith suggested.

Kaia laughed. "I feel so wanted!"

Symphany threw a pillow at Kaia and laughed.

Kaia said, "I'm going to stay here with Aaron if it's alright with the two of you." She looked at Keith and Symphany for their consent. "I need to be with Aaron. Plus you just moved into your place, Symphany. Enjoy having your own apartment for a little while."

Symphany reluctantly agreed. They all got ready to head over to Janice's house to tell her the news. And as Kaia watched Aaron prepare for the battle that lay ahead of him, she beamed with pride. She thought to herself, *"This man loves me. He really, really loves me. And I am so lucky to have him."*

She said a silent prayer of thanks and held Aaron's hand as they headed for Janice's house.

Chapter Four

Drama

As the elevator made the slow ascension to Janice's apartment on the fifth floor, Kaia felt a huge lump in her throat. She was scared to death. Aaron held her hand in his and he noticed that she was trembling. She looked at him with anxiety written all over her face and Aaron winked at her. "It's alright, Kaia," he said. "Don't be so nervous."

Kaia nodded and thought to herself, *"Easier said than done."*

As they stepped off the elevator and walked down the narrow hallway, Kaia recited a quick prayer under her breath. This was not going to be easy.

Kaia inserted her key in the apartment door and they all entered, only to find that Janice was not at home.

"Maybe she went to the store or something," Symphany suggested. "I'm sure she didn't go far so let's just wait for her."

Kaia had an idea. "Why don't I pack my stuff before she gets back?"

Aaron looked at Symphany and she shrugged her shoulders. "Do you think you should?" she asked.

Kaia sighed and put her hands on her hips. "Symphany, you know she's going to throw me out so I might as well get my stuff while I still can."

Symphany nodded. "Go ahead. I'll get everybody something to drink.

Aaron and Keith took a seat on the sofa. Keith stared at his brother for a few moments before he spoke. "Look, man, I hope you know what you're doing. How are you planning on supporting this kid?"

Aaron shot a look toward the kitchen to make sure that Symphany wasn't within earshot. "How do you think?" he asked, giving Keith a knowing look. "I'm gonna hustle again."

Keith shook his head. "Man, the crack game is gonna get you in trouble. I told you all that fast money ain't worth the drama that comes with it."

Aaron shrugged his shoulders. "Look, I gotta finish school. This is my last year and then I'll get my diploma. Once I have that, I can try and get a city job. But until then, I gotta do what I gotta do to make sure Kaia has everything she needs and the baby has everything he needs. I'm not gonna stand on the block all day and hustle. That's how people get caught. Sean told me he got a few connects whenever I'm ready to get on. I been thinking about it but I didn't have no reason to take his offer seriously until now." Aaron paused. "Why? Do you have a better idea?"

Keith shook his head. "Yo, if there's one thing I know for sure it's that you're gonna do what you wanna do, regardless. I just hope you're planning on staying with this girl and not just making both of your lives more complicated. Don't be one of these dudes out here with three baby's mamas by the age of 20."

Aaron smiled. "Nah, man, you don't have to worry about that. I know Kaia's the one."

"How do you know that?" Keith asked.

"Because she's nothing like these other girls nowadays. She was a virgin when I met her and that's rare nowadays. She don't have a reputation. Nobody can step to me telling me they had her. Plus she's smart, she's pretty, and when I'm with her I'm at peace. I love that girl. Just because we're young don't mean we can't recognize the real thing when we find it. You were my age when you got with Zenobia and you're still with her."

Keith nodded. "True. I guess you got it all figured out. Just be careful, man. I'm not going to tell you how to handle your business. Just don't bring none of that shit in our house. Weed is one thing but crack is something totally different. You don't shit where you sleep. Keep a separate lab for that shit. And be careful."

"I will. I got more to live for now."

Symphany returned with the juice just as Kaia reentered the living room with a suitcase in her hand. She set the suitcase on the side of the couch and sat next to Aaron.

They heard a key turn in the door and Kaia's heart thundered in her chest. Janice was home. Symphany closed her eyes and said a silent prayer. Janice was going to flip.

40

Janice entered the living room and saw her daughter, Symphany, and two young men she'd never seen before. The frown on her face sent shivers through everyone.

"What's all this?" she asked, looking at Kaia.

Kaia couldn't seem to bring herself to respond, so Symphany stepped in. "Hi," Symphany said. "This is Aaron, and his brother Keith."

Janice just stood and stared at everyone. She didn't move or say a word. Aaron shifted uncomfortably in his seat. Kaia looked at the floor as her hands shook from nervousness. Aaron finally broke the silence.

"Hi, Mrs. Wesley. It's nice to meet you. Kaia has told me a lot about you."

Janice continued to stare at him. "Who are you and what are you doing in my house?"

Symphany cleared her throat. "Miss Janice, please come and sit down. We have a few things to talk about."

Janice rolled her eyes and folded her arms across her chest. "I ain't sitting nowhere until somebody tells me what the hell all y'all are doing in my house."

Aaron noticed Kaia shaking, and reached over and held her hand. He looked at Janice and said, "Mrs. Wesley, I'm Kaia's boyfriend. I came over here with my brother after Symphany and Kaia stopped by our house this afternoon. I've been seeing Kaia for a few months now and I really care about her."

Janice scowled at Aaron. "How the hell you gonna sit in my house and tell me you been sneaking around with my daughter?" She looked at Kaia. "What did I tell you about having boyfriends? Not until you're grown and you move the hell out of my house, right?"

Kaia continued to look down and nodded her head.

Janice continued, "Well then who the hell is this fool and why the fuck is he sitting in my God damned living room?"

"With all due respect, Mrs. Wesley, there's no need to call anybody names. No one has disrespected you and we only want to talk to you about the situation at hand," Keith said, obviously trying to control his temper. Janice was getting on his nerves.

"What damn situation?" she asked, looking at Kaia.

Aaron squeezed Kaia's hand. Kaia found the nerve to speak.

"I'm pregnant."

You could have heard a pin drop in the silence that followed. Everyone looked to Janice for her reaction. She stood glaring at Kaia.

"What the fuck did you just say?" Janice asked as she advanced menacingly toward Kaia.

Symphany stood and blocked Janice's path to her friend. "Calm down and listen for a minute," she urged.

"I want this bitch to repeat what the hell she just said," Janice yelled, trying to push past Symphany to get to Kaia.

Aaron spoke up. "Please calm down, Mrs. Wesley. I love Kaia and I plan to take responsibility for her and this child. I don't want you to think I'm going to turn my back on her or the baby because..."

"She ain't keeping your fuckin' bastard baby!" Janice yelled. "The bitch is getting an abortion or I'm going to beat the muthafucka out of her."

Keith stood up. "Now you're out of line," he said.

"If your ugly ass don't get out of my face I'll cut you and your fuckin' hood rat brother. This is my God damned house. *You're* out of fuckin' line."

Symphany yelled over all the commotion. "Wait a minute!" Looking at Janice she said, "You need to calm down and listen."

Janice folded her arms across her chest and continued to stare at Keith. Keith stared right back.

Symphany continued. "Kaia does not want to have an abortion. Legally, you can not make her get one because she is over twelve years old. It's her decision. Aaron loves her and she loves him and they are willing to do whatever it takes to handle the responsibility. Now, this is your *daughter* sitting here!" Symphany pointed at Kaia who had begun to cry. "You need to stop insulting everybody and be there for your child. She needs you right now."

The living room fell silent again as Janice stared at Kaia with hate in her eyes. When she spoke she had the attention of everyone in the room, but she never lifted her gaze from Kaia.

"Let me tell your little ass something. All he wants from you is pussy. And you're sitting here believing all this bullshit he's talking about he loves you and he's gonna take care of you. You're stupid if you fall for that shit. He got what he wanted and now you want to have his baby." Janice paused and shook her head in disgust. "You have two choices. You can get rid of this bastard child you're carrying or you can get the fuck out of my house. But let me tell you one thing. If you keep this kid, don't ever speak to me again. As far as I'm concerned you'll be dead."

Symphany stood speechless and stared at Kaia's mother.

Keith spoke through clenched teeth. "How can you say that to her? That's your daughter for God's sake."

Janice's head whipped around and she glared at Keith. "You wanna know how I can say that to her? Because she's just like her damn father that's why. She don't appreciate shit. All these years I've been getting up everyday and working my fingers to the bone to keep a roof over her head. Anything she needed, she had it. Anything she wanted, I got it for her. All I asked in return was for her to respect me and follow my rules. Instead, she got knocked up by your low-life brother. Now she can do what I say or I wash my hands of her. And if you don't like it, you can kiss my muthafuckin' ass!"

Keith looked at Aaron. "I'm leaving before I hurt this woman," he said.

Aaron stood to leave with his brother and looked at Kaia. "Sweetheart, are you coming with me?"

Kaia stood with tears running down her face and nodded. "Yeah, I'm out of here." She looked at her mother and shook her head. "All my life you've treated me like you hate me," she said.

Janice looked Kaia up and down with a condescending gaze.

Kaia continued, "What did I ever do to you?"

Janice gave her an icy stare. "You were born."

Kaia grabbed her suitcase and headed for the door. As she tried to pass her mother to get to the door, Janice stopped her.

"No way are you walking out of here with the clothes I bought for you," Janice said, snatching the suitcase out of Kaia's hand.

Symphany protested, "Well, what the hell is she supposed to wear?"

"The clothes on her back," Janice answered. "And she's lucky I don't rip those off of her." She looked at Aaron. "Let this son of a bitch buy her some clothes since he's so damn responsible'."

Kaia opened her mouth to protest but Aaron stopped her. "Nah, sweetheart, don't waste your breath. I'll make sure you get some clothes. Let this bitch be miserable by herself."

"Word," Keith chimed in. "Let's go."

The three of them walked out of the apartment and pressed for the elevator. Symphany stood in the living room staring at Janice. She couldn't believe what she had just witnessed. Even the problems she had with her own mother didn't compare to this. She knew she was out of line to question Kaia's mother but she couldn't leave without asking her this question. "How could you do that to her?" she asked.

Janice stood her ground. "If you're gonna stand here and take up for that bitch, then you can get the fuck out, too." Janice stormed down the hall to her bedroom and slammed the door.

Symphany shook her head in disbelief and left to console her friend.

When the four of them arrived at Keith and Aaron's place, Symphany volunteered to make dinner for everyone. She went into the kitchen and prepared to make vegetarian lasagna. Keith sat on the porch smoking a cigarette with a Heineken in his hand. He needed to calm down after having resisted the temptation to beat the shit out of Kaia's mother. He had never been so tempted to knock a woman out in his life.

Aaron and Kaia retreated to what was now *their* bedroom and Kaia lay across the bed in the fetal position. Aaron lay beside her, facing her back, and stroked her hair. *In Living Color* was on tonight but there was nothing funny about the events of that day. He felt so sorry for Kaia after what he had witnessed. He whispered in her ear, "I love you, Kaia. Don't worry about nothing, okay?"

Kaia nodded but didn't move. She was overwhelmed by the day's events. Her own mother had said she should have never been born. Her own mother had thrown her out with no money and no clothes. Her own mother had told her she considered her dead. And it hurt. It hurt like hell.

"Try to take a nap, okay?" Aaron coaxed her to close her eyes and relax. He felt so responsible for this entire mess. He wished there was something he could say or do to right all that had been so wrong in Kaia's life. He felt helpless and he hated Janice for what he had witnessed earlier. "Kaia, I'm sorry."

Kaia turned over and faced him. "Sorry for what?"

"For everything. It's my fault you got pregnant because you kept telling me to pull out and I didn't listen. It was feeling so good that I couldn't control myself. And now, I got you kicked out of your mother's house and..."

"Stop right there." Kaia sat up. "*We* got into this mess. Both of us, together. And *we* will get through this together."

Aaron kissed her lips and held her in his arms. "I just don't want you to worry about nothing," he said. I know we made a mistake by getting pregnant so young, but I also know that we're soul mates." He smiled. "I've known that since English class, our freshman year. It just took me awhile to get you to see it."

Kaia smiled, too. "You were a real pest!"

Aaron laughed. He was glad to see her mood brighten a little. "I wasn't ashamed to admit that I had a crush on you." Aaron laid his head in her lap and kissed her belly. "And now look at how far we've come. Pretty soon there'll be a little Kaia or Aaron running around."

Kaia liked the sound of that. She stroked Aaron's head as he laid in her lap. "I have to go to the doctor soon."

"I know," Aaron said. They'll tell us if it's a boy or a girl, right?"

"I'm not sure. I think they'll let us know when the baby will be born, though."

They both sat in silence for a moment; each lost in their own private thoughts. Kaia spoke after a few minutes. "My mother really hates me," she said.

Aaron weighed his response before he spoke. "Your mother has a problem, Kaia. She has a lot of shit she needs to deal with before she can love anybody." He looked up at Kaia. "Has she always been like that?"

"Yup." Kaia sighed.

"Well, she'll come around eventually," Aaron said, rather unconvincingly. "But we don't need her. You'll see. I'm going to be all you need."

"Aaron, how are we going to support ourselves *and* a baby? I'll have to drop out of school and..."

"Oh no you're not," Aaron interrupted. He sat up on the bed and looked at her with an expression that told Kaia he meant what he was saying. "You're too smart to drop out of school. You came this far and you're going to finish. I'll watch the baby while you go to school."

"And what about you, Aaron? You've come a long way, too, so why should you have to drop out?"

"Because I'm a man, Kaia. And I have a big responsibility now. I'll watch the baby while you go to school and I'll study for my GED at night."

"You have this all figured out, don't you?" Kaia asked.

"Pretty much."

"Well then tell me what we're going to do for money. Where am I going to get clothes from?"

"Don't worry about that."

"Don't start keeping secrets from me, Aaron."

Aaron thought about it for a minute. She was right. They had never had any secrets between them and he didn't want to start now. But he didn't want to add to Kaia's worries by telling her that he intended to sell drugs to get money. He convinced himself that he would tell her when the time was right.

"I'm not keeping any secrets. Sometimes you just have to let a man play his position. I don't want to tell you exactly what I plan to do until I know for sure that it can be done. As soon as I have a definite plan, you'll be the first to know." Aaron kissed her nose. "Until then, you just make sure you eat right, get plenty of rest and don't stress nothing. Trust me, sweetheart."

Kaia still wondered what Aaron had up his sleeve. But, after the events that had transpired that day, she was too drained to push the issue.

Just then, Symphany called them into the kitchen to eat. They entered the living room and saw Keith sprawled out on the couch asleep. Symphany came out of the kitchen wiping her hands on a dishtowel.

"Alright, guys, I'm getting ready to get out of here," she said.

Symphany walked over and hugged Kaia. "It's going to be okay, honey. Janice is ignorant and we need to pray for her. I'll be back tomorrow with some clothes for you to wear until you get some of your own."

Kaia smiled. "You mean I'm going to be walking around looking like a superstar?"

Symphany pushed her playfully and laughed. "That's not such a bad thing is it?"

Kaia shook her head. "No, that's not so bad."

Symphany kissed Kaia and Aaron on their cheeks and headed for the door. "The lasagna is in the oven and the garlic bread is, too." She looked at Aaron. "Make sure she eats something."

Aaron nodded. "I will. Don't worry."

Symphany smiled. "I won't. I know she's in good hands."

Kaia's heart leapt as she watched her best friend hug the man she loved. She knew that from this day forward, she and Symphany would be closer than they had ever been. She felt blessed to have two people in her life who loved her as much as they did.

Symphany left to catch her bus and Kaia and Aaron helped themselves to the food she'd prepared. They returned to Aaron's room leaving Keith snoring on the couch.

Kaia fed Aaron some lasagna and giggled as the cheese dripped down his chin.

Aaron joked, "How are you going to raise a baby when you can't even get this right?"

Kaia smacked him playfully in the head.

They sat watching Def Comedy Jam and laughed until their sides hurt. That night, Kaia fell asleep in Aaron's arms and dreamed of a beautiful baby, a wonderful man, and a lovely house with a fountain in the yard.

Chapter Five

Life After Death

About a week after Kaia moved in with Aaron and Keith, Aaron awoke her with a kiss. "I have to take care of some business," Aaron said.

Kaia sat up and looked at him. "What kind of business?" she asked, her voice heavy with fatigue.

Aaron frowned. "I have to go talk to Sean for a little while about some things. It's no big deal."

Kaia's eyes narrowed as she stared at Aaron. "Sean is nothing but trouble, Aaron."

Aaron rolled his eyes. "Come on, sweetheart. Don't start. Sean has been my boy since junior high school. He ain't that bad."

"Well what do you need to talk to him about?" Kaia pressed.

"Just a few things. I'll be back home before you know it. Why don't you make lunch for me while I'm gone?" Aaron was trying to avoid telling her the truth.

Kaia didn't like the thought of Aaron being around Sean. Sean lived in the Stapleton Projects and had a reputation as a trouble making, drug selling, gangster. Aside from his reputation as a thug, Sean was also a ladies man. Sonia, a girl from Kaia's old neighborhood, was pregnant with his child and he was screwing Symphany as well. Kaia felt insecure with the idea of Aaron being close with such a character. What if he encouraged Aaron to have a chick on the side? The very thought of that sent chills down Kaia's spine.

Aaron noticed the disconcerting look on Kaia's face. "Don't worry, sweetheart. I promise I won't be gone long."

Kaia held his gaze. "I just don't like it when you're away from me for a long time," she said.

Aaron smiled. "I don't like it either," he said. "But pretty soon, I won't have to be away from you much at all. Just let me go and talk to Sean about a few things and before you know it, we'll be on *Easy Street*"

Kaia sat in silence as Aaron headed out the door. Once he was gone, she reached for the phone and called Symphany. She answered on the second ring.

"Hey, girl," Kaia tried to sound like this was merely a social call.

"Hey, Kaia. How's my future Godchild doing?"

"Symphany, this baby is still only the size of a pea. But I'm doing fine, thanks for asking." Kaia switched the phone to her other ear.

Symphany laughed. "What are you getting into today?"

Kaia shrugged. "Nothing."

"Wanna come with me to the mall? I need to find some shoes to match my birthday outfit." Symphany had just been on an expensive shopping spree. Courtesy of her secret occupation as Sean's drug trafficker.

"Yeah. I'll go with you. Meet me at the ferry and we'll take the bus from there."

"Girl, you go on and take the bus if you want. I got my friend's car today." Symphany looked out her living room window. She glanced across the street admiring the gleaming green Acura Legend parked at the curb.

"What friend?" Kaia's curiosity was peeked now. "And what kind of car is it?"

"Don't worry about it and you'll see when I get there to pick you up." The girls hung up and got dressed for their meeting.

Aaron got off the #74 bus on Broad Street in the Stapleton section of Staten Island. He looked up and down the block for his friend, Sean.

Broad Street was packed. It was a sunny September afternoon and the Black people came out like roaches. Cars and motorcycles were glistening in the summer sun and girls walked around wearing next to nothing. Aaron walked the long stretch of the block and greeted a few friends along the way.

He spotted Sean standing in front of the building wearing a blue Champion T-shirt and matching shorts. He walked over and they greeted each other with the handshake of the streets and commented on the asses of a few girls walking by in tight shorts.

"Let's get down to business," Aaron suggested after a few minutes of small talk.

"Aiight, then," Sean agreed. "What is it you need from me?"

Aaron put his hands in his pockets and looked at the ground. "I need some dough, man. Kaia's pregnant and her moms put her out. Now she's staying with me and it's up to me to make sure everything is taken care of." Aaron realized, as if for the first time, that he had so much responsibility resting on his young shoulders. He needed some money and he needed it fast.

Sean nodded his understanding and passed Aaron the blunt he had just rolled. As Aaron smoked, Sean laid down his offer. "Here's what I can do," he said. "Since you're my boy from way back I know I can trust you. Plus you already know the ropes from when you used to hang around with Wayne and them from the Hill. So I'm going to give you Jermaine's old spot to run."

Aaron and Sean had known Jermaine for several years. He was well known in Staten Island for being a hustler. It was that same rep that got him killed. Jermaine was making money when many weren't making any, and for that he was set up and murdered on a block in West Brighton -the same neighborhood in which he grew up.

"Well what do I have to do?" Aaron asked, passing the blunt back to Sean.

"Just come to my lab tonight and I'll go over everything with you. In the meantime," Sean pulled a wad of cash from his pocket and peeled off three hundred-dollar bills. "This oughta hold you until things start jumping off."

Aaron took the money and again they shook hands. They agreed to meet at Sean's place at around nine and Aaron returned home to Kaia with a new sense of hope. Everything was going to be just fine.

Kaia and Symphany cruised along the Staten Island Expressway headed for the mall. It was still very warm although the end of summer was approaching and the breeze from the open windows felt good.

"So what's up with you and Sean?" Kaia asked as an opportunity presented itself to find out what she needed to know.

Symphany kept her eyes on the road and smiled. "He's aiight. It ain't serious, though." As always, Symphany was careful with her words.

Kaia pressed further. "Why do you think Aaron would be going to see him today?"

Symphany took her eyes off the road and looked at Kaia briefly. "Well they're friends, right?" Symphany asked.

"Yeah, but today it seemed like he was going for a reason. Like it was business. Do you know anything?" Kaia needed answers.

"Nah, Kaia. I know what you know. Sean hustles. He's on some straight up money making shit. We could draw conclusions about what type of dealings are going on with him and Aaron, but why bother? Right now, you're pregnant with your soul mate's child, you got out of your mean mother's house, and you have enough to worry about. If Aaron says to relax and let him handle it, you should do just that. Let him handle his business. You work on taking care of your baby and finishing school."

Kaia let Symphany's words sink in. Symphany had always been wise like an old owl. Kaia decided to take her advice and she let herself enjoy the shopping spree with her friend.

The next six months were filled with joy for Aaron and Kaia. The baby was due in four weeks and Aaron had seen to it that they had everything any baby would need. He bought a crib, a changing table, a stroller, a swing, and more clothes than their child would probably ever wear. He gave Kaia money for bottles, bibs, pampers, rattles, and they soon realized that there was no need for a baby shower. Aaron got everything. Since there was nothing left to buy for the baby, Talia, Symphany, and Giselle agreed to alternate babysitting for Kaia once the baby was born.

Aaron bought a used car from a dealership on Bay Street. Kaia loved sitting in the passenger seat of their Mercury Sable while Aaron drove. Aaron promised that once she gave birth he would teach her how to drive. She was so proud to be with him. They were beginning to feel like a real family.

He went with her to every single doctor's appointment. When they went for the sonogram during Kaia's fifth month of pregnancy, Aaron was overjoyed at the sight of his baby's hands, feet and head. The doctor couldn't tell the sex of the child in Kaia's womb, but to Aaron it didn't make a difference. He was about to become a father and nothing in the world could take the smile off his face.

Kaia had returned to school in September and had continued to attend classes even as her stomach began to grow. She tolerated the stares from her classmates and teachers and heard the whispers as she walked through the halls. A few of her teachers complained that having her in their classrooms with a pregnant belly was a distraction for the other students. Teachers whispered about her in the hallways. They said she'd never amount to anything. She'd never graduate. She was just another statistic...a baby having a baby. But Kaia was proud...so very proud to be carrying Aaron's baby. She was proud because he loved her. He loved their baby. No one could make her see this as a hindrance. It just felt right. Kaia was again, on cloud nine.

She still had not heard from her mother. Neither of them had contacted the other. Nubia and Asha came by Aaron's apartment to see their sister once they heard the news. Asha reported that Janice was still stubbornly refusing to accept the fact that Kaia was having this baby and that Aaron would be a part of their family. In Janice's opinion, the child Kaia was carrying was a bastard and Kaia was a Goddamned fool. Nubia and Asha didn't tell Kaia that they, too, were embarrassed about her pregnancy. They didn't tell her that she had disappointed them and the rest of their "family". They didn't say that she was now, officially, the black sheep of their family. But, Kaia knew that was how they felt. She could tell by the fact that they never called her. They never came back to check on her. In the months that followed, Kaia never heard another word from anyone in her family. She felt abandoned again, and she was reminded of what an outcast she had always been to them. Kaia wished she still had her father around to shower her with love. Janice had subtracted hers from Kaia years ago. Now it seemed she had succeeded in convincing Nubia and Asha to do the same.

Now that she had entered her eighth month of pregnancy, the guidance counselor at Curtis High School had suggested that Kaia take home instruction. Now, a teacher came to their apartment each morning and taught her the lessons that she would have been learning in school. Kaia got home instruction five days a week from 9a.m. to 1:00 p.m. This allowed her time to get the rest that she so desperately needed since pregnancy was beginning to take its toll on her. Kaia found that she was always tired. She couldn't wait to have the baby so that she could feel like her old self again. The extra pounds she had gained made her feel like a fat cow.

Aaron did what he could to soothe her diminished self-image. Every chance he got her told her that she was the most beautiful woman he knew. Kaia knew he was bullshitting, but it made her love him more than ever. It seemed that Aaron was giving her all the love she had never received all of her life. It made her want to cry.

Aaron, on the other hand, was not without his share of dilemmas. Wayne, whom Aaron had implicated in the robbery months before, had been released from prison. Upon his release and subsequent return to the streets of Staten Island, he had learned of Aaron's newfound wealth, and Wayne wasn't pleased. He had voiced his displeasure to a number of people and this information had been relayed to Aaron.

Aaron had successfully steered clear of Wayne up to this point. He continued to hustle but kept a much lower profile. He had too much at stake to risk a run-in with Wayne. Aaron also kept the news about his beef with Wayne from Kaia. He didn't want to worry her during her final month of pregnancy. But Aaron worried about it plenty.

He had managed to secure a sizeable nest egg courtesy of his steadily increasing crack sales. He had lessened his chances of getting caught by not hustling on the street corner like so many of his peers. He operated by pager only. The crack fiends beeped him and he made his deliveries door to door. Aaron knew that by now, Kaia was aware of how he was making so much money. She was no fool. But he loved her for not questioning him about it. She never criticized him for it. She never mentioned it.

He kept his product at an apartment he subleased in the neighboring New Brighton projects. The $500 a month rent barely put a dent in his pockets. He had a nice amount of money saved, and once the baby was born he intended to take Kaia and the baby and move away from Staten Island. Aaron was uncomfortable with the idea of hustling so close to where he called home.

The one thing that brought him joy, aside from Kaia and his unborn child, was the fact that he had finally been able to bless Keith financially. His brother had sacrificed so much of himself so that Aaron would have all he needed. It felt good to be able to finally repay him. Aaron had given him the money to put a down payment on a car and now Keith was the proud owner of a Nissan Maxima. It warmed Aaron's heart every time he saw his brother behind the wheel of that car. No one deserved it more.

In Aaron's opinion, Kaia deserved the world. It was the night before Valentine's Day, and as he slid into bed beside her, he smiled. He was going to fill the house with roses, balloons, candy and jewelry for her. Nothing was too much for Kaia.

He pulled the covers back and kissed her belly. "Hi, little one," he said to the baby.

Kaia laughed. "Every time this baby hears your voice it starts going berserk," she said.

Aaron placed his hand on her stomach and felt his child moving around. "That's right, kick for daddy, baby."

He lay beside Kaia and kissed her. "I love you," he said. "Don't ever forget that, you hear me?"

"Yes," Kaia replied. "I love you, too. You know that."

"Nah, I don't know that. I need you to prove it."

Kaia giggled seductively as she stroked between his legs. Aaron smiled and made love to her as if it were the last time.

The wind outside whistled like a freight train as Aaron awoke the next morning. He pulled the comforter over him and Kaia and woke her with a kiss. She turned toward him and put her arms around his neck.

"Good morning, baby," she said in a voice that was heavy with sleep.

"Good morning to you," he said. "Happy Valentine's Day."

"Oh, I completely forgot, Aaron. I have to go to the mall and get you something." Kaia started to get out of bed, but Aaron pulled her back.

"Not now, you're not," he said with a smile. "Today, we're going to stay in bed all morning and fuck."

"Aaron!" Kaia laughed. "You're so nasty!"

"Yup, and you love it!" He licked his lips and rubbed his hands together as if preparing for a feast.

"You're right, I do love it," she said. "But it's our first Valentine's Day and I want to do something special for you."

"Then put your lips..."

"Aaron, stop being nasty! I'm serious."

Aaron laughed. "Alright, alright. Let's get dressed and go get some breakfast at Perkins."

Kaia smiled. "Last one dressed is a rotten egg!"

Perkins wasn't too packed when they arrived. They found an empty booth and sat and enjoyed an intimate breakfast. They talked about the upcoming birth of their child and about the latest gossip. By the time they finished eating they were both full and lazy.

As they drove away from the restaurant, Kaia stared out the passenger side window at the cloudy sky.

"Aaron," she said. "If I ask you something will you get mad at me?"

Aaron took his eyes off the road briefly and frowned at her. "You know I can't get mad at you, girl."

Kaia paused for a moment. "Aaron, when are you going to stop hustling?"

Aaron looked straight ahead. He knew he'd have to face this question sooner or later. But the truth was, money was better now than ever before, and things were only getting better. But he understood that this was not the life Kaia wanted.

"Kaia, I promise that once the baby is born and you graduate from school, I'll stop. I just want you to finish school."

Kaia prayed that he was telling the truth. She had a bad feeling about the amount of money he was making. For some reason, she was beginning to think that Aaron would eventually find himself in big trouble.

They rode the rest of the way in silence.

When they arrived at home, Aaron helped Kaia out of her coat and joined her in the living room.

"Sweetheart, don't worry about anything, okay?" He sat beside her on the couch. "I promise that I will get out of this when the time is right. You're having my baby, and you're going to be my wife. I'm going to take care of you and the baby always. You understand?"

Kaia nodded.

"Don't worry about anything. I will never be away from you, okay. Trust me."

"I do trust you, Aaron. I just worry about you that's all."

"You don't have to worry about me, okay? Just sit back and watch TV. I have to run out for a little while and when I come back I want to celebrate Valentine's Day the way I told you earlier."

Kaia smiled, naughtily.

Aaron leaned down and kissed her. Then again. Then again.

"I love you," he said.

"I love you, too."

Aaron grabbed his coat and walked out the door.

As Aaron stepped out of his car on the corner of Broad Street and Tompkins Avenue, he noticed Sean almost running in his direction. The look on Sean's face was one of deep concern.

"Yo, Aaron, man we got a problem," Sean said, looking around as if he were afraid of something or someone.

Aaron was worried now. "What happened?," he asked.

"Yo, man," Sean opened the passenger door of Aaron's car. "First let's get the hell out of here. We'll drive somewhere and talk on the way. The block is hot right now."

Aaron got back in the car and they pulled off in the direction of Bay Street.

"What's going on?" Aaron asked.

Sean shook his head. "Man, shit is about to go down out here. Your boy Wayne came out here earlier today. Talking about he heard me and you was boys so he figured he should tell me to relay a message to you. First of all he was like "be careful cuz you're hanging with a snitch." Then, after I told him to go 'head with that bullshit cuz me and you are boys, he said, "well then tell your boy to watch his back because I'm looking for him." He said to tell you that you won't live to see your baby born."

Aaron pulled into the McDonald's parking lot and parked in an empty spot. He turned the engine off and looked at Sean. "Now I gotta kill this nigga."

Sean nodded in agreement. "Seems like that's the only option now. It's kill or be killed." Sean lifted his shirt and pulled a .38 out of his waistband. "Keep this with you in case you run into that nigga."

Aaron took the gun and tucked it into his jeans. He shook his head and sighed heavily. He didn't need this right now. Kaia was due to give birth any day now. His baby was about to be born and he had assured Kaia that he would always be around. Now if he killed Wayne, and was faced with going to prison, Kaia would have to raise their baby by herself. Aaron was overwhelmed.

He started the engine and pulled out of the parking lot. Sean told him to drop him back off on Broad Street so Aaron headed back up the block. They spotted Sonia standing in front of Miller's pharmacy. Sean hopped out and hugged her, then walked back over to the driver's side of Aaron's car. He reached through the window and gave Aaron a pound. "You be careful, nigga, you hear me? Keep your eyes open."

Aaron nodded and pulled off. He was going to put an end to this shit immediately.

Kaia had fallen asleep on the couch after Aaron left. She awoke with a sharp pain in her stomach. Figuring it was a cramp, she took a deep breath until the pain subsided. Keith had returned home from work and she could hear him moving around in the kitchen. She stood up and began to walk towards the kitchen for some juice. But as she stood, a gush of water escaped her vagina. She looked down and found that her pants were soaked as if she had wet herself and there was a pool of water at her feet.

"KEITH!" she screamed

Keith came running into the living room, wearing a pair of jeans, Timberlands and no shirt and saw Kaia standing in a puddle. "What happened?"

Kaia looked scared. "Beep Aaron," she said. "My water broke."

"You're gonna have the baby now?" Keith now looked just as scared as Kaia. He stood holding a sponge in one hand and a glass in the other. He ran to the kitchen and grabbed the phone and frantically dialed his brother's beeper number. After paging him, he returned to the living room and found Kaia crying.

"What's the matter?" Keith asked her. "Are you in pain?"

"Yes," Kaia muttered through clenched teeth. "I want Aaron."

"I know, Kaia, I beeped him. I'm gonna call Symphany so she can meet us at the hospital. Where's your bag?"

"I don't want to leave without Aaron," Kaia said. She lay back on the couch.

"Girl, I like you a lot, but I'm not delivering your baby in this living room. Now we're going to wait for Aaron to call back and we'll tell him to meet us at the hospital. Then we're getting in the car and I'm taking you to the hospital."

Kaia didn't argue. She closed her eyes and prayed silently. *Hurry up, Aaron. I need you so bad right now.*

Aaron drove slowly along Targee Street looking for Wayne. He hoped to catch the son of a bitch off guard and shoot him at point blank range. It was time he became the hunter instead of the hunted. His pager vibrated on his hip. Stopping at the stoplight on Targee and Vanderbilt, he looked at his pager and saw his home phone number and the code '911' next to it. *'What's going on?'* he wondered.

Once the light turned green, Aaron pulled into the gas station and walked over to the pay phone outside. He dialed his home number and Keith picked up on the first ring.

"What's going on?" Aaron asked.

"Man, you're about to be a father, that's what's going on," Keith answered. "Kaia's water broke and she's having contractions."

Aaron's mouth fell open. "WHAT?!? She's in labor?"

"Yes, Einstein. She's in labor and I'm taking her to the hospital. Meet us there."

Aaron's heart raced. He was about to be a father. "How is she?"

"She's okay, but she's in some pain. Just meet us at Staten Island Hospital. We're leaving now."

"Alright. Yo, Keith..."

"Wassup, man?"

"Thanks a lot for this. I mean that."

Keith smiled. "Don't sweat it. Just bring your behind on to the hospital so you can see your baby born."

"Tell Kaia I love her."

"I will. See you in a minute."

"Peace." Aaron hung up the phone and turned to walk back to his car. When he turned around he was staring down the barrel of a Gloch 9.

Wayne stared icily at Aaron as he held the gun in his face.

"I never liked a snitch nigga," Wayne said menacingly.

Thoughts raced through Aaron's head at lightning speed. *Should I reach for my gun? Should I try to run?*

Figuring it was too late to do either of these things, Aaron stood still and stared at Wayne. "I didn't snitch on you, man," Aaron said, calmly.

"You was supposed to be my man and shit," Wayne continued. "Trusted you and shit. Now you act like you the man around here. Driving through like you running things. Fuck you."

Wayne cocked the gun and, as he did, Aaron reached in his waistband and pulled out his gun. Ducking behind the pay phone, Aaron opened fire at the same time as Wayne. They exchanged gunfire as people ran for cover. As Wayne tried to duck for cover, he was hit in the leg.

Seeing Wayne fall, Aaron took aim and shot him in the chest. As Wayne lay sprawled on the pavement bleeding, Aaron stood back and whispered, "Happy Valentine's Day, motherfucker!"

Aaron jumped back in his car and sped off down Vanderbilt Avenue and turned on Osgood. As the sirens blared in the distance, he felt no remorse. He felt nothing at all. It was kill or be killed and the best man won.

As he sped down the narrow block he noticed the sound of the sirens seemed to get closer and closer. Glancing in his rearview mirror he saw several blue and white police cars chasing him. Before he knew it there were police everywhere. They had him cornered and there was nowhere to run.

"Push, Kaia," Symphany coached her friend. She wiped the sweat from Kaia's forehead and told her to breathe. The nurse held one of Kaia's hands while Symphany held the other and together, they encouraged Kaia to push as the doctor instructed.

"Where is Aaron?" Kaia asked, breathlessly, during a break in contractions.

The nurse looked helplessly at Symphany. Kaia had been in labor for four hours and there had been no sign of Aaron. Symphany had run out of explanations and was now just as concerned as Kaia. "He'll be here, Kaia, but right now you have to push this beautiful baby of yours into the world. Now focus and try to remember to breathe like the nurse said."

Another contraction began as the doctor announced that the baby's head was beginning to crown. Looking at Symphany, he said, "Do you want to see?"

Symphany darted down to where the doctor stood and was frozen in astonishment. She could see the top of the baby's head poking out of Kaia's vagina. She was amazed.

"Kaia, I can see the baby," Symphany said.

Kaia managed a smile. "Can you tell it to hurry up?"

Symphany laughed. "Kaia, your baby has a lot of hair. So much curly hair."

As another contraction began, the doctor told Kaia to push long and hard. Kaia obeyed and after a few more strong pushes, the baby was born.

"It's a girl, Kaia," the doctor announced. Symphany stood with her hand over her mouth as the baby wriggled and cried. Kaia smiled, exhausted.

"Kaia, she's beautiful," Symphany managed, as tears fell from her eyes.

Kaia was teary-eyed, too. Her emotions were mixed. She was overjoyed at the birth of her daughter. But where was Aaron? What could have caused him to miss the birth of their child?

The doctor turned to Symphany. "Would you like to cut the cord?" he asked.

"Yes!" Symphany followed the doctor's instructions carefully and snipped the umbilical cord. The nurse took the baby to be weighed and cleaned up. Symphany went to her friend's side.

"Kaia," she said. "Aaron will be here soon, I'm sure. You did a really great job, girl. She's beautiful."

Kaia smiled through tears as the nurse brought the baby to her wrapped in a pink blanket. Kaia's face beamed. "Oh, she's so beautiful. She's so precious."

Symphany nodded in agreement. "Did you decide on a name?" Kaia stroked the baby's sleeping face. "Yes. Aaron wanted to name her Phoenix. I wanted to name her after his mother so we compromised. Her name is Phoenix Grace."

The nurse came to take the baby while the doctor prepared to perform an episiotomy on Kaia.

"Kaia, I'm going to go now and when you wake up in recovery, me and Aaron will be there, okay?"

Somehow, Kaia felt that Symphany was mistaken. She couldn't imagine what would make Aaron miss this moment but she had a feeling he would not be there when she awoke. She watched tearfully as Symphany walked out of the room.

In the waiting room, Keith was pacing back and forth. Talia and Giselle sat in the hard waiting room chairs and tried to concentrate on the small television instead of wondering where Aaron was.

Symphany entered looking both angry and exuberant.

"She had a girl."

Keith smiled. Talia and Giselle were overjoyed "Is Kaia okay?"

Symphany nodded. "Yeah she's fine. Where the hell is Aaron?"

Keith shook his head. "I don't know where he is. I beeped him so many times and he never called back. When I spoke to him, he said he was on his way. I don't know what could be keeping him. But I'm going to go home and see if he left a note or something."

When they all reached the lobby, they noticed Sean walking towards them with a sullen expression on his face.

"Yo, Keith, I gotta talk to you, man." Sean said, placing a hand on his shoulder.

"What happened?" Keith asked. "Where the hell is my brother?"

Sean's eyes were glued to the floor. He finally looked apologetically at Keith. "Yo, Keith, I've been trying to get in touch with you for hours, man."

Keith was puzzled. "Get in touch with me for what?" Just as the words left his lips, Keith's heart sank and he began to put two and two together. Aaron hadn't made it to Kaia's bedside. He hadn't returned Keith's calls. And now here was his friend telling him that he had been trying to find Keith for hours. Keith's heart thundered in his chest.

"Where's my brother, Sean?" he asked.

"He got locked up, man. He shot Wayne on Targee Street and 5-0 got him."

Symphany threw her hands in the air and flopped down in the nearest chair.

Keith stared at Sean in disbelief.

"Explain this to me, Sean. From the beginning."

Sean recounted the story to Keith as Symphany cried uncontrollably. How was she going to break this news to her friend? Giselle and Talia looked dismayed. They all knew this meant that they'd have to really help Kaia with the baby now that Aaron could be gone for a very long time.

When Sean finished telling Keith what had happened, Keith was like a zombie. He heard the voices of everyone around him but he wasn't listening. All he could think about was the fact that his little brother, whom he had promised his mother and grandmother he would take care of, was in jail for murder. His niece would probably have to grow up without her father. Kaia had nobody. How had he let this happen?

Symphany stood and walked over to the window. She collected herself and tried to get her emotions in check. She would have to face Kaia sooner or later. It might as well be now. But what would she tell her? What would Kaia do now? What about Phoenix? How had everything gone so wrong?

Kaia couldn't imagine what could have possibly caused Aaron to not show up. The baby cried softly in her arms and Kaia looked closely at Phoenix for any resemblance to her beloved Aaron. She held the baby's hand in hers and smiled. This child was their completion...the period at the end of their sentence.

'Maybe he decided that he doesn't want to be a father after all.' Kaia's thoughts raced as she thought of a possible excuse for Aaron's absence.

Just then, a nurse appeared in the doorway accompanied by Symphany. Kaia smiled at her friend, who stood in the doorway with tears in her eyes. Symphany managed a weak smile in return as she approached her friend's bedside and stroked her newborn niece's curly hair.

"Ms. Wesley, I will take the baby for her feeding so that you can have some time with your friend," the nurse said. As she lifted the baby out of Kaia's arms, Kaia noticed the knowing look the nurse exchanged with Symphany. Kaia sensed that something was wrong. Symphany sat beside her on the bed as the nurse exited the room.

Kaia wasted no time asking questions. "Where is Aaron?"

Symphany choked back the tears, which threatened to plunge from her eyes. She couldn't look at Kaia. She couldn't face her knowing that the news she had to tell her would destroy her.

Kaia noticed her friend's struggle and her heart began to beat audibly. Something was terribly wrong. "Symphany, where is Aaron?"

Symphany shook her head. She couldn't do this. Just as she was about to break down and cry, Keith walked in followed by Talia and Giselle. Kaia noticed his eyes were puffy as if he'd been crying. She sat up in the bed.

"Keith," she said in a voice barely audible. "Where is Aaron?"

Keith looked at Symphany and realized that the burden of delivering the news to Kaia, would fall on his shoulders. He walked over to Kaia and took her hand.

"Kaia, there's no easy way for me to tell you this," he began. His voice cracked and Kaia's hands began to tremble. Keith continued, "You have to remember that we need you to be strong for your baby."

Kaia was sick of the guessing game. "KEITH!" she yelled. "Where is Aaron? Tell me now!"

Keith took a deep breath. "Aaron was in Park Hill when I told him to meet us at the hospital. Wayne's out of jail now and he saw Aaron using the phone. After he hung up with me, the two of them had a shootout."

Kaia gasped and covered her face with her hands.

"Kaia, Wayne died at the scene. But Aaron is alright. He's in jail, though and he's being charged with murder." The room fell silent.

Everyone held their breath and waited for Kaia's reaction. She sat frozen with her hands covering her face for several seconds. Then she cried hysterically. It was a sound that made Symphany's blood curdle. Keith held Kaia in his arms and rocked her as she cried.

"Noooooo!!!! What am I supposed to do? What am I supposed to do?"

Nurses entered the room and attempted to calm Kaia down. Symphany cried as the nurses physically restrained Kaia, who was flailing wildly. Symphany wished she had warned Kaia sooner about the beef brewing between Aaron and Wayne. Symphany had heard that the word on the street that Aaron was in danger if Wayne ran into him. She had hoped it wouldn't come to this. But she was grateful for Kaia and the baby that Aaron had been the one taken away from the scene in handcuffs rather than a body bag.

"Kaia," Keith fought to keep his emotions under control. He had to be strong for Kaia. Aaron would want that. "Kaia!"

Kaia finally stopped fighting the nurses. Her body went limp and she lay on the bed in a fetal position. She moaned softly and tears cascaded down her face. "Aaron," she moaned. "Why did you leave me? Why did you leave me?"

Keith stroked her hair. "He didn't leave you, Kaia. He would be here if he could." He paused. "Kaia, me and you have to be strong for her. We owe it to Aaron to hold it together for the baby."

Kaia lay silent. Her body continued to be wracked with sobs and she shook uncontrollably. The nurse gave her two pills to make her sleep and Symphany and the girls stayed with her until she drifted off.

Kaia awoke an hour later with Symphany at her side. She hoped that when she awoke, she would find that it had all been just a nightmare. But it wasn't.

Symphany smiled reassuringly at her friend. "Hey, honey, are you alright?"

Kaia sat up slowly. "Can you call the nurse? Ask her to bring Phoenix." Her voice was flat, emotionless. Symphany had never seen her friend look so helpless. So lifeless. So empty.

Symphany summoned the nurse and asked her to bring in the baby. "Kaia," she said softly. "We're going to get through this. We're going to work together and we're going to get through this."

Kaia sat in silence. She didn't respond. So many thoughts were racing through her head all at the same time. When would she be able to see Aaron? How soon would he get out of jail? She had to find someplace to stay. There was no way she could return to Keith's house without Aaron. She didn't feel right burdening Keith with her and her child. She had no money. She had no plan. All she had was pain.

The nurse entered carrying the baby in a tight bundle of blankets. Symphany stood.

"Kaia, do you want to be alone with her?" she asked.

Kaia nodded and stared at the beautiful newborn in her arms. Symphany left quietly, followed by the nurse.

Kaia gazed at her child sleeping innocently in her arms. What a beautiful child they'd made. She caressed the baby's tiny hands as her eyes welled up with tears. "Hi, Phoenix," she said, her voice quivering. "Looks like it's me and you against the world."

She held the baby close to her and cried silently. She faced the fact that the weight of Phoenix's world was on her shoulders. She had a huge responsibility and a broken heart to match.

Kaia thought about Aaron's words. *'I will never be away from you.'* But he was. He was so far away from her and she had never felt so hopeless.

The raindrops tapped the windowpanes like the rhythm of drums. The stillness that echoed through the storm calmed Kaia. It was the day of Aaron's sentencing.

She wore her hair pulled back in a ponytail. Dressed in all black, she donned her shades and prepared to attend the hearing at which Aaron's fate would be decided. He had pled guilty to voluntary manslaughter and weapons possession. He had originally been charged with second degree murder but had copped a plea at the advice of his lawyer. The evidence against him was too powerful for him to try to beat it. He knew that even with the lesser charge of voluntary manslaughter he was still facing quite a few years behind bars. When Kaia had spoken to Aaron after she and the baby were released from the hospital, he had sounded defeated, crushed. He told her that he loved her and he didn't expect her to wait for him.

Kaia was angry with him and felt sorry for him at the same time. She was angry because his decisions had cost them both dearly. Now she was forced to take care of the baby by herself and find a way to survive. But she knew that he had good intentions. He thought he was doing the right thing and he stood by her when it seemed the world had turned its back on her. How could she hold that against him?

Symphany held baby Phoenix in her arms and spoke quietly to her friend.

"Kaia, the car is outside. Are you ready to go?"

Kaia continued to stare out the window and shook her head. "Can I have a minute?"

"I'll take the baby to the car. You take your time." Symphany left, shutting the door quietly behind her.

Kaia glanced around the room. This had been her haven. This room had been the place she'd given herself to Aaron - the place where they'd conceived their daughter. This home had been one into which Aaron had welcomed her with open arms. Now he was gone. And she could no longer remain there. She had decided to move out. It would be better that way. Keith had protested, but Kaia knew it would be easier without her being there to complicate things. She would miss this house as much as she missed Aaron. But she had to leave. She had to learn to stand on her own two feet.

Keith had given Kaia the money that Aaron had saved. Kaia wanted to share it with him, knowing that Keith was as important to Aaron as she was. But Keith wouldn't hear of it. So, Kaia took the money and used some of it to rent an apartment for her and Phoenix. She chose to remain on Staten Island so that Keith could maintain a close relationship with his niece and so that she could finish school. In four months, she would graduate from high school and Aaron wouldn't be there. Kaia felt so alone.

She opened the window and let the February air fill the room. The wind whispered in her ear and nudged her cheeks. The cold air filled her lungs.

And Kaia wept.

She wept because fairy tales do not exist. She wept for dreams unrealized. She wept because she'd yet to see a sky dipped in blue instead of gray.

Her tears were salty with the bitterness of heartache. Her body convulsed uncontrollably. Her hands trembled. The earth ceased to spin.

And she wept. All the while, wrapping herself in an invisible cocoon, determined to survive the storm.

PART TWO
Cocoon

Dangling upside down
Suspended in time
Encased in a shell called Seclusion
Imprisoned in my mind
Wrapped in invisible layers
Encompassed by the pain
Shrouded in uncertainty
Drenched by spiritual rain

Chapter Six

Everyday it Rains

Kaia tore open the envelope and clasped the letter tightly to her chest. She held it in front of her and looked at her name scribbled in Aaron's distinctive handwriting. She looked at the date in the upper right hand corner and her heart sank. *November 2, 1995.* It had been more than three years since Aaron's incarceration. She missed him like crazy.

She sat down on the sofa in her modest two-bedroom apartment on Trantor Place and read the letter from the man who still held the keys to her heart. Aaron's letters were like the sun breaking through the clouds to Kaia.

> *What's going on, baby girl? How are you? I'm alright, just a little upset because I lost an important basketball game today, but it isn't anything I can't get over. I received your letter about two days ago and I'm sorry I didn't get right back at cha, but a lot of shit been going on between the c.o.'s and the inmates that has had my head in the wind lately. Anyway, though. Other than all that bullshit, your letter brought smiles to my face as usual. If anything goes wrong at least I'm sure your letters will cheer me up some.*

Kaia smiled. Aaron's letters always made her heart break just a little and at the same time made her feel like the luckiest woman alive. It was often difficult for her to explain this range of emotions to her girls, but the feeling is one that all women who have ever loved a man doing time can understand.

> *It's good to hear that you're doing okay. I worry about you and Phe-Phe all the time. I hate that I had to miss so much of her life because of the stupid mistakes I made. Kaia, I want you to know that I am so ashamed of myself for being in here. This was never part of the plan. I wanted to be able to take care of you and Phe-Phe and*

68

to repay my brother for the sacrifices he made while raising me after my grandmother died. I never took into consideration the possibility that I could wind up in here. But as crazy as it sounds I don't know what I would do different if I had it to do over again. I don't know if I would have done anything different. No job would have paid me enough to do what I did for the baby before she was born. You know it and I know it. I don't have the cradentials (did I spell that right?) to get no good job and I don't have a diploma or nothing. I already had run ins with the law and nobody would have gave me a shot. I think we both know that. I did what needed to be done at the time and I thought it was the right thing to do. Now I see that it caused us more harm than anything and for that I am sorry. Far as that nigga Wayne is concerned, it came down to him or me and I don't regret the decision I made. I hope that don't make you look at me like I'm cold-blooded or nothing like that but that's how I feel. I'd rather be in this hell knowing I will see you and my baby someday than to be six feet deep never seeing you again.

I want you to know that I love you so much. You are a part of me. We're a family – me, you and our beautiful daughter. It hurted me when you brought her to see me and she didn't want to leave. She was crying and all that. I wish I could hold her at night till she falls asleep. I wish I could lay next to you every night and make love to you. Just don't disappear on me, Kaia. I love you and that would be the end for me if you dropped out of my life. I know I fucked up, and you deserve better than this bullshit. But please just stick it out with a nigga. I promise that when I do get out of this hell I ain't never coming back.

Did you hear from your mother yet? I know you said that I shouldn't blame myself for you and her not speaking but I feel that it has a lot to do with me. Before I came into your life I know you and her weren't close but at

69

least she was speaking to you. Now you don't ever see her or talk to her and Phoenix doesn't have a grandmother. I feel real bad about that. I know she's your mother but part of me hates her for what she did to you all those years. And now that your out there by yourself holding Phoenix down all by yourself I feel like shit knowing that you don't even have your mother to fall back on. But what pisses me off the most is knowing that in a way I proved her right. In a way I'm everything she said I was. I'm not there for you and the baby and she gets to have the last laugh. But I hope you know that I do love you more than you might even know.

I'm going to end this letter here before I really get depessed. I just want you to know that I love you and my baby. I miss both of you and I can't wait to be home with both of you. Please tell Keith, Sean and Symphony that I said hi and kiss my little princess for me. Kaia, just keep me in your thoughts. You're always in mine.

Love,
Aaron

Kaia wiped the tears that had fallen from her eyes. She missed Aaron more and more each day. She hated the fact that they had to be so far away from one another. She hated having to raise Phoenix by herself. She hated the fact that her mother had the satisfaction of knowing that Aaron was in jail. It only added insult to injury to know that Janice still had no desire to see her daughter or her granddaughter.

Kaia had managed to survive after Aaron's arrest, but it was no easy task. The money Aaron left behind was enough to last them for a long time. But, there had been times when Kaia had reached out to Keith or to Symphany when she needed them. Symphany had taken on the role of Phoenix's unofficial Godmother.   There had been many times that without being asked Symphany brought over cases of Similac and big boxes of pampers when Phoenix was a baby. Kaia was truly grateful to Symphany for that.   And Talia and Giselle helped out by babysitting whenever Kaia needed to go somewhere. She was able to complete high school by enrolling Phoenix in a day care program for unwed teen mothers. Her determination not to be a statistic propelled her forward. But, it wasn't enough for Janice.

Asha had tried, unsuccessfully, to patch things up between her sister and her mother. She invited both of them over for Thanksgiving dinner the year that Aaron was incarcerated, hoping that once Janice got a look at her beautiful granddaughter her cold heart would melt. Kaia arrived first and began helping Asha prepare the traditional dinner. Asha had gotten married (without even inviting Kaia to the wedding) and, for Kaia, having to watch the happy newlyweds paw at each other while she missed Aaron so terribly was almost too much to bear. Nubia came next with her boyfriend and Kaia couldn't help but notice that Nubia barely spoke to her and then occupied herself with something else. She didn't bother to introduce Kaia to her boyfriend and she didn't behave at all like it had been months since she'd last seen or spoken to Kaia. *'She still can't bare to have a conversation with me.'* Kaia thought. *'Some things never change.'*

Everyone played with gorgeous nine-month-old Phoenix and the mood was festive and warm. Until Janice finally arrived. Stepping into the apartment, she removed her coat and handed it to Asha. But when Janice turned and glanced around the living room and sighted Kaia and the baby, she snatched her coat from Asha and headed for the door.

Asha tried to stop her to no avail. As a last resort, she picked up Phoenix and followed Janice down the stairs until Janice stopped and faced her.

"Why don't you just look at your granddaughter? She's an innocent child? She has nothing to do with you being mad at Kaia!" Asha pleaded.

"I don't want nothing to do with your sister or her kid." Janice answered as she continued down the stairs.

Asha called her mother's name and Janice finally stopped her hasty descent.

"Give Kaia *some* credit! She graduated high school on time. That wasn't easy to do with a baby. She's got her own place. She takes good care of Phoenix. Why are you being so mean to her?"

Janice's voice shook as she spoke words that Asha would never forget and would never have the heart to repeat to Kaia. "That bitch is an embarrassment. She's nothing but a stupid girl who threw her life away over some nigga. Fuck her and keep that kid away from me. She made her choice. Let that son of a bitch be her family."

71

Janice turned and walked down the stairs leaving Asha standing dumbfounded in the stairway. She returned to the apartment and made apologies for her mother's behavior. But Kaia wasn't having it.

"Don't apologize for her, Asha. She's the only one that owes anybody an apology. She's the only person who should be saying they're sorry."

Nubia surprised Kaia by coming to their mother's defense. "Kaia, maybe she acts like that towards you because you made such a mess of your life. She's your mother and it's hard for her to sit by and watch you ruin your life with jailbirds, unwanted pregnancies and those trashy friends of yours."

Nubia's boyfriend looked at her like he had never seen this side of her before. Asha's husband shifted uneasily in his seat. All this family drama was not what he was accustomed to.

Kaia was seething now. All of the emotions she had felt over all of the years of her life began to resurface. This was her sister. And the woman who had just left was her mother. Yet, here they were condemning her for making mistakes. None of them were perfect. But right now Nubia sounded like she was on a pedestal and Kaia had every intention of knocking her off.

"Oh, I see, Nubia. You mean to tell me that Janice has every right to judge me because I fell in love with Aaron and when I found out I was pregnant I decided to keep my baby rather than kill her like she wanted me to? Is that what you're saying?'

Nubia shook her head. "What I'm saying is…"

"What you're saying is bullshit!" Kaia was outraged. She finally had the chance to say what she'd been holding in for years and no one was going to shut her up. "Janice has had it in for me since the day I was born, Nubia. That's why she killed Daddy. He wouldn't treat me like shit so she stuck a knife in his chest."

Nubia really thought that her sister had lost her mind. "What are you talking about, Kaia? You've been brainwashed or you're on drugs. Which is it? Janice stabbed our father because he was beating her ass…"

Asha tried to interrupt. She didn't want all of this being rehashed in front of her new husband. "Can't we just have dinner like a normal family and…"

"Normal family?!?!?!?!?" Kaia laughed out loud at the absurdity of the statement Asha made. "Who in this family is normal? Is it you, Asha? Is it you, Nubia?" Looking directly in Nubia's eyes, she continued,

"Neither one of you was there the day that she killed him. I was. I heard them arguing and I ran in their room to tell them to stop it. Janice slapped me so hard that I fell to the floor and that's when Daddy swung at her. He was defending me, like any father would. But what kind of a mother slaps their child in the face and then runs to the kitchen and grabs a knife? What kind of mother stabs that child's father right before her eyes? Daddy wasn't even touching her when she stabbed him. He was drunk , Nubia, and she had wounded him in the face. Daddy was rolling around on the floor in pain when she stuck that knife in his chest. He never even saw her coming!"

It was Nubia's turn to be outraged now. "How dare you make up lies like that, Kaia!"

"I'm not lying, Nubia. Why do you always follow Janice and believe everything she says? She's even got you believing that I ruined my life and that's not true. My life is what I made it. I am fine with the fact that I had a child before I turned 18. I am fine with the fact that her father is locked up. I am fine with the fact that I didn't get to go to college and marry a man with a PHD. I will never have 2.5 kids, a house with a picket fence and a dog in the yard. That's not my story. But don't you or your mother try to put me down because I didn't live my life according to *your* plans. Everybody makes mistakes, Nubia. Even you. Does it mean that you're better than I am just because you didn't get pregnant in high school? You were still fucking!"

Asha's husband gasped and excused himself from the room. He retreated to the kitchen. He had heard enough. Nubia's boyfriend tried to hide the smirk on his face. This was his first time meeting Kaia and he liked the fact that she was putting her condescending sister in her place.

Kaia wasn't finished. "Just because you didn't' get pregnant doesn't make you superior. And just because you hang around with shallow gold-digging females, doesn't mean that my friends are trash. Don't forget where you came from, sisters." Kaia looked at Asha to let her know that she was referring to her, too. "And before you judge me, take a step back and look at your own skeletons in your own closets." Kaia gathered her and her daughter's belongings. She'd rather spend the holiday alone than with these people who were supposed to be her family.

Kaia tried to keep her game face on but both Asha and Nubia could tell she was hurting. As she put on her coat and walked towards the door, Kaia paused and turned to face her sisters. "And for the record, what I told you about the day Daddy died was not a lie. Someday, maybe your mother will tell you the truth. Until then, you can believe what you want. But all I ever did wrong to any of you was to be myself. Maybe, if I had sisters I could confide in or a mother that I could talk to...just maybe I would have taken a different path in life. But it's easier to call me the black sheep than to sit and think about what you could have done differently. Happy Thanksgiving." And she was gone.

That was the last time Kaia had seen her mother and she had made up her mind that she would make it on her own. But the pain never subsided. It just got pushed to the back of Kaia's mind.

But one thing that never got pushed to the back of her mind was Aaron. Kaia thought of him constantly. She felt guilty for the situation he was in knowing that he did it for her and Phoenix. She felt sorry for him knowing that he had already missed out on important events in his daughter's life – her first crawl, her first step, her first words, her first tooth – and knowing that he would miss out on countless others in the years remaining in his sentence. (Aaron had been sentenced to five years, but could be released on parole in three and a half years with good behavior. He had originally been charged with second degree murder and criminal use of a firearm. At the advice of his attorney, Aaron pled guilty to a lesser charge - manslaughter - and the firearm charge.)

When a caterpillar begins its transformation from an unsightly worm to a colorful insect, it first wraps itself in a cocoon to protect itself from outside forces. Kaia did the same. She wrapped herself in motherhood, work and a rigorous daily routine. She wrapped herself so tightly in these things that she became numb, frozen, anesthetized. Her days consisted of routine and her evenings consisted of waiting by the phone for Aaron's collect calls or writing him letters to keep his spirits up. One weekend a month, she traveled to visit Aaron in the upstate New York Correctional facility in which he was caged. Her life was Aaron. Her life was Phoenix.

Kaia was a terrific mother despite her own lack of a suitable one. She doted on Phoenix and put her all into the roll of motherhood. Phoenix was a beautiful child with Aaron's cocoa complexion and Kaia's long, thick hair. Phoenix was her everything. But aside from Phoenix, Kaia's life was void of joy. There was a blank space where her happiness should have been. There was a vacancy in her spirit that had long been empty. And instead of tending to it, she tried her best to ignore it, filling it instead with the rigors of motherhood and work.

So as a caterpillar begins its metamorphosis and retreats into the confines of a cocoon, Kaia retreated into her own safe haven. One of loneliness and seclusion. A cocoon in which, despite the sadness, she felt security. And though she tried to remain distant and inaccessible to anyone outside of her small circle of friends, she would soon find that into the midst of her secluded world would come another storm.

Chapter Seven

Illusions

Kaia stepped off the elevator on the third floor of the office building in which she worked. Located at the corporate complex known as the Teleport, the company she worked for was a reputable securities firm in Staten Island. She worked as a receptionist and enjoyed the lack of overwhelming responsibility. All she had to do was smile pretty when clients or visitors came in and transfer calls to the appropriate desk. She signed for deliveries and spent much of her day reading, which had always been her favorite pastime. The job paid well and allowed her to shower Phoenix with every luxury a little girl could dream of. Kaia had a good amount of money in the bank, a decent job, a nice car and a precious daughter. She was not exceedingly happy but she was content. Her joy came whenever she was able to visit Aaron in upstate New York's Greene Correctional Facility.   In the meantime, she kept busy with Phoenix and her job.

She walked through the double doors leading to the reception area and sat down at her desk. Sorting through the mail she clicked on her computer and logged into the system. As the morning progressed, she greeted the numerous executives as they reported to work and answered countless phone calls. It wasn't until lunchtime that she got a welcome break from the monotony.

Deciding to take her well-deserved break, Kaia headed to the section of the grounds where smoking was permitted. While she was not a habitual smoker, she decided to indulge in a cigarette for a change. She got one from one of the other receptionists and headed outside.

While standing in the shade puffing away, she noticed a young man standing on the other end of the courtyard. From a distance she couldn't be sure whether she had seen him before but she couldn't help noticing his confident stance. He finished his cigarette and stomped it out. He began walking in Kaia's direction and to her surprise she felt a chill at the thought of being close to him.

As he drew nearer, Kaia couldn't help but stare. Noticing this, he held her gaze as he continued to stride in her direction. Before long, the two were standing nearly face to face as Kaia's heart thundered in her chest. Extending his hand in greeting, the gentleman never took his eyes off hers. Kaia shook his hand and allowed him to hold onto hers as she continued to take in his unforgettable features.

His eyes were a shade of brown similar to Autumn leaves. His smooth skin was the sexiest hue of caramel she'd ever seen. Kaia noticed his jet-black hair was coarse yet possessed a natural curl. His eyebrows were the deepest shade of black and were thick and rich. His short, neatly trimmed goatee barely disguised a scar that began at his right cheekbone and ended at his chin. And his lips were kissable, decadent. She had never been so taken back by any man's looks before.

By the standards of many young ladies her age, he was not what one would consider gorgeous. But to Kaia he was breathtaking, and she couldn't stop staring. He had style. Not the type you see in magazines featuring black male models wearing white boy's clothes. Not the cleaned up version of Hip-Hop style that's displayed in ads for the clothing lines of rap moguls. This man had a style all his own. He held her gaze and her hand as boldly as a man who possessed all the charm in the world and a bank account to match. Kaia didn't have a clue as to who he was, and still she was smitten. Swept off her feet by a roughneck stranger who had only held her hand and never uttered a word.

Finally releasing the grip he had on her hand, the stranger smiled at Kaia and she felt her heart melt. She also felt a tap on her shoulder and turned around to find her friend smiling slyly at her.

"See something you like?" Giselle asked. Kaia rolled her eyes playfully at Giselle and stomped out her cigarette. She felt a twinge of embarrassment for having been caught staring at the mysterious stranger before her.

"I can see you've met Eric." Giselle smiled at her friend's obvious interest in the new employee.

"Hi, Eric. Nice to meet you." Kaia knew that if she was White her face would have been red with embarrassment.

"Nice to meet you, too, Kaia."

Kaia and Giselle looked stunned. " How did you know my name is Kaia?

Eric smiled at the puzzled expressions on the faces of the two women. Part of him wanted to continue the guessing game he was playing with them but he decided not to.

"I'm a friend of Keith's."

Kaia's mouth fell open and Giselle looked away in amazement. Staten Island really was too damn small! Everybody knew everybody.

Kaia was visibly shocked. "Why don't I remember you?" she asked.

Eric smiled. "We never met."

Giselle's nosy ass had enough of the guessing game. "Then how do you know who she is?!?" she demanded.

Eric explained, "I saw you with Keith's brother Aaron a couple of times around the way. I knew you were his girl and I always thought how lucky he was." Eric looked suggestively at Kaia and for moments you could have heard a pin drop.

Finally he stepped back and said, "Okay, ladies. Enjoy your lunch." Looking at Kaia he said, "I'll see you soon."

As she watched him stroll confidently across the courtyard, Kaia fought off the urge to chase after him.

"Talk about chemistry!" Giselle said.

Kaia frowned and shook her head. "Chemistry my ass! I'm taken remember?" she said.

"Yeah but you ain't dead!" Giselle reminded her.

"Come on now, Giselle. He knows Aaron. Any X-rated thoughts I had a minute ago went out the window as soon as he told me that."

"Well then you need to dive out that window and get 'em, girl. That boy is *fine*!"

Kaia laughed. "Giselle, you're too much." Kaia envisioned Eric's sexy ass and mentally agreed with her friend. He *was* fine. "Who is he anyway?"

Giselle smiled mischievously. "He's some new guy working in the mailroom at that insurance company in building two. He just started last week."

"And how did you meet him so fast?" Kaia asked.

"I met him on the elevator. I knew I hadn't seen him before and I introduced myself. You would meet new people, too, if you would stop being so anti-social!"

Kaia took offense. "I'm not anti-anything. I just like to stay around people I know, that's all."

Giselle shook her head disapprovingly. "Come on, Kaia, you never go anywhere, you never want to do anything, you never want to meet anyone, you never..."

"Alright, alright, I get the picture!" Kaia sighed. "I guess I just feel guilty since Aaron is locked up. It seems like I should be holding him down, you know what I mean?"

Giselle shook her head. "You *are* 'holding him down', Kaia. You handle your business like a woman twice your age. You work hard everyday, you take care of your baby, and you write to Aaron and go see him every chance you get. But you're human, girl. How long has it been since you had a man touch you?" I'll tell you how long it's been. Since Aaron got locked up - that's how long it's been, Kaia, and you're depriving yourself of what's natural."

Giselle paused when she noticed that Kaia seemed to be considering her words. "Let me ask you a question, Kaia."

Kaia looked at Giselle. "What?"

"Do you think Aaron would be "holding you down" if you were locked up and he was in society?"

Kaia gave this some thought. Aaron was her heart but she wasn't sure that he could be faithful to her for all these years if she was the one behind bars. But she loved him so much that she couldn't bring herself to admit this to Giselle.

"That's not the point, Giselle." Kaia answered. "I don't want to be involved with anyone right now. I need to focus on raising Phoenix the best way I know how. I'm not concerned about this other cat."

Giselle smiled mischievously. "That's not how it looked a minute ago. Wait till I tell the crew that you finally got your groove back."

Kaia tapped her friend playfully and they headed back toward the office building.

The van rolled through the streets of Upstate New York filled with women en route to visit their loved ones in correctional facilities. The van would make a number of stops at various prisons in close proximity to one another, dropping the women off for their six hour visits and returning to pick them up when the visits were over.

The women had an unspoken bond between them, sharing the long ride from New York City each weekend. Most of them lived within the accessible boroughs (Manhattan, Queens, Brooklyn, and the Bronx). But for those who lived in the outer borough of Staten Island, they had to meet the van at one of the stops along its route. So Kaia and Phoenix left Staten Island at 5:00 in the morning and caught the Staten Island Ferry to downtown Manhattan. Then they took the subway to 125th Street and Lexington and caught the van bound for the Upstate prisons. The ride Upstate was about 3 hours long and many of the women and children, including Kaia and Phoenix, took this opportunity to catch up on sleep. But not before tying their hair up in scarves to protect their flawless hairstyles.

The driver announced the first stop. "Greene." Kaia awoke the sleeping Phoenix and gathered her belongings to begin the visit. She entered the facility, locked her purse in the locker and proceeded to the correction officer's desk. There, she showed her ID and filled out the visitor's form. She handed over the package she had brought for Aaron and watched while the officer examined its contents. Next came the metal detectors which she and Phoenix were required to pass through. Finally gaining clearance to enter the visiting room, she and Phoenix passed through two sets of doors to a visiting room filled with plastic chairs and vending machines. They found a table in the corner and waited for Aaron to come through the door where the inmates came in.

Moments later, Aaron made his entrance. Dressed in his prison-issued jumpsuit, he looked so much older and more mature than the eighteen-year-old young man who had entered this hell three years ago. He was heavier now from years of lifting weights and playing basketball. He had a more confident swagger than he once did and his face told the tale of a man who had lived a hard life. But he was still *fine!*

He strode over to the table where Kaia and Phoenix sat and that familiar smile graced his chiseled face. Kaia rose to her feet and hugged her man, holding him as if she'd never let go. Aaron held her just as tightly all the while smiling over her shoulder at his beautiful baby girl. Phoenix smiled back and Aaron felt his heart melt. After sharing kisses with Kaia, Aaron sat and stretched out his arms. Phoenix ran to him and threw her arms around his neck.

"Daddy!!" she exclaimed. "I miss you, Daddy."

Aaron's eyes began to water. Kaia smiled at the sight of father and daughter bonding under such grim circumstances. Phoenix curled up in her father's lap and lay her head against his chest. Aaron cradled her like that for the rest of the visit.

Looking at Kaia he said, "She's getting so big." Kaia could tell by the look on his face that Aaron wanted nothing more than to be home with them. She understood his pain because she wanted him home just as much. Aaron stroked Phoenix's hair as she snuggled against his muscular chest. He winked at Kaia and smiled again.

"You look as beautiful as ever, Miss."

Kaia returned the smile and was grateful that he had noticed. She always wore her best outfits when she came to see Aaron. She knew that he replayed each visit over and over in his head after he returned to his cell. She wanted all his thoughts of her to be at times when she looked her best. Today she was wearing a pair of skintight jeans with a sheer blue blouse. She had gotten her hair and nails done the day before. Her eyebrows were waxed to perfection and her makeup was flawless. Phoenix, too was dressed in one of her cutest outfits. She wore a baby blue Guess jumper with a white turtleneck underneath. Her cute little baby blue Weeboks completed the outfit.

"You don't look so bad yourself, handsome."

Aaron smiled. "Wait till I get out. Then I'll be able to show you 'handsome'." He paused and held Kaia's gaze for a few moments. "Yo, I can't wait to take you out to dinner or something like that when I come home. I want to see you get all dressed up and put your hair up and everything. I miss going places with you, Kaia."

Kaia smiled. "In a minute, baby. Soon you'll be back home where you belong and we can go out every weekend if you want to." She tried to sound optimistic to lighten the mood.

Aaron shook his head. "Kaia, it's like hell in here, girl."

Not knowing what to say, Kaia opted to just listen without speaking. Aaron had never spoken so candidly about what it was like for him in prison. Usually when she asked him he would remind her that he was a man and he could handle it. She had pressed him at times to tell her if he was having fights or if what she had seen on prison documentaries on cable TV were accurate portrayals of the real thing. Each time, Aaron had evaded her questions with a grin, telling her not to worry about him. He could handle himself in there.

Aaron continued, "I stay to myself, you know what I'm saying? I don't get in no real beefs because I don't fuck with nobody in here. Nobody really bothers you as long as you don't give them a real reason to. I had one fight the whole time I've been in here. That was with some Puerto Rican dude who tried to tell me I couldn't use the phone. Even that wasn't nothing cuz they wound up transferring him out. But lately...maybe it's because I'm *real* homesick right now...the holidays are coming, my baby is three years old now and I want to be home spending the holidays with her and you...all I know is my temper is real short all of a sudden. I find myself looking around my cell wondering how the fuck my life got so messed up and hating myself for being in this place. I sit around and think about you and about Phoenix and I wind up crying like a little bitch. I just want to be home, man."

A tear fell from Aaron's eye and slid down his left cheek. It was the first time Kaia had ever seen Aaron cry in all the years that she'd known him. Aaron discreetly wiped his face, obviously not wanting to be seen showing emotion in front of the other inmates in the visiting room. Kaia sat speechless listening to Aaron share what it was like for him. She wanted to break down and cry but fought back the tears that threatened to plunge from her eyes. She needed to be strong for Aaron. He needed her right now.

"Aaron, I know this shit ain't easy for you. I know it's not. I sit up at night sometimes and cry because I know it can't be easy for you." Kaia's voice cracked with emotion but she was determined not to break down in front of Aaron. "I know it's fucked up that you have to spend the holidays in this place. I know it's fucked up that we can't wake up together on Christmas morning and watch Phoenix open her presents together. But all of that will happen for us. It's not going to be like this forever."

Aaron nodded and managed a slight grin. "I know. I guess I sound like a real punk talking like that, huh?"

Kaia could tell that Aaron was actually embarrassed that he had shown weakness in front of her. "Shut up, Aaron. Me and you have been through all types of shit together and you're worried about whether or not you sound like a punk for telling me exactly what I've been wanting you to tell me all these years? Come on now, we're bigger than that."

Phoenix lay in Aaron's arms stroking his face as if in awe of her good-looking father. Aaron smiled at his little princess and then looked into Kaia's eyes. "Yo, I love the shit out of you, girl." Don't forget that, you hear me?"

"I love you, too, Aaron. You don't have to worry about that." Kaia reached for his hand and held it in hers.

Aaron sat with his daughter in his lap and the love of his life at his side and realized how lucky he was. It had been three years already and the remainder of his sentence could range anywhere from six more months to two more years. Kaia had been there through it all...bringing Phoenix to see him as often as possible. Phoenix had gotten to know her father through these visits, and Aaron was grateful to Kaia for making the long journey upstate each month. Those visits were like oxygen to Aaron. They made his life worth living despite his circumstances. It was through those visits that he was able to witness his daughter's transformation from a newborn to a walking and talking toddler. He loved Kaia for that. He loved her more because he had never heard one report of her ever messing with any other guy while he'd been locked up. His brother and Sean gave him constant updates on Kaia and Phoenix's well being. There was no question in Aaron's mind that he would marry her as soon as he tasted freedom.

Kaia pulled out a deck of cards and smiled playfully at Aaron. "Come on, boy. Let me show you how much I've been practicing."

Aaron smiled back and rubbed his hands together. "Show me whatcha got!"

Arriving home after her visit with Aaron, Kaia's spirits were lifted. She took off Phoenix's coat and her own and hung them in the closet. While Phoenix went to her room to play with her favorite dolls Kenya and Addy, Kaia decided to call her friends. Maybe they could all get together for some much-needed bonding.

Kaia had to admit that she missed the vibe of all her girls being together. In high school they saw each other every day. But after graduations (some graduated later than others but they all graduated), they found themselves wrapped up in their own lives. It was a rare occasion that got them all together.

Symphany was the first one that Kaia called. Kaia hadn't heard from Symphany in weeks. Symphany was always on the go so no one thought anything of her disappearances anymore. But the last time Kaia had spoken to her, Symphany had told her about her plans to move into her own home, and she had done just that. Symphany had recently purchased a nice house on Regis Drive and she had yet to invite the crew over to see the place. Kaia waited anxiously for Symphany to answer the phone.

Finally, Symphany answered amid the sound of "C.R.E.A.M." by Wu Tang Clan blaring from what sounded like twenty speakers. "HELLO?" Symphany screamed over the volume.

"Girl, turn that shit down!" Kaia had to scream through the receiver.

"HOLD ON," Symphony lowered the volume on her Sony entertainment center equipped with 16" speakers. "Hello?" she finally returned to the phone.

"Girl, what's up?" Kaia asked, sitting down on her couch and curling her feet beneath her.

"Hey, Kaia! What's going on with you?" Symphony sounded happy to hear from her friend.

Kaia laughed. "Nothing new. I should be asking you that question since you're the one moving into a new house on Regis Drive!"

"Girl, please. All this moving is making me sick. You never realize how much stuff you have until you move."

"Where are you working at these days?" Suddenly, Kaia wondered how Symphony could afford to buy a house at the age of twenty-one. To Kaia's knowledge, Symphony had *never* had a job. Not in high school and not after graduation, either. But, surely Symphony must have landed a big job if she could afford to buy a house! Lately, Kaia had wondered more and more how Symphony managed to have so much money at her disposal. Something wasn't adding up.

"Working?"

"Did I stutter? How do you afford to live on *Regis Drive*?" Kaia couldn't hide her thirst for details.

"You're asking an awful lot of questions. Who you working for at the Teleport? Barbara Walters?" Symphony stretched out on her chenille sofa.

Kaia was undaunted. "Ha, ha, ha. You're funny. Really, Symphony, why are you being so secretive?"

"Cuz I have to be careful what I say these days, that's why. I'll tell you, but not on the phone. What are you doing later on?"

Kaia seized the opportunity. "Well, how about we all get together and have drinks or something? I can call Talia and Giselle and we can meet somewhere."

"Wow, what is this a reunion?" Symphony laughed. She missed times like this when her friends would hang out and catch up on each other's lives. She certainly had a lot more to tell them now. She looked around her new home. She was proud of what she had managed to accomplish and this was the perfect setting for her to tell them what was on her mind. She said, "Alright, Kaia, round up the girls and come to my house at nine o'clock."

Chapter Eight

Revelations

Kaia packed Phoenix an overnight bag and dropped her off at her Uncle Keith's house. Phoenix loved to hang out with her fun-loving uncle and he doted on her as if she were his own. Kaia hadn't taken him up on his offer to baby-sit anytime she needed a break. This was the perfect opportunity.

Kaia drove over to Talia's house on Union Avenue. Talia's father had died two years earlier and left enough money to his wife for her to finally afford to move out of the projects. Talia said it was the one thing he did right his whole life. Now, Talia and her mother shared a cozy two-story house on the relatively quiet street. Talia was waiting on the steps and walked over when Kaia pulled up in the Sable.

"Wassup, girl?" Talia fastened her seatbelt and checked her reflection in the mirror. "Did you get in touch with Giselle?"

"Yeah, we have to go and pick her up now." Kaia headed for Giselle's apartment in Arlington.

They sang along to "One More Chance" by the Notorious B.I.G. as they drove along. Kaia pulled up in front of 35 Holland Avenue where Giselle was leaning on the fence smoking a cigarette.

"Get yo ass in the car," Talia playfully ordered her friend.

"Hold your horses. Do you like these boots? I just got them yesterday." Giselle sauntered over to the car.

"Damn, Giselle, say 'hello' before you start bragging for a change." Kaia was letting Giselle get on her nerves already.

"Meeeow!!" Giselle hissed at Kaia and they all broke out in laughter.

"Let me turn this shit up before I put her behind out of my car." Kaia laughed, reached for the radio dial and blasted Mary J. Blige's "Be Happy" all the way to Symphany's house.

They pulled into the driveway and Giselle could hardly wait until Kaia put the car in park before she bolted toward the front door. Talia and Kaia exchanged glances that said it all. Giselle couldn't hide her enthusiasm. When Symphany opened the door, they stepped into what looked like money and smelled like a long story. Everything was plush and pricey. Statuettes and authentic masks and swords that looked like they'd been bought in the islands or the Motherland. Plush carpet so thick you felt elevated. Cashmere throws and exotic plants. It made them all wonder how Symphony could afford to live so lavishly.

"Wow." Giselle broke the silence.

"Exactly." Talia's chin hit the floor.

"Where did you get all this stuff, Symphany?" Kaia cut to the chase.

"I knew y'all were going to act like reporters as soon as you came in..." Symphany protested.

"Ain't no reporters, Symphany! We're family, right?"

Symphany couldn't help but smile at them. Since graduating high school, they hadn't all gotten together as often as they would have liked. Kaia was a busy mom and Talia was a full time student at the College of Staten Island studying to be an accountant. Giselle had so many men to juggle and they all had lives of their own. But Symphany realized how much she had missed them. They hadn't changed a bit. "I missed y'all. Come inside, let me show you around and then I'll play "20 Questions" if that's what y'all want to do."

She didn't have to say it twice. The girls followed her like obedient school children through all the rooms of the split-level home. They noticed that each room looked tastefully decorated...perhaps professionally decorated. After the tour, the girls settled in the dining room in high-backed mahogany chairs. The matching table was the resting-place for the glasses of wine each girl was given as Symphany played hostess. Giselle was the first to break the ice.

"Symphany, we don't mean to be nosy or anything, but..."

Symphany interrupted. "I know you're curious and I'll tell you what you want to know about me. You're my *friends,* and I trust you. But you have to swear that you'll keep your mouths shut. Nobody repeats shit that gets said in this house tonight. Deal?"

"Deal," came the chorus.

Symphany continued. "We always used to say that the four of us are like a fist, right? Well, here's the test." Symphany took her seat at the head of the table and began her tale:

Y'all know I didn't grow up like any of you. Talia always had her moms. Giselle has family all over Staten Island. And, Kaia, even though

*your moms is fucked up – no disrespect – but
you had Aaron and now you have Phoenix.
Well I always had nobody but me. My mother
worked about 20 hrs a day to feed me and my
brother. Then he got locked up, and it was me
and me alone. The streets raised me. I
learned the art of survival. That's how I got
introduced to the game.*

*I started cutting class with Sean when we first
got together in junior year. That's when he was
hustling for Big Dog in the Hill. Sometimes I
went with him to places to pick up shit or drop
off shit and he showed me the ropes. Made me
like his right hand chick or whatever. The sex
was good, but it didn't take me long to realize
that he wasn't the settling down type. After all, I
knew Sonia was pregnant with his baby when I
started messing with him. That showed me a
lot right there.*

Kaia shifted uneasily in her seat. She had always been
uncomfortable with Symphany's relationship with Sean. Even though
Symphany was her partner in crime, Sonia was cool, too. Kaia always felt
caught in the middle. Symphany continued:

*Anyway, since we had formed a business
relationship and a personal relationship, when
the personal part fell away the business
continued. When I moved out of my mom's
house, I started making runs for him. Down to
VA and back. A couple of times I even got to go
to the islands for him. All I had to do was
pretend to be a young lady on vacation with my
man. I would usually travel on the weekends
and none of you even noticed I was gone.
Everyone was busy with their own life. It was
perfect. The money was good and I liked the*

*travel. Aaron would meet me at the airport to
make the exchange and...*

"Aaron? What do you mean Aaron?" Kaia couldn't believe her ears. Symphany had known all of this and had never shared one detail with Kaia. Not once had Symphany ever let on that she was so much a part of Aaron's hustling lifestyle.

"Kaia, let me finish, please." Symphany continued...

*Aaron would meet me at the airport and we would make
the exchange. He would take the product so his
workers could package it and distribute it. I would take
the money to Sean and Big Dog.*

*Well, about three months before Aaron got bagged, Big
Dog got mirked over some stupid dice game. That
meant that Sean was now the new "Big Dog", Aaron
was Top Dog and I moved up in the ranks, too. So
money was flowing, things were jumping off and then
BOOM! Aaron gets bagged.*

*So, after Aaron's sentencing, me and Sean went on as
best we could. By then, we had all made a nice amount
of money. The difference between me and Sean is that
I saved my money. I figured as long as I could pay the
rent for the apartment I had, I was good. Now, I have a
nice nest egg and I was able to buy this place. I bought
my first home while I'm still in my early twenties. To
me, that's quite an accomplishment. Sean ain't making
the same money we made in the beginning. Aaron
was forced to get out of the game by getting locked up.
I decided that now it's time for me to get out of the
game before I get forced out of it the same way Aaron
did. This is my official retirement party so to speak.*

Symphany paused.

*Anyway, Sean is still running things out here. All the
spots in Stapleton, Park Hill, and West Brighton are his.*

> *Aaron might take New Brighton when he comes home.*
> *That is, if he still chooses to hustle..."*

Kaia had heard enough. "Symphany what do you know about "when Aaron comes home"? How can you sit there and tell me that all of this time, you were involved with all of this and you never told me shit?"

Symphany tilted her head to the side like she was confused by her friend's anger. "Kaia, it wasn't my place to tell you nothing that Aaron didn't choose to tell you himself..."

Kaia wasn't having it. "What do you mean it wasn't your *place* to tell me, Symphany??? I ASKED YOU!!" Kaia's voice echoed off the walls in the spacious dining room. "You said that you only knew what I knew. What type of tricky language is that?"

Talia came to Symphany's defense. "Kaia, you act like you didn't know that Aaron was hustling. Why are you acting so shocked?"

Kaia glared at Talia. "Because I didn't know that one of my "friends" knew so much about my man and I never knew shit."

Talia held Kaia's gaze. "Perhaps you should be mad at your man, then."

Silence filled the room. Kaia let Talia's words sink in. Despite the fact that she was pissed, she had to admit that Talia had a point. Talia and Symphany waited for Kaia's reaction. Giselle held her breath and waited for the fireworks.

Like a cat pouncing on its prey, Talia sunk her claws in deeper. "Wasn't Aaron the one who owed you and explanation? I'm not saying that Symphany wasn't wrong for not mentioning her secret career to us – especially since we're supposed to be friends..." Talia shot Symphany a sideways glance. "But you can't be mad at her for not telling you what your man was up to. If I knew I probably wouldn't have told you either."

"Well, Talia, that tells me a lot about you." Kaia was tight! She couldn't believe Talia was taking up for Symphany. "I always thought that friends don't keep secrets. First, I find out that my best friend has been selling drugs and trafficking them from state to state. Then, I find out that she knew more about Aaron's business than I *ever* did. Maybe I'm naïve, Talia, but I thought Aaron was doing low-level hustling. Symphany's making it sound like they had some "New Jack City" shit going on. Aaron has been 'Nino Brown' all this time and I knew nothing." Kaia felt deceived.

Talia was unfazed. "I still think that you should be mad at Aaron for that. He's the only one who owes you an explanation for what he was doing. Symphany wasn't hiding the fact that he was a drug dealer from you. You already knew that. She just never told you exactly how much money he was making."

Giselle's antennae went up. "Yeah. Exactly how much money *was* he making, Symphany?"

Symphany scowled at Giselle. "What difference does that make, Giselle?"

Giselle stuck to her guns. "Well it made a difference between you renting an apartment and buying a house, didn't it?"

Symphany ignored her. "All that matters, girls, is that I am not going to hustle anymore. I'm retiring. Kaia, I apologize if you feel that I should have told you what Aaron was up to. But, I honestly didn't think it was my place to tell you if he didn't tell you himself. Believe me, if I had a feeling that he was holding out on you financially, I would have told you. But he got y'all that car and he bought everything Phoenix needed before she was even born. So I stayed out of it. You knew he was making money. Maybe you didn't know all the details but there are some details you wouldn't want to know. Trust me. I would have told you if I thought he was disrespecting you in any way, Kaia. You have my word on that."

Despite her anger, Kaia was somewhat soothed by Symphany's words. She knew that her friend had her best interests at heart. But it still disturbed her that Aaron had been so involved in the crack game. "How can you decide what I should and shouldn't know, Symphany?"

"I'm just saying that Aaron did right by you. He wasn't fucking around behind your back. He was taking care of you. I didn't think it was my place to tell you that he had beef with "so and so" or that he shot at "so and so". That was for him to tell you."

Kaia had to admit that Symphany made sense. Aaron was the one who owed her his honesty. She smiled weakly at Symphany. "No more secrets, bitch."

Symphany laughed and the other girls breathed a collective sigh of relief. "I promise no more secrets."

Giselle still hadn't gotten an answer that she considered satisfactory. "Good, so you can stop keeping a secret about how much money you have in the bank."

Symphany turned and looked Giselle directly in the eyes. "Girl, sometimes you get on my last nerve."

"All I'm saying is why tell half the story? Just tell us how much money you have." Giselle had absolutely no home training.

Symphany sighed. She always gave much thought to what came out of her mouth. She pondered the question for a moment. Noticing that Giselle was still waiting for an answer, she continued. "I said there would be no more secrets so I will tell you that I made enough money to let my mother quit that fucked up job she had. I can afford to take some time to decide what I want to do with my life and that's just what I'm going to do." She hoped that would end the questions. She had no such luck.

Talia nodded her head. "Symphany, can I borrow $20?" she joked.

Symphany threw a dishcloth at her friend and invited them into her living room. The girls stretched out across the sofa, chaise lounge and the thick carpet as Talia rolled a blunt. "Where did you get this weed, Symphany? In Jamaica?" Talia was on a roll with her comedy routine.

"Nah, Bahamas!" Symphany shot back as she stuck her middle finger up at Talia. Symphany couldn't help feeling elated that her girls were all together. Just like the good ole days! They got high as they discussed the events unfolding in each other's lives. Talia was almost done with college. Talia was now in her third year at the College of Staten Island. She was a bright girl and she had the world at her feet.

Giselle was still juggling men. She had seven of them – one for each day of the week. She even called them "Monday", "Tuesday", "Wednesday", etc. When Kaia asked her how she kept their names straight, Giselle told her that she called them all "boo". The girls laughed at Giselle's scandalous ways. That girl would never change. She told them about her mother's continuing battle with alcoholism and the girls listened sympathetically. Giselle's two younger sisters still lived in their mother's house. But Giselle had turned 18 and never looked back. She never concerned herself with how her sisters handled things at home. As far as she was concerned no one had helped her when *she* was suffering with an alcoholic mother and she didn't' care how they dealt with it, either. Sisters or not, they were on their own.

Symphany was embarking on a new phase in her own life. The only one who seemed to not have much to share was Kaia.

91

Kaia told her tale of motherhood and work. She told them about her job and recounted some of the funny things Phoenix had said or done. But there wasn't much else to discuss. "I went to see Aaron today," she offered. She detailed their visit and how she looked forward to his calls and letters. But she noticed that her friends were staring at her like she should have more to tell.

Symphany tried to sound optimistic. "Good. I know he was glad to see you and Phe-Phe."

Giselle wasn't as nice. "That ride is too damn far to be going up there every month. You and Phoenix should just wait until that nigga gets home to do all that family bonding. That's all your life consists of! Going up north to visit your incarcerated boyfriend. Being a single mother juggling career and family. Waiting by the phone for collect calls that you have to bust your ass to pay for. Sitting at the mailbox waiting for a kite. Where the hell is the fun?"

Kaia was offended. She had never noticed how pathetic her life must seem. Why was everyone acting like it was a crime to love her man and to wait for him to come home to her? "I have fun," she responded, trying to sound convincing. "Being a mother is fun. So, fuck you, Giselle!"

"That's just what you need, girl. Some sex!"

"Giselle mind your business. I don't need..."

"Did Kaia tell y'all that she's about to cheat on Aaron with this *fine* brother from the office?"

"What?!?!?" came the chorus.

"Giselle, stop lying. I just *met* the guy last week for God's sake."

Giselle continued. "And you should have seen how speechless she was! I think this one is going to make her forget about Aaron altogether."

Talia smiled as Kaia blushed. "Tell us, Kaia. Who is the mystery man at work? Ain't nobody gonna tell your secret."

Giselle laughed and Kaia felt like strangling her. "I did <u>not</u> meet anybody who would take my mind off of Aaron. I met a guy *briefly* the other day..."

"Tell them how fine he was!" Giselle wasn't letting Kaia take the easy way out.

"Giselle..." Kaia couldn't finish the sentence.

"Kaia was kicking it with this cutie the other day. His name is Eric and he's one of Keith's friends..."

"KEITH?" Symphany and Talia cut Giselle off mid-sentence.

"Kaia, are you crazy? You can't do your dirt so close to home, girl!" Talia was very surprised at Kaia's brazenness.

"Tell the *whole* story, Giselle. You're making me sound like an idiot." Kaia sat back and listened to Giselle give a more accurate account of her meeting with Eric.   When she was done, everyone smiled mischievously.

"Kaia, you only live once you know?" Talia pried.

Symphany felt differently. "She's already waited three years for Aaron. Why start messing up now?"

"It's not about messing up, Symphany," Giselle countered. "Kaia is only 20 years old. She's young, pretty and smart and she deserves to have a life. I'm sick of hearing about women wasting time on men who wouldn't waste their time on them. Kaia, I'm not saying that Aaron is a bad guy or anything. I think he's a good man. But he made the decisions that got him locked up. He got locked up for something *he* did...not you. Why are you living like a convicted felon when you're not one? Going up north through metal detectors. Subjecting Phoenix to all of that negativity. It just ain't right."

Symphany shook her head in disagreement. But she could tell that Kaia was being persuaded.

Kaia spoke up. "So what do you think I should do, 'Miss Know-it-all'?"

"Go out with the guy," Giselle prodded. "Have a drink or two with the guy. Get to know the guy. And if you really like him, fuck the guy and tell him to keep it on the hush."

"Giselle!" Kaia was embarrassed again.

Talia agreed with Giselle. "For real, Kaia. You can still be Aaron's girl and have fun at the same time. You have to be true to yourself. Aaron would *not* go out of his way to be faithful to you if you were locked down. Don't deprive yourself, girl. Live a little."

Kaia let her friends' advice sink in.

Symphany, who was happy not to be the one in the spotlight anymore, sat in her favorite chair and enjoyed the blunt that was passed to her. The girls smoked and drank until the wee hours of the morning. They reminisced about old times and discussed how they would be spending the upcoming holidays. After agreeing to call one another the next day, the girls parted company and retreated to the confines of their individual cocoons.

Chapter Nine

Enemies in Disguise

Talia and Symphány were in a fierce competition for Phoenix' attention. The girls had gathered at Kaia's house on a frosty December evening. It had become a routine for the four of them to get together one weekend each month and catch up on each other's lives. On this Friday evening, Symphany was putting Kaia's hair in neat cornrows while Talia kept Phoenix entertained.

"See, Symphany, I told you she likes me better than she likes you." Talia was convinced that she was the child's favorite playmate.

"Shut up, Talia," Symphany said. "She only keeps coming to you because I'm busy with her mama's hair. But as soon as I'm done she'll be shutting you down. You'll see."

Talia laughed. "Don't be jealous, girl. I just have that magic touch."

As the girls chuckled and Phoenix played with Talia, Symphany noticed a void. "Where is Giselle?" Like Judas at the Last Supper, Giselle was nowhere to be found.

Kaia shrugged. "She called me last night and said she was going to Brooklyn early this morning to see her cousin and then she'll come by later on."

Talia frowned. "Where in Brooklyn?"

Symphany had a similar question. "What cousin?"

Again, Kaia shrugged. "All I know is that she said she was going to see her family. I don't get involved in Giselle's business. She probably has a new man in her life."

Talia was right on cue. "Speaking of which, what's up with you and Eric?"

Symphany nodded emphatically. "Word. I know you went out with him a couple of times. Any sparks?"

Kaia smiled. She would never admit to her friends that Eric had her feeling brand new. In fact, he was the reason she was suddenly keeping her hair and nails in top condition. Kaia still loved Aaron and had every intention of being with him when he got out. But in the meantime, Eric was keeping her warm...and making her hot.

95

"He's real nice. We went to the movies twice and he took me out to dinner at this nice restaurant in New Jersey."

Symphany knew Kaia very well, and she knew men even better. "So, let's see...the dinner at the nice restaurant in New Jersey was the third date. Which means he got some ass, right?"

Kaia was shocked at Symphany's accuracy.   "Shut up, Symphany!" Talia and Symphany laughed.

"Let me guess. He took you to The Loop, right?" Symphany asked, smiling as she remembered the last time she'd been to that same hotel.

The doorbell rang and Kaia was grateful for the interruption. She opened the door for Giselle and returned to her seat on the floor between Symphany's legs. Symphany continued to braid Kaia's hair as Giselle hung up her coat.

"So, what have you been up to all day, missy?" Talia couldn't hide her suspicion. Giselle looked a little on edge.

"I went to Brooklyn to see my cousin." Giselle poured herself a glass of Hennessy and sat down on the loveseat. Talia noticed that Giselle wasn't her usual talkative self. Usually, Giselle would have been telling some long, detailed story of how her day had gone. Instead, she gave a very uncharacteristic one-sentence response.

"I didn't know you had a cousin in Brooklyn." Symphany had also picked up on Giselle's unusual behavior.

Giselle rolled her eyes. "She just moved up here from North Carolina, that's why. What were y'all talking about when I came in? Everyone was laughing a few minutes ago."

Symphany noticed that Giselle had very slyly changed the subject, but decided not to press it any further. "Kaia was just telling us about her dates with Eric."

Kaia laughed. "No. *Symphany* was just telling us about my dates with Eric. She seems to be psychic all of a sudden so I'll let her finish telling it."

Symphany laughed. "Just tell us this, Kaia. Was it good?"

Kaia laughed at her nosy friends and decided not to keep them in the dark. "Yes, I slept with him. Yes it was at The Loop, Symphany. Yes, it was good, and no, he didn't make me forget about Aaron."

Talia giggled. "I bet you forgot about him until you finished getting your groove on."

High fives and giggles erupted across the room. Phoenix looked around at her mother and all her friends having a good old time. She curled up on Talia's lap and got comfortable.

Talia teased Symphany. "See? I told you she likes me more than she likes you."

Symphany rolled her eyes. "Kaia, your daughter better not expect Christmas gifts from me this year."

Kaia laughed. "Symphany, she's three years old! When she turns four she'll start liking you."

Talia laughed, too. "Yeah, right. Why don't' you start making some babies of your own?"

Symphany sucked her teeth. "I don't need that much responsibility. I can hardly keep myself out of trouble."

Giselle agreed. "I hear you, girl. Me, either."

Symphany finished the last braid in Kaia's cute new hairstyle. She turned her attention to Giselle as Kaia got up to stretch her legs.

"Giselle, what's your cousin's name?"

Giselle was caught off guard. "What cous...oh...her name is Alicia."

The phone rang and Kaia made a mental note to tell Giselle that she could tell she was lying after she answered the phone. "Hello?"

Kaia sat through the recording notifying her that she had a collect call from and inmate in a correctional facility. She waited for the voice prompt and accepted Aaron's call.

"Hey, baby," Kaia was so happy to hear from Aaron. He hadn't called much in the past few days.

"Hey," Aaron sounded upset. "When are you bringing Phoenix up here?"

Kaia was caught off guard. Aaron wasn't being his usual lovey-dovey self. "What's the matter with you?" she asked.

"What the fuck do you *think* is the matter with me, Kaia? What would be the matter with you if you were locked up and you found out I was fucking around behind your back, huh? How would that make *you* feel? I KNOW you didn't think you could hide some shit like that from me, did you? And if I find out that nigga was around my daughter I'll be right back in here for another body, you hear me?!?"

Aaron was enraged.

Kaia stood frozen in shock. How had Aaron found out? He was yelling at her like he never had before. Symphany heard Aaron yelling through the phone and looked at Kaia with a puzzled expression on her face. She gave Kaia a "what happened?" look. Kaia shook her head that she had no idea.

"Aaron, what are you talking about? I ain't messing with nobody and..."

"Don't fuckin' lie to me, Kaia. Don't play games with me. I don't care what you do anymore. Just don't have them lame ass dudes around my daughter. Word is bond, Kaia. Keep them niggas away from my baby. Just let my brother bring her to see me from now on and stay the fuck out my face!" Aaron slammed down the phone in Kaia's ear.

Kaia trembled in shock. She couldn't believe what had just taken place. How had Aaron found out? Who would have told him? Kaia felt her world crashing down around her.

Talia rushed over to Kaia's side. "Kaia, what happened? Why was Aaron yelling like that?'

Symphany and Talia tried to calm Kaia down as she cried nonstop. Giselle took Phoenix, who had fallen asleep, and carried her to her bedroom to tuck her in.

Between sobs, Kaia told her friends about her conversation with Aaron. Symphany shook her head in disgust. "Who else knows about you and Eric besides us, Kaia?" Symphany hated how Staten Island was such a small world. You couldn't get away with *anything* in this borough without somebody finding out about it.

Kaia shook her head. "I haven't told anybody but y'all. The only people who know are in this house right now."

Giselle spoke up as she came back in the room. "What about Eric? How do you know he didn't tell Keith?"

Talia and Symphany exchanged glances. "That's a possibility, isn't it?" Talia asked gently.

Kaia held her head in her hands. "I can't believe he would do that. Eric wouldn't do that."

Giselle continued. "Kaia, you don't know *what* Eric would do. You hardly know him. It's possible that he told Keith. It's possible that he told somebody else. The bottom line is that somebody sure blew up your spot. Now what are you going to do?" Giselle flopped down on the couch and folded her arms as if she were watching a really good episode of *The Young and the Restless*.

Symphany shot Giselle an evil look. "Why the hell are you being so mean?   She don't need to hear that shit right now."

Giselle didn't appreciate Symphany's tone of voice. "I wasn't talking to you, Symphany. So mind your business. I'm trying to help Kaia face reality..."

"Fuck reality! She's your friend and all you can say is "now what are you going to do?" And you have a whole lot of nerve saying that she hardly knows Eric. You 'hardly know' most of the men you mess around with!"   Symphany was pissed off at Giselle.   Kaia was obviously distraught and Giselle was making matters worse.

"You know what, Symphany? •Fuck you!" Giselle grabbed her coat and stormed out.

"And fuck you, too!" Symphany yelled after her.   Looking at Kaia she said, "I'm sorry, Kaia, but she made me mad..."

"Don't apologize, girl. Cuz, if you didn't tell that witch something I was damn sure going to," Talia piped in.

Kaia couldn't' care less about Giselle's bruised ego at the moment. She was busy wondering how Aaron had found out and what her next move should be. She cried on Talia's shoulder uncontrollably. Giselle's words echoed in her head. *'Now what are you going to do?'*

The next day, Kaia made the trip upstate to visit Aaron at Greene. She sat in the waiting room nervously waiting for Aaron to come down. On the three-hour long drive upstate, Kaia had cried and lamented over how she was going to face Aaron. He had, after all, been her only family for so long. He had loved her and taken care of her when no one else had. She knew he had every right to feel betrayed. But she hoped to make him understand that she still loved him.

Kaia prayed that Aaron wouldn't refuse her visit. She had seen other inmates refuse to see their relatives and girlfriends despite the fact that they'd traveled for hours to get to the prison. She hoped Aaron wouldn't be that cruel. She only wanted the chance to talk to him. She felt that if he would just hear her out, he might understand why she did this.

By now, all the other inmates were seated at tables with their loved ones. Kaia was the only one still sitting alone. She said another silent prayer that Aaron wouldn't deny this visit. As if in answer to her prayer, the door swung open and in walked Aaron. He looked menacing and Kaia could see the vein in his neck throbbing. She knew him well enough to know that meant Aaron was pissed off.

He walked over to her table and sat across from her. He made no attempts to be in any way affectionate. Kaia decided not to ask for a hug and risk setting him off. She smiled weakly.

"Hi," she said. Aaron ignored her but stared at her with contempt.

Kaia tried again. "I didn't think you were coming down to see me."

Aaron continued to stare at her. "I wasn't coming down," he said through clenched teeth. "But my man said it would be grimy to do that to you after you came all the way up here. So, what did you come up here for and why didn't you bring my daughter?"

Aaron wasn't even trying to hide his disdain. Kaia disgusted him. All of his problems had been because of her. He started hustling again to provide for Kaia. He let go of countless girlfriends to be with Kaia exclusively. He had planned to marry her as soon as she came home, and she had betrayed him. He would never forget that.

Kaia was trembling. She had never been the target of Aaron's rage before. She had never seen him be so cold and she didn't know how much more of it she could take.

"I didn't bring Phoenix because I thought we should talk in private today," Kaia explained. "Aaron, what made you flip on me like that yesterday? I don't know what you heard but..."

Aaron slammed his fist on the table and the Correction Officer loudly warned him to quiet down. Aaron scowled at Kaia. You know exactly what I heard, Kaia!" Aaron was enraged. "Don't you?"

Kaia was shaking like a leaf now. She felt all the stares from the other inmates and their inmates. "Aaron, I..." she stammered.

"Kaia, don't sit in my face and act like you don't know what's going on. You know that I'm not this mad for nothing." Aaron looked away and Kaia thought she detected a tear threatening to fall. He turned back to her and shook his head in disbelief. "You fucked him, didn't you, Kaia?"

"Who, Aaron? What are you talking about?" Kaia tried to act innocent.

Aaron was losing his patience. He wiped the tear that fell from his eye and the vein began to throb in his neck all over again. "Okay, since you want to play games with me..."

"Aaron, just tell me who told you this nonsense!" Kaia pleaded.

Aaron tried to read her face. "You really think you're fooling me, huh? So, tell me this," he began. "Why would Giselle make up some story about you messing around with my brother's man Eric, huh?"

Kaia gasped. *Did he just say 'Giselle'?*

Aaron continued. "This is your friend. Your pal. Why would she tell me that the mother of my child is out there in Shaolin fucking my brother's friend? Why would she tell me that you and him met at your job and that you couldn't wait to sex him? She told me all about the times she tried to convince you that you should wait for me to come home..."

"What?!?" Kaia couldn't believe her ears. She half-listened as Aaron told her about the letter he received from Giselle. She wrote to him and told him that she always admired him for dropping out of school and putting his life on the line to hustle and take care of Kaia and Phoenix. She included her phone number and asked that he call her. She claimed she had some serious things to discuss with him and she'd rather not do it in a letter. Aaron had called Giselle to find out why Giselle was so determined to contact him. Giselle suggested that she come and visit with him face to face.

Kaia heard Aaron's voice like a distant murmur as she put all the pieces together. Giselle had been the one who encouraged her the most to go out with Eric. Giselle had been the one who was most interested in how much money Aaron, Symphany and Sean had made. Giselle was the last one to arrive at Kaia's house the night Aaron called and went berserk. And Giselle was the one who had been so callous with Kaia's feelings after she hung up the phone. It had been Giselle who told Aaron about Kaia and Eric. Giselle had not been in Brooklyn visiting some mystery cousin. She had been upstate visiting Kaia's man.

Kaia was fuming now. So was Aaron. They sat in silence for minutes that felt like days. Finally, Kaia spoke.

"Aaron, she is lying to you. The bitch is lying, can't you see that?" Kaia was in tears now. The reality of the situation struck her like a ton of bricks. Giselle had snitched. Aaron knew the truth.

Aaron shook his head in disbelief. He wanted Kaia's words to be true. But he knew in his heart that they weren't. He spoke softly to the woman he still loved despite his pain. "Kaia, I know you did it. It don't even matter no more." Aaron massaged his temples trying to alleviate some of the pressure he was feeling. All of this was too much to take. "Just keep the car and whatever money is left. But I don't want to see you again."

"Aaron, don't do this to us..."

"Nah, Kaia. YOU did this to us." Aaron looked her dead in the eyes and spoke with malice in his voice. "Don't come back up here again, you hear me? Just tell my brother to bring Phoenix to see me until I get out. I don't want to see your face anymore." Aaron rose from the table and walked away as Kaia cried, begging him to hear her out. She didn't care that all of the inmates and their visitors were staring at her. She didn't care that she must look like a fool to the correction officer who escorted Aaron back to his cell. She only cared that the love of her life had walked away from her.

And just like that, he was gone.

The ride back to Staten Island seemed to take days. But it had actually only taken 3 hours for Kaia to find herself on the Staten Island ferry heading home. She couldn't help recalling the time she and Aaron had taken the ferry to Manhattan on the Fourth of July the summer they met. She remembered how romantic it had been. How she and Aaron kissed and held hands the whole way there. It all seemed so long ago, and Kaia felt the tears in her eyes as she reminded herself that they would never be together like that again.

But by the time the ferry docked in Staten Island, Kaia's heartache had slowly morphed into rage. She went into the terminal and used a pay phone to call Symphany. After explaining to Symphany what had happened, Kaia headed to the parking lot and climbed in her car. She looked in the rearview mirror at her reflection and noticed how puffy and red her eyes were. All that crying and all she had to show for it was a broken heart and swollen eyes. She vowed to herself that she would get back at Giselle, and it was a promise she intended to keep!

She drove along the Staten Island Expressway without realizing that her speedometer showed that she was going 80mph. All she could focus on was the look on Aaron's face during their visit. He hated her and it showed. Kaia hated herself for hurting the one person who had loved her unconditionally. She had betrayed him and she convinced herself that she deserved the treatment she'd received from him. Aaron had done nothing wrong. All he'd ever done was to take care of Kaia and provide for her and Phoenix. Kaia told herself that she had blown her only chance at real love. And the tears began to flow once more.

Arriving at Symphany's house, Kaia got out of the car and headed up the driveway. Before she reached the door, Symphany had opened it and held her arms open to embrace her friend. Symphany could tell that Kaia had been crying and she wanted to do was to comfort her.   Kaia hugged Symphany and realized for the first time that Symphany really was her best friend.   She entered the living room and saw that Talia was sitting on the couch. Kaia waved to her, too drained to make small talk. Talia patted for Kaia to sit beside her.

"Come on in, girl," Symphany coaxed. "I made you a drink to relax you. Sip on that while you tell me the story one more time. I can't believe Giselle would stoop this low."

Kaia shook her head as if she, too, was in a state of disbelief. "I told you everything there is to tell. In a nutshell, Giselle wrote to Aaron and told him that she needed to talk to him about something important. She wound up going to visit him on Friday when she told us that she went to see her cousin. Then she told him that Eric and I have been sleeping together and that she tried to convince me to wait for Aaron to come home..."

"That bitch is lying!" Talia was outraged.

Kaia agreed. "I know she is and I told him that. But he doesn't want to hear anything I have to say. He doesn't believe me. She told him that she couldn't understand why I would betray him after all he did for me and Phoenix. Now, it's over between me and Aaron. He told me not to come back to see him anymore. He wants Keith to bring Phe-Phe up there from now on."

Talia was shocked. "But, Kaia, why would Giselle do this? What does she gain by telling Aaron that you slept with Eric?"

Kaia shrugged her shoulders. "I've been trying to figure that out since I left the prison. I don't know why she did this."

Symphany did. "I'll tell you why." Symphany shook her head in astonishment as all the pieces of the puzzle began to fall into place. "When we sat in this very house last month and discussed my life of crime, who was the one that showed the most interest in how much money me and Aaron had made?" Symphany paused to allow her friends

103

to catch on. When their facial expressions told her that they understood, Symphony continued. "Giselle has always been a materialistic bitch. Knowing that I have all this money is enough to turn her green with envy. But knowing that Aaron had just as much money and that he's on his way home to you was probably more than she could stand. So she decided to break you guys up and try to get with him herself."

Talia nodded in agreement. "Isn't she the one who told you to get with Eric in the first place?"

Kaia couldn't believe this. "Yeah, but she started telling me that before we found out about Symphony or Aaron's money."

Talia countered, "But she *really* started trying to convince you after we found out. That has to be it. There's no other explanation for her to do this."

Kaia guzzled the rest of her drink and placed the glass back on the coaster. "Let's stop wondering and go find out. I want to see this bitch face to face.

Symphony grabbed her keys. "I'll drive."   They piled into Symphony's car and headed for Arlington.

BANG! BANG! BANG! BANG! BANG! Kaia and Symphony pounded on Giselle's apartment door. "Open the door, you two-faced bitch. I know your devious ass is in there, so come out and face us like a real woman would!"

Talia kicked the door while Kaia and Symphony banged on it. They had been assaulting Giselle's apartment door for more than 10 minutes and there was no answer. Kaia's rage intensified the longer she was forced to wait. She knew Giselle was in there. And she *had* to confront her now!

"OPEN THE DOOR, GISELLE!" Kaia's yelling echoed off the walls in the hallway outside Giselle's 8th floor apartment. Nosy neighbors looked through their peepholes to see who was causing all the confusion. An older woman opened her door and angrily glared at Kaia, Talia and Symphony.

"She must not be home. All that banging ain't necessary," the woman stated, nastily.

"You mind your fuckin' business and close the door," Talia spat at her. Symphany's head whipped around in surprise. She couldn't believe that the normally quiet and calm Talia was cussing at this old woman. She smiled proudly. Obviously, Talia still had a little "hood" in her.

Kaia kicked the door angrily. Talia continued her tirade, since the woman hadn't closed the door. "You shouldn't complain about the noise. Complain about having a nasty bitch for a neighbor. One that goes behind her friend's back and tries to fuck her man!"

The older woman gasped.

"Yeah," Talia continued. "Surprised, huh? She's a stank, nasty, low-down BITCH, and if I were you, I'd hold tight to my man."

Shaking her head, the woman retreated to her apartment, leaving Kaia and her two henchwomen to proceed with the destruction of both Giselle's reputation and her apartment door. Kaia panted as she screamed obscenities at her former friend.

"She ain't' coming to the door, Kaia. The bitch is scared. We'll catch her, don't worry." Symphany and Talia walked toward the elevator, until they noticed that Kaia wasn't following them. Talia spoke up. "Come on, Kaia, let's go."

Kaia leaned against the wall for support. "She took it all away from me, Talia. I have to get that bitch. Kaia shook her head in frustration. "I have to get her back."

Symphany walked back to where Kaia stood. She wrapped her arm around Kaia's shoulder and guided her friend down the hall. As they boarded the elevator, Kaia cried softly.

"We'll get her, Kaia," Talia assured her. "Don't worry."

Inside her apartment, Giselle watched from her terrace as Symphany, Talia and Kaia headed to the parking lot towards Symphany's green Ford Explorer. She was scared to death. Aaron had *promised* that he wouldn't tell Kaia about their conversations. He swore that he wouldn't reveal who had given him the information on Kaia and Eric. He vowed to keep it a secret. But Giselle had never considered the possibility that he would lie. Now she looked like a two-faced witch who'd spilled the beans on someone who was supposed to be her friend. Now she looked like a snitch.

Giselle had secretly envied Kaia for a long time. From the moment she began to date Aaron, Kaia had talked about how sweet and romantic he was. Giselle, herself, had never looked twice at Aaron while they were in school. Not until he started going out with Kaia and spending so much time with her. Giselle's lack of love in her poor excuse for a family made her desperate for attention and affection. Her lack of a father figure caused her to seek love from boys at a very early age. Giselle had become promiscuous during junior high school and found herself labeled a 'ho' by the time she reached high school. For that reason, guys never took her out or wined and dined her. They didn't buy her thoughtful gifts on her birthday. Most of them had no idea when her birthday was.

So when Kaia and Aaron started reading books together, meeting in the park and going to the zoo, Giselle was beside herself with envy. In her opinion, Kaia had always had it easy. Even though she had it hard at home, everyone who had no respect for Giselle had always respected Kaia. It sickened Giselle that while most teenaged mothers struggled with absent fathers and the responsibility of finding a place to stay, Kaia had Aaron galloping to her rescue. Aaron had given Kaia all the things that Giselle wanted for herself. Giselle had always wanted a man who would buy her a car, give her money, and take her shopping. When she found out that Kaia had also snagged Eric, it was too much for Giselle to bear. She found herself despising Kaia's luck. Giselle had spotted Eric first and he'd shown no interest in her. But then she'd found him gawking at Kaia and Giselle was furious.

She had decided the time was right to drop Aaron a few hints that his girl had strayed. But Giselle never counted on Aaron going back on his word. Now she had lost Kaia as a friend. And Symphany and Talia would certainly never speak to Giselle again, either.

But, perhaps most devastating, was the fact that Giselle was unsure whether or not Aaron would fall into her hands like she'd planned. She had hoped to deliver the news to Aaron and appear compassionate. She went on and on about how highly she thought of him and how she couldn't stand to see Kaia make such a fool of him. The truth was, as soon as she'd learned of the large amounts of money that Aaron and Symphany had made hustling, she decided to make her move. There was no way she was going to sit by and watch Symphany *and* Kaia live in the lap of luxury.

Sitting in the dark in her apartment in case the girls came back, Giselle recalled how handsome Aaron was on the day of their visit. Giselle hadn't seen him in three years, and the pictures Kaia showed her didn't do him justice. Aaron was no longer the tall, slim boy she remembered. Now he was a very muscular, toned replica of his older brother. Aaron's sexiness had Giselle practically melting as they discussed Kaia's indiscretions. She knew that he was hurt by her revelations but she hoped he would turn to her for comfort. However, Aaron hadn't called her like he promised he would. She wondered whether she'd hear from him at all.

Her next hurdle was facing Kaia. It was inevitable since they both worked in the same office complex and lived within minutes of one another. How was she going to defend her actions? Giselle closed the curtains and plotted her next move.

Keith accepted the collect call from Aaron and listened as his brother told him about Kaia. He couldn't believe his boy Eric would cross the line like this. And Keith was also surprised at Kaia. But he had warned his brother about these young girls who seem so sweet. He'd seen how that sweetness could turn bitter.

"Well, man, it seems like you made up your mind, huh? You ain't dealing with her no more?" Keith asked.

"Nah, man. I can't trust her now." Aaron wished things were different but Kaia had crossed the line. He had been the only man in her life...the first to ever make love to her. Now her image was tainted in Aaron's eyes, because another man had been intimate with her. The thought of that made him sick.

Keith agreed. "Once a girl starts trickin', ain't no turning back. Kaia should have never started hanging with them girls she rolls with." Keith recalled the stories he'd heard about Giselle and her trifling ways. He wondered why she had stabbed her friend in the back like she did. "What's up with this chick who told you all this shit? What do you think she's up to?"

Aaron laughed. "She probably thought I would dump Kaia and start going with her. I'm going to use her dumb ass for more information until I get out. Then I'll probably hit it and diss her afterwards."

Keith laughed, too. "Just make sure you put on a condom on with her. We both know she's been around." Keith was glad to hear his brother laugh. He knew this whole thing had taken its toll on him.

Aaron's pressure rose everytime he thought of Eric touching the mother of his child. "All I know is when I see this nigga Eric, it's on."

Keith nodded in agreement and switched the phone to the other ear. "Word, Aaron, let me handle that. I'm gonna take a ride over to the Rendezvous to have a talk with that nigga." The Rendezvous was a bar located on Targee Street in Park Hill. Eric was a regular there on the weekends when the crowd was a who's who of Shaolin. "I'll find out what the deal is with him and Kaia."

"Yo," Aaron rubbed his head, which had begun to ache from all the stress of the past few days. "Tell that nigga to stay away from my daughter." All he had left to keep him sane for the remainder of his sentence was Phoenix. Aaron couldn't handle the thought of another man playing daddy to his baby girl.

"Definitely," Keith affirmed. "Yo, man, keep your head up in there. Don't let this shit get to you too much." Keith knew Aaron had enough to worry about without adding Kaia to the list.

"Easier said than done. Peace."

As he hung up the phone, Keith thought about how he'd felt the first time he had his heart broken. His heart went out to his little brother because, in addition to the pain, Aaron also had to deal with the fact that he was behind bars. Keith could only imagine how helpless Aaron must feel. He headed out the door and prepared to face Eric.

Chapter Ten

Suffocating

Keith walked into the Rendezvous and immediately spotted Eric at the bar. He strode over to his buddy and tapped him on the shoulder.

"Wassup, man?" Eric extended his hand to Keith. Keith didn't take it.

"Wassup with *you*?" Keith countered. "What's this I'm hearing about you fucking my brother's girl?"

Eric was caught off guard. Kaia claimed that their relationship was supposed to be a secret and that was fine by Eric. He didn't want beef with anybody over some ass. So how the hell had Keith found out?

"What? Keith, don't come at me like that." Eric sipped his drink, trying to hide his nervousness.

Keith towered over Eric. "I'm coming at you like that, nigga." The other patrons turned in the direction of Keith's booming voice. Keith was obviously pissed off.

Eric stood and faced Keith eye to eye. "Yo, check it. I'm a grown ass man! I'll go where I want, I'll do what I want, and I'll mess with who I want. You don't come questioning me about who I'm dealing with!" Now it was Eric's voice that was booming.

"Oh, word?" Keith smirked. "You're a 'grown ass man' now, huh? Were you a grown ass man when my brother put you down with his operation? Were you a grown ass man when you came to my baby brother and told him your ass was broke and couldn't find a job? Now you gonna bite the hand that fed your ass by messing around with his girl while he's locked down?"

Some of the older men in the bar shook their heads in disapproval. Eric had broken a code that said you never mess around with your friend's girl. Especially if your friend is locked up and can't do anything about it.

Eric had no rebuttal for what Keith had just said. He knew that what he'd done was wrong. He wasn't going to play himself further by trying to defend his actions. Plus he didn't want to go toe to toe with Keith. Him and Aaron had a lot of clout in the streets. Eric stood silent.

109

He never saw the punch coming. Keith knocked the spit out of Eric's mouth with a hard right hook. Eric was sprawled on the floor of the bar, as commotion and pandemonium filled the place. He did hear Keith's cryptic warning, though.

"Do this for me and my brother, man. Stay away from my niece. You can mess with Kaia now if you want. My brother is done with her. But do yourself a favor and don't go nowhere near my niece. Otherwise, I might have to give you a matching cut to the other side of your face."

Keith stormed out with steam flowing from his nostrils. He started his car and headed to Kaia's place.

Kaia, Symphany and Talia were sitting in her living room with Phoenix when Keith rang the bell. Kaia opened the door and Phoenix ran to her uncle with outstretched arms. Keith scooped up his niece and kissed her. He greeted Symphany and Talia and reached into his pocket and handed Phoenix a five-dollar bill. Turning to Kaia, he asked, "Can I talk to you in private for a minute?"

Figuring that she knew what Keith wanted to discuss, Symphany leaped to the rescue. "We'll take Phoenix to the store and let her buy something with all that money she has now." Symphany winked at Talia and the three of them walked out the door. Kaia and Keith sat down.

Kaia decided to cut to the chase. "Look, Keith, I know that Aaron told you what happened. I want you to know that I do love your brother and I'm sorry that I..."

Keith held up his hand to cut her off. "Kaia, I don't even want to hear all of that because that is between you and my brother. I'm just here to tell you that I'll be taking Phoenix upstate to see him from now on. I'll probably just pick her up the night before so that we can get an early start the next morning. I was thinking that I'll probably go on Sunday so just have her packed on Saturday night." Keith rose to leave.

Kaia was dumbfounded. She had always thought of Keith as a part of her family and here he was treating her like a stranger. She knew that he was Aaron's brother, not hers. But, it still hurt to see that the line had been drawn and sides were already being taken.

"Keith, can you understand that I was lonely and..."

110

Again, Keith cut her off. "Kaia, I don't have nothing to say about that. Just so you know, I had a talk with your boy Eric and I told him that he better stay away from Phoenix. Now I'll tell you. Aaron understands that it's over between you and him and he can't dictate who you see. But he wants to make it clear that he don't want Eric around her. Please respect him on that. If you're having company or something, bring my niece to me. I'll take care of her whenever you need me to," Keith said as he turned and walked out the door.

Kaia stood in the doorway and watched as Keith drove off. She felt like everyone and everything had been taken from her. Giselle wasn't her real friend. And thanks to her, Aaron was not a part of Kaia's life anymore. Keith, the only family Kaia felt she had for so long, was against her. She hadn't heard from her sisters in months and her mother still hated her. Kaia found herself wondering if she could take another day. She felt like giving up.

She saw Symphany and Talia leading a happy Phoenix back home. Phoenix had a small brown bag that was filled to the rim with candy and she ran to her mother with a huge smile on her face. "I got candy, mommy!" Kaia smiled and reminded herself that this sweet little girl was the reason she couldn't give up on life. But Kaia was beginning to wonder if she was destined to be miserable all her life. She couldn't recall one moment of peace that hadn't been shattered by pain.

Phoenix ran to her room and Kaia and her friends sat down in the living room.

Talia looked around the room. "Did Keith leave already?"

Kaia nodded. "He came by to tell me that Aaron wants him to bring Phoenix upstate to see him from now on. I've been officially kicked out of the family."

Kaia forced a smile, but Talia and Symphany could tell that it hurt her to speak those words.

Kaia continued. "What else is new, right? First I got kicked out of my family. Then I kicked out of Aaron's. This just might be one of those Guinness World Records."

Talia was sympathetic. "Kaia, Aaron will come to his senses over time. I think he's still recovering from the shock of all of this. Don't worry. Everything will work itself out."

Kaia wasn't so sure. "What makes you think that, Talia? Since when has everything worked out for me? There has never been one point in my life that things worked out for me. First my father died and left me to live with a woman who hated me...and she just so happened to be my mother! Then I wind up pregnant in high school so my mother kicks me out penniless and with nothing but the clothes on my back. My sisters don't call me, don't write to me...not even a card at Christmastime. I wasn't even invited to Asha's wedding!

Then my man gets arrested on the day I give birth to my daughter. I meet another guy who I hope can make the time go by faster until I see Aaron again, and one of my "friends" rats me out. Now I'm an outcast once again. I was an outcast in my family. I was an outcast in school. Now once again, I'm an outcast...but this time it's with the man I really love. Where's the silver lining in that cloud, Talia?"

Silence cloaked them. No one seemed to know what to say. Kaia fought back tears. She was sick of crying.

Symphany had never seen Kaia so defeated. "Girl, fuck Aaron. To hell with him, Giselle, your mother, your sisters, your old teachers...fuck all of them, Kaia! If you go through life looking at yourself through their eyes, you will *never* be good enough." Symphany knew how it felt to be alone even when you were in a room full of people.

She continued. "I used to measure myself according to other people's opinions of me. But then I realized that if you keep doing that you will never learn to love who *you* are. Not who other people want you to be. Your mother wanted you to be a certain way. But it's not her life to live, it's yours. As a parent, her job was to provide for you and to love you whether you make mistakes or not. She didn't do that, so that's something she's got to answer to God for. Don't carry that around with you like it's your burden, Kaia. If you do it will consume you, trust me."

"How do you forget that your mother doesn't love you? How do you forget that, Symphany?" Kaia was searching for answers that had eluded her all her life.

"Kaia, you have to learn to not give a damn whether she loves you or not. Listen, what I'm saying is this: your mother may not love who you are, Aaron may not love you anymore. Giselle may hate your guts. But that's their problem. You have to learn to like yourself. When you learn to like yourself it doesn't matter if someone else doesn't like you. You won't give a damn, because you know it's their problem, not yours. You have to like spending time with yourself, and then you'll begin to love yourself. That doesn't mean that you're conceited or that you think your shit doesn't stink. It means that you are not defined by other people's definitions of who or what you are."

Talia nodded in agreement. "That makes sense, Kaia. Nobody is perfect. We all make mistakes. Maybe getting pregnant in high school was not what you planned. But sometimes things don't work out like you planned. That doesn't make you a bad person. It makes you human. And you know what? Other people may look at the situation and dislike you because of that. So what! That doesn't mean that you should feel bad about yourself. You have to learn to let that shit bounce off of you."

Kaia let her friends words sink in while she poured them each a glass of wine. Symphany was busily twisting an 'L' while Talia spoke. Finally, Kaia sat down on the couch and curled her feet beneath her. "It's just that sometimes all this shit feels like it's too much for me to handle. I feel like talking to a "mother" sometimes, you know? Then I realize that I don't have one, and I can't help but wonder if there was something about me that made her dislike me so much."

Symphany passed the blunt to Talia and spoke. "I used to wonder the same thing, Kaia. My mother was never home. She was always working. When my brother got locked up, she worked even more hours. I took that to mean that she didn't see any reason to be at home with me. We didn't' need the money *that* bad. I used to wonder why she never came to my school plays and why she never took Christmas Day off or Thanksgiving. I felt like everyone else in the world had their moms, but mine was too busy with work to care about me and what I was doing. Maybe that's why I started with the drug game. I made money and I was able to make all the pain go away by making more money. But that just made the pain fester like a disease. Eventually, I had to come to grips with who I am. Then I realized that my mother had no idea what a cool daughter she missed out on raising!" Symphany laughed and so did Talia and Kaia. The mood had been lightened somewhat.

Kaia inhaled the ganja and exhaled. "So, you think that all of this is going to make me stronger? Is that what you're saying?"

Talia nodded. "I think this will make you invincible."

Symphany agreed. "Kaia, if you learn to look at your reflection in the mirror, and say 'Hey, girl! I love you like crazy!!!' and mean it, you will be free. For the first time in your life."

And at that moment, Kaia decided that was what she wanted more than anything. To be free.

Stepping off the #46 bus at the Teleport, Giselle scanned the parking lot for Kaia's car. She had remained cooped up in her apartment all weekend, in fear for her safety. Kaia sounded like she meant business when she'd come by. She had also left several very scary messages on Giselle's answering machine. So today, Giselle wasn't taking any chances.

Strolling toward the building, she fingered the box cutter in her coat pocket. She had no intention of being caught off guard. Too bad she never noticed the two ski-masked individuals creeping up on her from behind.

BOOM!

The first individual caught her with a mighty blow to the back of the head, knocking her to the ground. Even in her foggy daze, Giselle immediately wished she hadn't worn her stiletto boots to work that day. Perhaps then she could have tried to run. But already the two masked bandits had set to work, ferociously punching her in the face. They stomped her in the face with their Timberlands, all the while calling her every obscenity known to man. The merciless beating continued until the guard at the security gate saw what was happening.

"HEY!" he yelled. "I'm calling the police!"

Giselle knew that one of her eyes must be swollen shut, since she couldn't see out of it. But as she looked out of the other eye, trying to figure out who her attackers were, one of them spat in her face. Standing over her, both of her attackers laughed. Then one said, "That's what you get for fucking with Kaia, bitch!"

Then they both took off running toward South Avenue.

The guard noticed them slip into a waiting green Ford Explorer. He ran over to where Giselle lay brutalized on the ground. "Be still, m'aam. The police are on their way."

Giselle sat on the ground, looking like the loser in heavyweight boxing match. *'Kaia had gotten her revenge.'* She thought. *'Now, let's see who gets the man.'*

PART THREE

Butterfly

you've condemned me since i first crawled
slow on my belly
crucified and despised me
like I had committed a felony
abandoned me emotionally,
unleashed the very hell in me
made me ugly like you said i was
when all you did was yell at me
caused me to withdraw
and to retreat within the shell in me

never believed that i could re emerge
 triumphant and unbeaten
that i could spread my wings and fly
when you thought I'd been defeated
you made me cry and can't tell me why
you taught me to accept mistreatment

despite the tears and all my fears
my bitter life is now sweetened

through hatred and lies
I still survived
now victory is within my reach

a butterfly
who died inside
is finally at peace

Chapter Eleven

Emerging

Keith looked across the table and smiled proudly at his brother. It was so good to see Aaron dressed in civilian clothes rather than the prison-issued jumpsuit he'd become accustomed to seeing him in. Aaron was tasting his first bit of freedom in years. It was February 4th, 1996 and he was finally a free man. He was overjoyed by the idea that he had made it home in time to celebrate his daughter's fourth birthday with her. This would be the first time he'd ever been able to do that. Aaron was reminded of the contrasts of that day. Valentine's Day was the day that his princess was born. It was also the day that he'd taken Wayne's life and began his incarceration.

Keith couldn't stop smiling at his brother. It was so good to have him home that Keith felt like a kid again. He hadn't realized how much he'd missed Aaron. But now that he was a free man, Keith realized just how much better life was going to be.

The first place Aaron had wanted to go after they'd reached Staten Island was to Perkins. Aaron told his brother that over the years he had longed for some pancakes from Perkins countless times. And now, as he sat with five large fluffy pancakes in front of him, it was Aaron's turn to feel like a kid again. He reflected briefly on how determined he was to never return to prison.

As Aaron dug in to his meal, Keith finally broke the silence.

"Did you tell Kaia that you were coming home today?"

Aaron shook his head and continued to chew on the mouthful of syrup-soaked pancakes he'd just shoveled in. "Nah."

Keith sipped his coffee and smiled at his brother. "Why not?"

Aaron wiped his mouth with his napkin and sat back in the booth. "Why should I have told her I was coming home? It's not like we're together anymore."

Keith nodded in agreement. "That's true. But don't you think she would want to know that you've been released?"

Aaron turned his attention back to his food. "I don't want her to know. I'd rather just show up. You know...catch her off guard."

117

Keith wondered if Aaron would reconcile with Kaia now that he was home. Keith thought to himself that it wouldn't be a bad idea for the two of them to work things out. He had always liked Kaia, and whenever he imagined having a sister-in-law, Kaia was the first person to come to mind. But, she had hurt his brother deeply. Keith wasn't sure that Aaron would ever get over that.

Aaron looked at Keith and sighed. "What do you think is going on with her and that guy Eric now? I know you handled him, but does he still mess around with Kaia?"

Keith shook his head. "Not that I know of. I haven't seen them together or heard anything about them. Phoenix would have told me if anything was going on. You know that girl loves her daddy to death!"

Aaron smiled at the thought of Phoenix. He missed his baby girl tremendously. "Today is Monday, right? That means Kaia's at work now, so Phoenix is probably in school. I'll go by Kaia's tonight after I get some sleep in a real bed."

Keith agreed. "Yeah, and a real shower, too. At least now you don't have to worry about dropping the soap!" Keith laughed at his own joke.

Aaron gave his brother the finger and added, playfully, "That was never a problem for me. Them dudes in there know who to mess with. Now, if *you* had been locked up, you might have had some problems." Aaron smiled as he shoved more food in his mouth.

"Yeah, right!" Keith threw his napkin at his brother as they shared a laugh.

The person who had just walked in the door diverted Keith's attention. Before he could alert Aaron, Giselle was at their table practically squeezing Aaron to death.

"AARON! When did you get home? Why didn't you tell me you got out?" Giselle was practically in Aaron's lap. She was hugging him so tightly that he looked helplessly at his brother. Aaron finally managed to release himself from Giselle's death grip. "I just came home today, Giselle. How are you doing?"

Giselle smiled at Aaron as if they were long lost soul mates. "I'm fine now that you're home."

Keith wasn't sure how much more of this he could stomach. "Giselle, what brings you in here so early in the morning all by yourself?" he asked.

"I'm here with my friend Danielle." Giselle gestured to a table in the corner where a Puerto Rican girl was sitting alone. "We can join you if you want."

Aaron nearly choked on his coffee. "Nah, that's alright, Giselle. Maybe some other time. We were just on our way out."

Taking his cue, Keith summoned for the waitress and requested their check. While he walked to the counter to pay, Aaron stood and put on his coat while Giselle continued pressing him.

"Aaron, how come you didn't contact me after I came to visit you?" Giselle asked as soon as Keith was out of earshot.

Aaron sighed heavily. He hadn't been on Staten Island for more than an hour and he had the misfortune to run into Giselle so soon. He decided to try and spare her feelings.

"I don't know, Giselle," he began. "What you told me caused me a lot of grief. You know how I feel about Kaia..."

"I know how you *felt* about Kaia," Giselle corrected him. "But that's all changed now, right?"

Aaron was surprised at how guilt-free Giselle sounded. After all, she and Kaia had been friends for a long time. The fact that Giselle could betray her and not feel bad about it, made Aaron's antennae go up.

"Look, Giselle, I'm sorry I didn't write to you or call you. My head was messed up over the whole situation. But, I do appreciate you telling me what was going on. Nobody wants to be made a fool out of. So, thank you for looking out for me."

Giselle didn't like the way this was going. Aaron was trying to brush her off. She decided to make things a little interesting. "Well, I saw her with Eric last week and they looked very happy," she lied. "Maybe all of this worked out for the best."

Aaron was clearly hurt by what she'd just told him, but he refused to give Giselle the benefit of seeing that. Prison had taught him how to camouflage his emotions.

"Good. I'm glad she's happy. Thanks again for doing me that favor."

Aaron walked past her before Giselle could respond. She turned around in time to see his back as he and Keith walked out the door.

Kaia returned to her desk to find the phone ringing. "Albanese, Poonwasi and Moore Securities, how can I help you?"

"Hello, can I speak to Kaia Wesley, please?" the female voice on the other end asked.

"This is Kaia speaking. Who's calling?" The voice sounded vaguely familiar.

"Kaia, this is Giselle. Don't hang up. I have something to tell you."

Kaia wanted nothing more than to slam the receiver down in Giselle's ear. Since Symphany had arranged for two of her younger cohorts to beat her up, Giselle had not returned to work. She had quit her job and Kaia hadn't heard from her since. But here she was calling her after so many months had passed. Kaia smelled a rat.

"What do you want?" she demanded.

Giselle put the first part of her plan into action. "Aaron asked me not to tell you this..."

"AARON?" Kaia was playing right into Giselle's hands.

"Yes, Kaia. Aaron didn't want me to tell you that he's home. He came home yesterday and when we woke up this morning, I begged him to call you. He told me that he has nothing to say to you. But for Phoenix' sake, I think everyone should put everything behind them and we can all move on." Giselle paused, waiting for Kaia's reaction.

She didn't have to wait long. "You're saying that Aaron is out of jail?" Kaia struggled to keep her voice under control as her hands trembled in anger.

"Yeah," Giselle answered innocently. "He came to my place last night as soon as he got to Staten Island. I thought for sure he would come to see you and Phoenix first, but he told me that it's over between you and him. We were in the shower together this morning and I kept reminding him that he has to put your daughter first. I don't know if he's going to take my advice or not, but I thought you should at least know that he's home."

Kaia slammed the phone down and grabbed her coat. She stormed into her boss' office and feigned illness. She explained that she would be leaving early and her boss agreed. By the time she reached the elevator bank, her tears had already begun to fall. Giselle had obviously called to rub salt in Kaia's wounds. Kaia had hoped that somehow she and Aaron would work things out. But it was Giselle's bed that Aaron had spent his first night home in. Not Kaia's. The thought of Aaron showering with Giselle was enough to make Kaia nauseous.

She walked through the parking lot in a daze. Reaching her car, she started the engine and peeled out of the Teleport headed for Symphany's place.

Giselle hung up the pay phone and slid back into her seat in the booth across from Danielle. She wished she could have seen Kaia's face, but hearing the shock in Kaia's voice was reward enough. Soon, she hoped, Aaron would be in her arms where he belonged.

RING! RING! RING! RING! RING! RING! RING! Someone was frantically ringing Symphany's doorbell. She ran down the stairs with her ivory silk robe swinging behind her. She opened the door only to find Kaia crying in a heap on her porch.

"Kaia? What the hell happened, now? Get up. Come inside." Symphany pulled Kaia to her feet and ushered her into her home. She helped her weepy friend out of her coat and into the kitchen. As Symphany brewed some water for tea, she listened to Kaia's recap of the phone conversation she had just had with Giselle. As Symphany listened she became angrier and angrier.

"Kaia, she's probably lying." Symphany hoped that this was all a cruel joke. "Don't let her get you all upset."

Kaia shook her head. "I bet he did sleep with her, Symphany. He hates me and he wants to get back at me."

Symphany placed the aromatic peppermint tea in front of Kaia and took a seat beside her. "Girl, Aaron don't want Giselle. Believe me! If she's telling the truth, then he probably just hit it and that's that. He don't want her."

Kaia wasn't so optimistic. "If she's lying, why hasn't he called me? Why didn't he tell me that he was coming home?"

Symphany thought about it. "I don't know why. But I think you should wait to hear his side of the story before you jump to conclusions."

Kaia sat back in the chair and folded her arms across her chest. "I'm not going to beg him, Symphany. He said it's over between us, right? He had Keith coming to my house every month to pick up Phoenix and take her upstate. I was banned from visiting him. He never called me or wrote to me...all of his letters are addressed to Phoenix and she can't even read yet! He kicked me out of his life and I will not allow him to see that he's hurting me. The best revenge is to be happy, right?"

Symphany nodded her head in agreement. "What are you going to do?" she asked.

Kaia bounded off the couch. "I'm going to NuStyle to get my hair done. Then I'm going to get my nails done. If I'm going to see Aaron, I want him to see what he's missing."

Symphany stood up. "Well, in that case, I might as well get my 'do' touched up, too. Call Lisa and Crystal and tell them we're on our way!"

NuStyle was packed! T.T. was busy gelling some girl's ponytail with almost a whole jar of gel! Crystal was busy working on one of her legendary haircuts. Everyone knew that Crystal worked wonders with a pair of scissors! Lisa was perfecting one of the flyest weaves Kaia had ever seen. Suzanne was at the sink washing an older woman's hair. The radio blared Hot 97FM and the mood was upbeat.

With each of them having several customers ahead of them, Kaia and Symphany took seats at the front of the shop and continued to discuss the situation at hand.

Kaia handed Symphany a crumpled up piece of paper. "All the drama with this nigga and my family got me so stressed out that I'm writing poetry! Can you believe it?

Symphany laughed and opened up the paper. She read the poem Kaia had written and the surprise was evident on her face.

Reflecting I can see it all so clear

The drama

The violence

The whole atmosphere

Unnurtured, unnourished, unattended, unborn

Forecasted, foretold, 'forementioned, forewarned

Long gone

I revisit the exhibit of my torn and broken spirit

And imagine what would have happened

If of my own ship I'd been captain

I reminisce on what once was bliss

Filled with gifts, sealed with a kiss...

Then I dwell on what was my hell

As my belly swelled to the toll of bells

And it seemed like only yesterday

When the child in me went out to play

And returned to the bed which I had made

And in which I was forced to lay

Only to find that if I pray

Trouble don't last always

Symphany looked at Kaia. "Girl, this is good. When did you learn to write like this?"

Kaia took the paper back and sucked her teeth. "Girl, please! This ain't nothing. I write all the time but it's just for fun."

Symphany shook her head. "Nah, Kaia, for real. That's really good. You should keep writing. Use that gift, girl."

Kaia shrugged her shoulders. Her mind drifted back to Aaron, and Symphany could see her friend's sadness written all over her face.

"Kaia, do you think Aaron kept in touch with Giselle after the two of you split up?" Symphany asked.

"I don't know. I never heard from Giselle after Ruthie and La-La beat her ass. She changed her phone number after that. And I didn't talk to Aaron, either. He stopped writing and calling. So, I have no idea what's been going on between them."

"Kaia, do you think Aaron kept in touch with Giselle after the two of you split up?" Symphany asked.

"I don't know. I never heard from Giselle after Ruthie and La-La beat her ass. She changed her phone number after that. And I didn't talk to Aaron, either. He stopped writing and calling. So, I have no idea what's been going on between them."

A tall guy wearing a Starter jacket entered the shop selling CD's. Symphany and Kaia looked over his merchandise and Symphany purchased one with old school jams. Once he moved on to the other customers, Symphany picked the conversation back up where they'd left off.

"Do you ever regret ending things with Eric? I mean it's not like you and Aaron got back together. So do you ever feel like you should have tried to make it work with Eric?"

Kaia gave this question some thought before answering. "You know, at one point I did feel stupid for not seeing Eric anymore. I liked him a lot. He was a gentleman and he treated me very nice. But, I never felt for him the way I feel for Aaron. Even though he called me and still wanted to see me after that whole episode between him and Keith, it was just too much for me to handle at that time."

Symphany couldn't resist the urge to giggle. Kaia seemed to miss the joke. "What's so funny?" she asked.

Symphany composed herself. "Keith is gangsta. I can't believe he punched Eric in the face like that. He didn't have to lay the man out in the Rendezvous!"

The girls shared a laugh at Eric's expense. They continued to discuss Aaron and his newfound freedom throughout the process of getting their hair done. Three hours later, they were finally done. Kaia had gotten a cute updo that complimented her eyes, while Symphany opted for a wrap.

As they walked out to the car, Kaia stopped in her tracks and looked at her friend.

"What happened?" Symphany asked, wondering why Kaia had paused so suddenly.

"I want to say 'thank you' for what you told me after Aaron broke up with me."

Seeing the puzzled expression on Symphany's face, Kaia continued.

"You told me that my mother may not love me, and Aaron may not love me anymore. Giselle may hate my guts. But that's their problem. You told me to learn to like myself because then it won't matter whether or not anyone else likes me. That advice helped me to learn to love myself. And ever since then, I get up and look in the mirror and I say 'Good morning. I love you, girl!' And I mean it. It may sound dumb. But I really feel better ever since I listened to you. So thanks."

Symphany felt emotional. "Wow. That's a big compliment, Kaia. I'm glad that it helped you because you're going to be tested now that Aaron is home. This is going to be a test of your self-confidence and your self-esteem, because Aaron probably looks better than ever. You *know* these chicks out here can't wait to get their hands on him. So hold on to your love of self, girl. You're going to need it."

Kaia nodded in agreement, climbed into the passenger seat of the Explorer and smiled. She looked at her reflection in the mirror and said, "I may not have Aaron. But I still look good!"

They exchanged high fives and drove off to pick Phoenix up from the babysitter

---

After picking up Phoenix, Symphany drove back to her place where Kaia's car was still parked. Kaia loaded Phoenix and her belongings into her car and bid farewell to Symphany. Then she headed home.

En route to their apartment building, Kaia struck up a conversation with Phoenix.

"So, how was school, baby?" Kaia looked at Phoenix sitting comfortably in the back seat. Phoenix was enrolled in a private preschool for gifted youngsters. Kaia loved the fact that her child had such a thirst for knowledge, and Kaia encouraged it.

Phoenix stared out the window and answered, "Fine. I got to be the attendance monitor today."

Kaia smiled. "Wow! That's wonderful, Phoenix! What does the attendance monitor do?'

Phoenix beamed. Making her mom proud was always a treat. "You have to bring the attendance sheet to the office. But you only get to be attendance monitor if you're good."

Kaia parked the car and continued congratulating Phoenix on her accomplishment. They piled out of the car and unloaded all of their belongings. They began to walk toward their building when Kaia noticed a familiar form sitting on the steps. As they got closer, she was able to make out who it was and her heartbeat quickened. It was Aaron.

Before she knew it, they had reached the steps and Phoenix, realizing for the first time that the person sitting outside their building was her father, ran like Flo Jo and leaped into her daddy's arms.

"Daddy, daddy, daddy!!!! When did you get here?" Phoenix couldn't hide her enthusiasm.

Aaron fought back tears of joy as he hugged his daughter as if he never wanted to let go. "I got home today, princess. And I've been waiting all day to see you."

'Liar!', Kaia thought to herself. *'Daddy got home last night, not today. And he was too busy screwing Giselle to come and see us.'*

"Can you stay, Daddy? PLEASE?" Phoenix had Aaron in a vice grip and wouldn't let go.

Aaron finally met Kaia's gaze. He couldn't help noticing how stunning she looked. Her hair was perfect and she smelled so sweet. He wanted to tell her how pretty she still was, but his pride got in the way. He looked at the ground instead. "Hello, miss."

Kaia's heart melted like the wicked witch of the west. She missed him so much. "Hello, Aaron. Welcome home."

"Mommy, can Daddy stay, pleeeaaaase?" Phoenix begged.

Aaron tried to intervene. "Phe-Phe, your mother is probably tired from working..."

Kaia interrupted, "No, Aaron. Don't be silly. Please come inside." Without waiting for an answer, Kaia led the way to her door. As she unlocked her apartment door, Phoenix filled her father in on her new status as her class' attendance monitor.

Kaia led the way inside. Phoenix wouldn't leave her father's side. "Come on, daddy. I'll show you where my room is." Phoenix took Aaron by the hand and led him down the hall to her room. Kaia hung up her coat and sat on the couch, trying to collect herself. She hadn't expected to feel so vulnerable when she saw Aaron. He was so handsome. And the situation with Eric must have really stressed him out, since he looked like he'd taken his frustrations out on a heavy bag or some weights. He was rippling with muscles, and he smelled so delicious. Kaia fanned herself to cool her hormones down.

'Pull it together, Kaia!' she thought to herself. *'Don't let him know you're suffering. He left you, remember? He's with Giselle now. It's over.'*

She got up and went to the kitchen just as Aaron and Phoenix returned from the tour. "Can I offer you something to drink?" Kaia asked.

Aaron declined and sat down at the table. "I hope you're not mad that I came by unannounced," he began. "I knew you'd be coming home around this time and I just wanted to see Phoenix."

Kaia cringed. Did he have to remind her that it wasn't her that he'd been so anxious to see? "No, I'm not mad."

Aaron pressed further. "I guess you'll be expecting company soon, so I'd better get going." The thought of Eric being close to Kaia still sent Aaron's blood pressure soaring. Knowing that if Eric happened to show up while Aaron was there, he would beat his ass, Aaron felt he should leave. He rose from his seat, but Kaia stopped him.

"I'm not expecting company, Aaron. You can stay if you want." Kaia was falling apart inside. What she wanted to say was *'Forget about Giselle! Please don't ever leave.'* But she was too proud to beg.

Aaron sat back down, much to Kaia's relief. She sat down opposite him and took a sip of her Corona. "How does it feel to be home?" she asked.

Aaron smiled. "Feels pretty good." Looking at Phoenix he said, "I missed her so much." A thought struck him and he excitedly suggested it to Kaia. "Since you have to work tomorrow, why don't I take Phoenix home with me? That way I can spend time with her tonight and I'll take her to school in the morning."

Kaia was dumbfounded. Surely, Aaron wasn't suggesting that she allow Phoenix to spend the night at Giselle's house! "Where is 'home' for you these days, Aaron?" she demanded. Kaia was ready for a fight.

Aaron looked confused at her change in demeanor. "I'm staying with my brother until I get a place of my own. She can sleep with me and I'll drop her off at school in the morning." Imagining Kaia with Eric, he spitefully added, "I'm sure you could use some privacy."

Kaia noticed the edge in his voice and decided to ignore it. By now, Phoenix was already running to her room to pack her overnight bag, so Kaia agreed. She rose from the table to help Phoenix, but Aaron stopped her.

"Kaia, can I say something to you before I go?" Aaron looked at Kaia with sincerity.

"Of course," she responded.

Aaron began, "I know that me and you haven't been on the best of terms lately. But you are a really good mother. Any blind man could see that. I wanted to say that I appreciate you taking such good care of her all these years by yourself. I know that wasn't easy. And now that I'm home, I plan to be a damn good father to her. So, what I'm saying is we should try to let bygones be bygones for Phe-Phe's sake."

Kaia was touched. "I agree." She couldn't help wondering if Giselle's pleading had made Aaron suggest this.

Just as she was about to bring up her conversation with Giselle, Phoenix reentered the room with her bag packed. "I'm ready, Daddy!" she announced merrily.

Aaron rose and took her bag. "Okay, baby, let's roll." Turning to Kaia, he said, "Thanks."

Kaia kissed Phoenix goodbye and watched as she and Aaron disappeared down the hallway. They exited the building and Kaia's heart began to melt once more. Aaron was a hard habit to break.

Chapter Twelve

Metamorphosis

After leaving Kaia's place, Aaron took Phoenix to McDonalds on Forest Avenue. He realized that something as normal as taking your child to the golden arches was a first for him. Most parents take for granted the little moments that they have with their children. But Aaron loved every minute of it. He had daydreamed about taking her to the movies or to the store. And now that it was reality, Aaron felt like the luckiest man alive.

Aaron had really bonded with Phoenix during his monthly visits with her. It was during those visits that he would hold her in his arms as a newborn infant. Then he observed her as a toddler roaming the visiting room under his watchful eye. But during the ride to McDonald's, Aaron finally got the chance to *bond* with Phoenix. For Aaron, the fact that he was driving again was a big enough thrill. But getting a chance to listen to Phoenix' narration of the people and places in her neighborhood made Aaron grateful that Kaia had raised her so well. Phoenix was a perfect lady, and Aaron was so proud of her, and she of him.

They stood in line holding hands. Phoenix already knew what she wanted. She always ordered the Happy Meal with chicken McNuggets. "Daddy, make sure they give us Sweet and Sour sauce. Last time me and Mommy came here they didn't give us any and when we got home I had to use ketchup. Yuck!" Phoenix shuddered at the memory.

Aaron laughed at how dramatic his child was. She reminded him of Kaia in so many ways. She was petite just like Kaia. Her long, thick hair, which Phoenix wore in several ponytails, had also been inherited from Kaia. Her eyes were just like Kaia's, and she had also inherited her flair for the dramatics from her mother. Aaron smiled to himself at the thought of someday having a son with characteristics similar to his own. But he had always hoped to have Kaia bear all of his children. That idea was beginning to fade to black.

The door swung open just as Aaron reached the front of the line. He ordered Phoenix' meal and one for himself and paid the cashier. After

129

receiving his change and his food, Aaron turned around and came face to face with Eric.

Time stood still, and the rage which Aaron had managed to somehow suppress all those years resurfaced. Eric, seeing that Aaron's face was taut with anger, prepared himself for battle. He hadn't realized that the man in front of him in line was Aaron. Nor had he realized that Aaron had been released. But Eric had not forgotten the wrath of Keith, and he figured that if Aaron was any comparison to his brother, Eric was in for a fight.

Aaron looked Eric over from head to toe, all the while scowling menacingly. Eric stood his ground and met Aaron's gaze.

"Peace, Aaron." Eric and Aaron were about the same height, but Aaron had an obvious weight and muscle advantage. Patrons in the restaurant, who had noticed the tense body language between the two, waited anxiously to see who would throw the first blow.

Aaron ignored Eric's greeting. His fisted right hand begged to connect with Eric's jaw. But, in his left hand Aaron held Phoenix' hand. He looked down into her innocent eyes and recalled how much of her life he had already missed. He realized that growing up without his own father had left him feeling angry, unwanted and incomplete. He definitely didn't want Phoenix to feel that pain. He reminded himself that he had once made the mistake of causing bodily harm to another individual, and that decision had cost him four years of his life – and Phoenix' life as well. He recalled the fact that he'd been given 2 years probation. Getting arrested now would put him in violation and he could possibly be returned to prison.

All of these thoughts swirled through his mind as Aaron stared icily at Eric. Finally, he said, "Yo, just move out of my way and when you see me, walk the other way from now on."

Eric wanted to say something. He wanted to tell Aaron that he knew he had made a mistake by getting involved with Kaia. He wanted to apologize and to assure Aaron that he and Kaia were a thing of the past. But, the threatening glint in Aaron's eyes warned Eric that this wouldn't be wise. Instead, he stepped aside and watched in silence as Aaron exited with Phoenix in tow.

Once outside, Phoenix looked up at her father innocently. "Who was that, daddy?" she asked.

Aaron took deep breaths to try and abate his anger. He had wanted to pummel Eric mercilessly. But he was convinced that he'd done the right thing. Forcing a reassuring smile, he scooped Phoenix into his arms and answered her. "Nobody, princess. He's nobody."

Kaia awoke the next morning and began to prepare herself for work. It felt strange that Phoenix wasn't there. The two of them had established an early morning routine together. Usually, Phoenix would set the table while Kaia prepared breakfast. Today, Kaia realized, was the first day she had ever awakened without her daughter being present in the apartment.

Kaia was saddened by the thought that Aaron's homecoming was not at all what she had envisioned during the years he'd been incarcerated. She had planned on waking up in his arms like she used to. She had planned on making love to him like never before and bringing him breakfast in bed. She had imagined that when he referred to "home" it was her apartment – *their* apartment – to which he'd be referring. But none of this was true, and Kaia couldn't shake the melancholy mood she was in. As she applied her mascara, she listened to Mary J. Blige softly crooning '*My Life*' and she sang along.

'*If you look at my life ~ And see what I've seen ~ la da da da da....*'

The phone ringing jolted her out of her thoughts. She walked into her bedroom to answer it, all the while hoping that it would be Aaron. Kaia would gladly call in sick in order to spend the day in bed with him. But, she had no such luck. It was Asha's voice she heard when she answered.

"Kaia, Janice had a heart attack last night."

Kaia's heart paused. "WHAT?"

Asha's voice trembled slightly as she spoke. "Kaia, Nubia was over there yesterday talking about what you said about daddy..."

"Nubia confronted her *now* about killing Maurice? Why did it take her all these years to do that? We had that conversation years ago!" Kaia was so shaken by this turn of events that she had to sit down. She plopped down in the recliner with her mouth agape.

"She didn't *confront* her, Kaia. She just told her what you said," Asha corrected her. "And murder is not something you just bring up in a conversation. I guess Nubia was waiting for the right time to mention it.

Anyway, Janice got all upset and kept ranting and raving about how crazy you are. She kept saying that you're just like him...just like daddy. Then she gripped her chest and fell out of her chair."

Kaia gasped. "She's still alive, ain't she?" Kaia couldn't stand the suspense.

"She's hooked up to all these machines, Kaia. They won't say for sure whether or not she's going to make it. All they keep saying is, 'We're running tests'."

Kaia managed to write down Janice's room number at St. Vincent's Hospital, despite how shaken she was. Immediately, Kaia dialed Keith's number.

A very sleepy (and sexy) sounding Aaron picked up on the fourth ring.

After audibly clearing his throat, he answered, "Hello?"

"I'm sorry to call you so early. My mother had a heart attack last night." As she talked, Kaia threw her keys into her purse and hurriedly began to dress.

Aaron was awake now. "Word?" As he sat up slowly, trying not to wake Phoenix, he wondered if this was good news or bad. Janice was no prize in his eyes. But he understood that she was Kaia's mother, so he sympathized. He knew all too well how much pain that kind of loss could cause. "Is she aiight?"

Kaia unplugged her curling iron. "I'm on my way to the hospital now. I just wanted you to know so that you can tell Phoenix' school how to reach me if there's an emergency. Can you tell them to beep me if anything happens, please?"

Aaron reassured her, "I got this. Don't worry about Phoenix. Go see about your moms."

"Thanks, Aaron."

"Don't thank me. She's my daughter, too," Aaron corrected her.

"But let me ask you one more thing before you go."

"Yeah?" Kaia asked.

"She does her own hair, doesn't she?" Aaron looked at Phoenix, who was sprawled out across Aaron's king-sized bed. Her hair was fanned out across the pillows, and Aaron wondered if it had grown overnight. Yesterday, her hair had been neatly twisted into cute ponytails. Before they'd gone to bed, Phoenix had taken all of the barrettes out of her hair, and now it didn't even *slightly* resemble its

132

previous appearance. He wondered if he should use a brush, a comb, or a weed-whacker. "Where did she get all this hair, Kaia?"

Kaia laughed at Aaron's dilemma and he chuckled along with her. Kaia said, "Now you see why I wake up so early in the morning. All that hair takes a lot of time to tame."

Aaron was glad to hear Kaia laugh. She had sounded so scared and worried when the conversation began. "Nah, but for real," he said. "Don't worry about Phoenix. I'll drop her off at school and I'll pick her up, too. Then when you get home tonight, you call me and I'll bring her home. Okay?"

Kaia admired the fact that Aaron seemed to take his responsibility seriously. He sounded like he had everything under control. Aaron had always been her rock. *'Who else could make me laugh when I just found out that my mother had a heart attack?',* she thought to herself.

"Okay." Kaia hung up the phone and rushed to the hospital.

Aaron wondered for a fleeting moment if he should stop by St. Vincent's and check on Kaia after he dropped Phoenix off at school. But he quickly dismissed the notion, telling himself that it was not his responsibility to look after Kaia anymore. That was Eric's job, now.

Kaia speed-walked through the corridors of the hospital, looking for Janice's room number. The lady at the patient information desk had informed Kaia that Janice was in the coronary ICU. But every room that Kaia passed contained a patient who appeared to be near-death. Kaia wondered if that was Janice's case as well.

As she rounded one corner, Kaia spotted the room that corresponded with the numbers she had scribbled on the paper she held in her hand. She slowly approached it, afraid of what she would find inside. As she entered the room, she observed Nubia weeping openly. Asha had a grim look on her face as well. As Kaia walked further into the room, she could see what all the commotion was about.

Janice looked ashen and gaunt. There were tubes everywhere. Machines hummed, buzzed, beeped. It all seemed like a nightmare. Janice lay on her back with her eyes closed.   The IV dripped an unidentified liquid into her veins, and Kaia felt sick to her stomach.

Asha saw her sister's turmoil and spoke soothingly to her. "They have her heavily sedated. But, she wakes up every now and then. Talk to her, Kaia. She can hear you."

Nubia continued to weep as Kaia slowly approached her mother's bedside. She felt conflicted. The woman lying before her had never been nice to her. But this was her mother. And Kaia felt that somehow an unfillable void would be left if Janice died.

A tear rolled down Kaia's cheek as she took Janice's hand in her own. Not because of the pain of seeing her mother so ill. But because it was the first time that Kaia could ever recall having held her mother's hand. Kaia had never felt her mother's hands in her own before, and the realization of this and the pain of all the years of distance between them suddenly seemed too much for Kaia to handle.

"Mommy?" Kaia called to her mother in a voice barely audible. She had never called Janice "Mommy" before. But at that moment, Kaia wanted nothing more than to have a mommy.

Janice stirred slightly. Kaia called to her again.

"Mommy. Please wake up."

Janice opened her eyes slowly. It seemed to Kaia that Janice must have used all of her bodily strength to open her eyes. She was so weak. Janice turned toward her daughter. Seeing for the first time that Kaia was the daughter who held her hand, Janice pulled her hand away. She seemed exhausted after she withdrew her hand, breathing heavily.

Kaia was stunned. She looked at her sisters with incredulity. "Did you see that?" she asked. Neither Nubia nor Asha spoke up. But they had both witnessed their mother's rejection of Kaia. The problem was, both of them were speechless.

Kaia wasn't. She glared at her mother, but Janice had turned her head in the opposite direction, refusing to look at Kaia.

"Janice, you took your hand away from me with the last ounce of strength you had left. Why? Why do you hate me so much?"

Janice did not answer Kaia. Instead she continued to stare at the wall.

Kaia fought back the flood of tears that threatened to plunge forth at any moment. She would not give Janice the satisfaction of seeing her cry. She looked to her sisters once again for some sign of support, sympathy...anything! Kaia found none.

Locking her sights on Janice, Kaia spoke with clarity and firmness in her voice. "All my life, I never wanted anything more than I wanted your love. I wanted to feel like I belonged. I wanted a family. And I never understood why you couldn't just love me. Or at least fake it! You couldn't even pretend. You couldn't even *hide* your hatred. And now, death is knocking on your door and you *still* can't stop this madness. So now I realize that you will never love me. And you know what, Janice? I don't give a fuck."

Asha gasped. "Kaia..."

But Kaia was far from done. "That's right, Janice. I don't give a fuck what you feel anymore. And I wish that I didn't waste so many years trying to please you. I remember everything, Janice. I remember all the times you called me a bitch, when I was too young to even know what that was. I remember all the times I came home from school and tried to start a conversation with you. I would ask you how your day was or tell you that I passed a midterm, and you ignored me every single time. You pretended not to hear me and you treated me like I was invisible. Do you know how I felt all those years living with you and your hate and knowing that you killed my father?!?"

Nubia jumped to her feet. "Kaia, have you lost your mind?!?"

Kaia spun around and faced her sister. "Have *you*? Have you lost your ability to think for yourself? Open your eyes, Nubia. Your mother is a murderer. She killed our father!" Turning back to Janice, Kaia's voice rose higher. "Tell them! Tell them what happened."

Janice finally turned and met Kaia's gaze. The hatred in her eyes as she looked at her daughter was so evident that Asha had to look away.

"I don't care how you look at me," Kaia continued. "You don't scare me anymore. You can't scare me into silence like you did when I was four years old! Admit it. For the first time in your life, admit that you killed him, Janice!"

Janice continued to stare at Kaia with disgust. Nubia and Asha waited for an answer. Kaia waited for closure. After clearing her throat for what seemed like hours, finally Janice spoke.

"I should have killed you're stupid ass, too."

Asha was visibly shocked. Nubia stood still and silent. Kaia shook her head in disdain.

Kaia's mouth formed a sadistic smile. "But you didn't kill me, Janice," she said. "And I'm still living. You can't stop me from living. I will continue to live my life and be happy for as long as I can. Just to spite you! I don't care if you never see your granddaughter. You would only ruin her. She's beautiful, she's smart and she is loved. I love my daughter. And you know why I can love my daughter after all the years of bullshit you put me through? Because I love myself. I *love* Kaia Wesley. So, I don't need your love. You can keep it."

Kaia turned on her heels and stormed out of the room. She had almost reached the elevator, when Asha called after her. But Nubia was hot on Asha's heels.

"Let her go, Asha! What kind of daughter would treat their mother like that when she just had a heart attack?? Let that bitch go to hell!"

Kaia stopped dead in her tracks and spun around.

"Fuck you, too, Nubia. Fuck you! And Fuck your mama, too! You can both go to hell!"

Nubia shot back. "Why did you have to do this now, Kaia? She could die in there, and here you are bringing up something that happened almost twenty years ago."

Asha couldn't believe her ears. "Nubia, Janice *killed* our father! I don't care if it happened 50 years ago! All these years, Janice lied to us. Kaia was a child when daddy died and she had to deal with this shit all these years, Nubia."

Nubia shook her head vehemently. "She didn't have to do this today. She didn't have to come in here and make a scene while our mother is hooked up to all those machines."

Kaia had enough. "I'm not going to sit here and debate with you, Nubia. I told you she killed him and you didn't believe me. So fuck you. But think about this when I'm gone. The same disease that is killing Janice as we speak, is going to kill you, too if you're not careful. I'm not talking about heart failure. I'm talking about hatred, Nubia. Evil. Negativity. Open your eyes, bitch, before you wind up old, lonely and miserable just like her." She looked from Nubia to Asha and back again. "This whole family can kiss my ass. I won't be part of this nightmare anymore."

Kaia stepped onto the elevator, leaving Nubia and Asha standing speechless.

Kaia stood on the porch of Keith and Aaron's home frantically ringing the bell. After leaving the hospital, she realized that she had only minutes before Phoenix was dismissed from school. Knowing that Aaron was picking her up, Kaia drove around Staten Island trying to come to grips with the episode which had just unfolded at the hospital. She had replayed the scene over and over again in her mind and she still couldn't get over Janice's nerve. Kaia was shaken, and now as she stood in front of Aaron's house she wanted nothing more than to get her daughter and go home. Kaia just wanted this day to end.

Finally, Aaron opened the door. He stood before Kaia shirtless and sexy. But she was too distraught to notice. "I came to pick up Phoenix," she explained, her voice shaky and uneven.

Aaron could tell that something wasn't right. "Come in," he instructed her.

Following his instructions, Kaia entered the house and immediately memories of a happier time in her life came flooding back. Nothing had changed. It was all exactly as she remembered seeing it on her last day there. She looked around for her daughter, but Aaron must have read her mind.

"Keith went to pick her up from school. He's taking her to the mall afterward because she told him that she wants a leather coat for her birthday."

Kaia looked quizzically at Aaron. "A leather coat for a four year old? Isn't that a bit too much?"

Aaron nodded in agreement. "That's what I tried to tell him. But Keith enjoys spoiling her so there's no point in arguing with him." Aaron sat on the sofa and patted the cushion next to him, signaling to Kaia that she, too, should sit.

Kaia sat beside Aaron. She tried to get her mind off of the events of earlier in the day, but she couldn't. Sensing this, Aaron spoke up.

"What happened at the hospital?" he asked.

Kaia was stunned by his accuracy. "How did you know something happened at the hospital?" she asked.

Aaron shrugged. "The only time I've ever seen you look this lost was when your moms kicked you out. The only people who cause you this much grief are your family." Aaron saw a few tears fall from Kaia's eyes despite the fact that she tried to turn her face so he wouldn't notice. "Is your moms alright?"

137

Kaia composed herself. She willed her emotions under control and nodded. "Yeah, she's fine. The problem is that I made the mistake of thinking that since she's practically on her deathbed, she would want to make amends with me. But, instead she told me she wished she would have killed me when she killed my father."

Aaron was amazed. "She said that to you?" he asked incredulously.

Kaia nodded. She took a deep breath and recounted the episode for Aaron. He listened intently, his sympathy evident on his face the whole time.

When Kaia was done, she sat there battling her emotions and telling herself not to cry. She felt that if she did, it would mean that Janice had gotten to her – that Janice had won, and she didn't want that to be true.

Aaron smiled at her. "So, you finally told her to kiss your ass, huh?"

Kaia smiled, too. "Yeah. It was long overdue."

"So how do you feel?"

Kaia wasn't sure of the answer to that question. "I don't know," she began as she fought the tears. "I feel alone. I feel tired of all the fucked up things that have happened in my life."

Aaron felt guilty for all the pain he knew he had caused her. But before he could say anything in response, Kaia spoke once again.

"I feel angry that my father was taken from me. I feel betrayed that my mother never met me halfway. I feel sorry for myself, Aaron. I feel like happiness is never mine for long."

Kaia didn't fight the tears anymore. She didn't try to pretend the pain was bearable. She gave in to it, and she cried for herself. She cried for the life that she'd lived when she didn't want to live anymore. She was tired of fighting.

Aaron understood. He had witnessed the cruelty of Kaia's mother and the distance of her sisters. He understood the pain that she was in and he wanted to relieve it. Without thinking about it, Aaron reached for Kaia. He pulled her towards him and she didn't fight. She gave in. When he embraced her, his arms felt safe. Kaia allowed Aaron to hold her as she cried. He held her until he, too, was crying. He felt sorry for all of her pain. He felt powerless to ease it. But when he held her face in his hands, he felt like he could erase all the bad memories in her life. He felt like he could somehow make it all right. And he kissed

138

her. Slowly. And Kaia didn't resist. In fact, she kissed him back with so much passion that Aaron lost himself. He forgot about Eric and the fact that she'd betrayed him. All he knew was that this felt right.

He slipped his hands underneath her sweater and gently caressed her. It felt so good to feel her skin again, and Aaron whispered to her softly. "I miss you so much, Kaia." He wiped the tears from her face and kissed her eyelids delicately.

Kaia was euphoric. She ran her hands across his muscles as he began to undress her. Once he'd gotten her sweater over her head, he found her lips once more and began to kiss her. He unbuckled her belt and kissed her neck. Kaia was now reaching in his pants for the part of him that had eluded her for too long.

And just when they were ready to throw caution to the wind and give in to their ecstasy, the door swung open and Phoenix and Keith stood before them.

Kaia rushed to grab her clothes and Aaron fought to fasten his pants. Keith, seeing that he had clearly interrupted, tried to usher Phoenix back outside. But Phoenix wasn't having it.

"Daddy, you kissed mommy?" she asked. Aaron looked to Kaia for help as she pulled her sweater back on. Phoenix turned to Kaia. "Why did you have your clothes off, Mommy?"

Keith chuckled under his breath as Aaron and Kaia squirmed.

"You're not helping us, Keith!" Aaron reprimanded his brother.

"I'm sorry, y'all. That's why they make bedrooms with doors. Yours even has a lock on it, Aaron," Keith teased.

Kaia's face was red-hot from embarrassment. Just when she thought she would die from humiliation, the doorbell rang. She tried to fix her hair as Keith opened the door.

Everyone's expression changed when they saw Giselle standing at the door.

"Well, looks like I got here just in time," Giselle said, with a smile. "The gang's all here!" She walked in, uninvited and smiled at Phoenix. "Hi, honey."

Kaia turned to Aaron with pain etched in her face. She had allowed herself to forget that Aaron was with Giselle now. But the truth was staring her in the face now. She grabbed Phoenix' hand and walked out the door.

Aaron called after her, but Kaia kept walking. He began to chase after her, but Giselle blocked his path.

"Aaron, we need to talk," she said. "And it can't wait."

Keith couldn't stand Giselle. There was something about her that rubbed him the wrong way. But, Aaron was a big boy. He would have to see Giselle for who she really was on his own.

"Yo, Aaron, go ahead and handle your business. I'm going to the gym. Peace." Keith walked out just as Kaia's car pulled away from the curb. He climbed into his own car and sped off.

Aaron turned towards Giselle and the vein in his neck began to bulge. He was about to put an end to her games once and for all!

Chapter Thirteen

Lessons

Giselle felt like a schoolgirl, sitting on the sofa with her hands folded innocently in her lap. Aaron towered over her and from the look on his face, she could tell he meant business.

"Yo, what the hell possessed you to come to my house without calling first?" he demanded. "You know the phone number, so why didn't you use it?"

Giselle batted her long eyelashes and feigned innocence.

"Aaron, I wasn't planning on coming over here. But I was in the area..."

"For what?" Aaron wasn't letting her off so easily.

This caught Giselle off guard and she chastised herself for not anticipating this question. "Well...I...I went to the...um..."

"Stop lying, alright?" Aaron was growing impatient. "I see right through you." Aaron sat beside her on the sofa and looked her in the eye. "I don't know what you expect from me, Giselle, but it ain't gonna happen. I'm glad that you told me about Kaia and Eric, but that does not mean that I intend to get involved with *you* now."

"Aaron, why not? It's not like Kaia cares about what you do anymore..."

"See? That's what I'm talking about," Aaron interrupted. "Every time you talk to me about Kaia, you're saying something bad. First you told me about her cheating on me. And - I can't lie to you - that made me wonder what kind of friend would betray her girl like that. I definitely benefited from your deceitful ways., but..."

"I'm not deceitful, Aaron. I told you about Kaia because I like you as a person and I didn't want to see her make a fool of you." Giselle realized that she was sinking fast.

"That's bullshit." Aaron had decided that the only way to deal with Giselle was to be blunt. "You're jealous of Kaia. You always have been. I noticed it years ago when you used to come over here to see her. Whenever she showed you something I bought for her or whenever she told you about someplace that I had taken her, you always had something sarcastic to say. Or the look on your face would tell it all. I even told her that you were jealous of her once. And she told me I was crazy. But now look at you. You broke us up and here you are trying to sink your claws into what she no longer has."

Giselle was crying now. Sometimes the truth hurts. "Aaron, that's not true. It's not like that at all."

Aaron shook his head. He felt a little sorry for Giselle. She had lost her friends and now he had to destroy her hopes of having him, too. "Well, the bottom line is this. I still love Kaia."

Giselle's mouth fell open. "You're a fool, then. And you're stupid if you think she's going to leave Eric."

Aaron was unfazed. "I don't expect her to do that. But I can't help how I feel. And as long as I care for her like I do, I'm not going to lie and say otherwise." Aaron saw the defeated look on Giselle's face and decided to soften his approach slightly. "Giselle, I could have fucked you and then shitted on you. A lot of my boys told me to do just that. But I wouldn't want anybody to do that to Phoenix. And you shouldn't want that for yourself, either. You should care enough about yourself to not want somebody to use you. I'm a man, and a man is going to do whatever you let him do. But this ain't right. And to be honest with you, I'm sick of seeing you causing Kaia pain. She's had enough of that to last her a lifetime."

Giselle sat in silence, letting Aaron's words penetrate. She knew it was wrong to want what someone else has. But it seemed that Kaia had all the luck. Giselle was tired of being a plaything to the men in her life. And she had hoped that Aaron would see her as more than that if she told him the truth about Kaia. But it seemed like that was not going to happen.

Deciding to hold onto the little dignity she had left, Giselle rose to leave. "Aaron, Kaia will break your heart and you'll see that she's not the one who deserves to be with you."

Aaron opened the door for Giselle and gestured for her to go. "Kaia *already* broke my heart, and I still love her. I'm sorry if that's not what you wanted to hear."

Giselle walked out the door and Aaron closed the door behind her. Now, he had to make things right with Kaia.

Kaia pulled up in front of her apartment building and put her car in park. After turning off her radio, she and Phoenix stepped out of the car and headed home. Kaia noticed that her daughter had been unusually quiet during the ride home, and she hoped the scene she'd just witnessed wasn't too traumatic for Phoenix. Kaia realized that she would have to figure out a way to explain to Phoenix why she'd found her parents on the verge of a no-holds-barred sex session.

But Kaia was also still reeling from the sight of Giselle at Aaron's home. She showed up without calling first, which Kaia assumed was fine with Aaron. It sure didn't appear that Giselle needed an invitation to pop up whenever she felt like it. *'But why did Aaron kiss me?'* Kaia wondered. *'Why is he making this harder for me to deal with?'*

While she contemplated these questions, Kaia noticed a person sitting on the steps in front of her building. For a fleeting moment, she thought it was Aaron. But as she got closer, she realized it was Keith. He stood and handed Phoenix three shopping bags.

"Hey, princess. You left so fast that you forgot your stuff." Phoenix took the bags and thanked her uncle. Kaia forced a smile and hoped that Keith would be on his way now. She was in no mood for pleasantries.

Keith had another agenda. "Can I talk to you, Kaia? I promise not to take too long."

Kaia nodded and led the way to her apartment. Once inside, Phoenix took her loot to her room to begin hanging everything up. She had convinced her Uncle Keith to buy her a black leather coat, as well as five new outfits to go along with it! She even had a pair of Timberlands to match. Phoenix was somewhat relieved that her mother seemed mentally preoccupied. That meant that she wouldn't have time to lecture Phoenix about asking Uncle Keith to take her shopping.

Kaia opened two beers for herself and Keith and they sat down at the table in her kitchen. Keith wasted no time getting to the point.

"Kaia, I know that you and Aaron don't need me to butt into your relationship..." he began.

Kaia corrected him. "We don't have a relationship anymore, Keith. Giselle made sure of that."

Keith nodded in agreement. "Yes, she did. And that's basically what I need to talk to you about. I know it's really not my business, but what's up with you and my brother? I know the two of you still care about each other."

Kaia forced a laugh. "Well, how did you figure that out, Keith. Was it the fact that we got caught with our pants down in your living room today?"

143

Keith chuckled, too. "You have to admit that was pretty funny."

Kaia smiled. "Yeah, you only think it was funny because you aren't the one who has to explain this shit to Phoenix!"

Keith sobered slightly and said, "That is part of what I have to discuss with you." Kaia was all ears now, as she tried to imagine what could have made Keith get involved in his brother's personal life.

Keith continued. "Ever since I started taking Phoenix upstate to see Aaron, me and her have gotten really close. She asks me a lot of questions about you and Aaron that she's to afraid to ask you herself."

"Like what?" Kaia interrupted.

"Like why you stopped going to visit Aaron; why you don't hang around with Giselle anymore; why Aaron stopped calling all the time. But today, she asked me why Aaron lives with me and not with the two of you."

Kaia felt stupid for underestimating her daughter's perceptiveness. "What did you tell her?"

"I told her that sometimes grown ups need a break from each other but that doesn't mean that they don't care about each other anymore. She thought that since Aaron lives with me that she would have to choose between the two of you."

Kaia was shocked. "Why would she think that?"

Keith shrugged. "I told her that was never going to happen. I told her that Aaron will always love her and that you will too, and just because you two may not love each other anymore, that doesn't mean that she has to choose."

Kaia nodded her approval. "And what did she say then?"

Keith laughed. "She said she understood and everything was fine after that. Then we walked in on you two getting busy."

Kaia laughed, too. "Damn, Keith. She must think that everything is fine between Aaron and me now. I should go and talk to her."

Keith shook his head. "What are you going to say, Kaia? It seems to me like you and Aaron aren't' even sure what's going on."

Kaia had to admit that Keith had a point. She couldn't explain to Phoenix what she wasn't sure of herself.

Keith reassured her. "I think she'll be fine. Just try not to confuse her anymore than she already is. If you and Aaron want to make this work, then go for it. But if not, just do what you have to do to make it all easier on her."

144

Kaia nodded again. "Thanks, Keith."

The doorbell rang, and Kaia rose to answer it. It was Symphany, and Keith resembled a dog in heat as he all but drooled on himself.

"Hey, handsome!" Symphany greeted Keith with a Colgate smile.

"Hello, gorgeous." Keith was obviously smitten. "You're looking good as usual."

Kaia tried to resist the temptation to gag from all the flirting going on, as she opened a beer for Symphany. While Symphany took a seat at the table next to Keith, she noticed how despondent Kaia appeared.

"Wow. It looks like you had a rough day."

Kaia nodded and let out a deep sigh. "You couldn't imagine what a miserable day I've had." Kaia proceeded to fill them both in on everything. She told them about Janice's heart attack and the scene at the hospital with her sisters. She ended with her near-passionate encounter with Aaron and Giselle's unexpected entrance.

Symphany was blown away. "Girl, you know what you need?" she asked, after marveling at Kaia's bad fortune. "A vacation!"

Kaia laughed. "Yeah, well who has time for that?"

Symphany wasn't laughing. "We do. It's Friday. That means that you're off until Monday morning. In fact, that's why I came over here. I have to go to Atlanta for the weekend to tie up some loose ends. Why don't you come with me and relax. Then we'll come back on Sunday night and you can call in sick on Monday to unpack. Aaron and Keith will watch Phoenix this weekend, right, Keith?" Symphany flashed one of her irresistible smiles and Keith was putty in her hands.

"Of course. Kaia, I think you should go."

Kaia gave it some thought. "This is kinda sudden, Symphany. I can't afford..."

Symphany wasn't trying to hear Kaia. "It's about time you did something spontaneous, and don't even think about money, because this trip is on me."

Kaia shook her head. "No, I can't let you pay for me to fly down to Atlanta, Symphany."

Symphany was unrelenting. "Look, you can either come with me and have a blast or stay here and feel sorry for yourself. I think you've had a rough time for the past few months. You should take a break."

Keith agreed. "Kaia, honestly, I think you should go. It's only for the weekend and you need to get your mind off this shit." Keith figured

Aaron could use some time alone with his daughter and Kaia could use a break from all the mothering she'd been doing for Phoenix. "Don't worry about Phoenix. You know she's in good hands."

Kaia sipped her beer and looked from Keith to Symphany and back again. "Okay. Let me go pack."

Symphany beamed. "I'll call Talia and tell her to start packing, too." Kaia left the room to tell Phoenix of her plans. As Symphany began to dial Talia's number, Keith walked up behind her and stopped her. Symphany turned around and the two of them stood eye to eye.

Keith smiled. "Since I helped convince your friend to go with you, I need to ask you for a favor in return."

Symphany smiled flirtatiously and said, "What might that be?"

Keith took her chin in his hands and caressed it. "Let me take you out one night. Let me get to know you a little better, that's all."

Symphany didn't budge, although she was very attracted to Keith. "What about your girlfriend Zenobia? I told you I don't deal with guys with baggage."

Keith understood where she was coming from. "I know. You told me that several times. But I'm not with her anymore. We went our separate ways a few months ago. So now what's your excuse?"

Symphany didn't have one. So she said, "When I get back, you've got yourself a date."

Keith kissed Symphany's hand and smiled as he headed for Phoenix' room to help her pack her things.

Symphany dialed Talia's phone number.

"Girl, pack your bags. We're going to Atlanta!"

About an hour later, Keith arrived at his own doorstep with Phoenix in tow. As they entered the house, Aaron emerged from his room looking like he was on his way to a Phat Farm photo shoot. He wore dark blue jeans with a cream-colored sweater bearing the Phat Farm logo. On his feet he wore chocolate brown Timberlands and a chocolate brown suede jacket sealed the deal. He looked delectable.

Keith noticed that his brother had gotten a fresh haircut and that he smelled of the cologne *Fahrenheit*.

Keith smiled, knowing that his brother felt good after a day of pampering himself. It had been years since he'd seen Aaron look so good.

"Looking good, brotha!" Keith couldn't stop smiling at Aaron.

Aaron, however, was trying to figure out why Phoenix was with Keith instead of at home with her mother. The puzzled expression on his face brought Keith out of his trance.

Phoenix ran to her father and Aaron scooped her up in his arms and hugged her. Keith said, "Your baby girl will be staying with us this weekend."

Aaron smiled at the idea of having Phoenix over for the weekend. But his curiosity was getting the best of him, especially since he had been on his way to see Kaia when Keith arrived. "Why does Kaia need us to watch her this weekend? Does she need time to be with Eric or something?"

Keith seemed surprised by Aaron's question. "Kaia went with Symphany and Talia to Atlanta. I brought Phoenix' stuff over there earlier. Symphany came by while I was there and she saw how upset Kaia was. Symphany has to go to Atlanta and handle some business so she paid for all of them to go down there and get their minds off of everything."

Aaron couldn't hide his disappointment. It was evident on his face. "Oh. So I guess there's no point in me going over there, huh?"

Keith shook his head. "Nah, they left for the airport already. What were you going over there for?" Before Aaron could answer, Keith began to grin. "Were you trying to finish what y'all started in here today?"

Aaron kissed Phoenix and put her down. He took her coat to the closet and hung it up. Then he took his own coat off and hung it up as well. "It doesn't matter what I was going over there for. She ain't there, so forget it."

Keith noticed the edge in Aaron's voice and he knew that his brother wasn't happy. "Yo, I don't know what you meant about that Eric comment, but I just left Kaia and Eric is not the one who's on her mind. She doesn't seem to have feelings for him. It's you that has her going through it."

Aaron walked into the kitchen and poured Phoenix some milk to go with the Oreos he'd just given her. Phoenix sat down at the table to enjoy her snack and Aaron joined his brother in the living room. He sat across from Keith and sighed.

"Keith, that girl has me real confused right now."

Keith couldn't remember ever seeing his brother look so lost. "Confused about what?"

Aaron sat back in his seat and shook his head in anguish. "It's like, I know she played me when she started messing around with Eric. And she lied to me about it on top of everything. When I was locked down, I didn't want nothing else to do with her. But then when I saw her...it's like she still makes me feel like I did when I was that little boy in the park who was crazy about her. And I wasn't expecting that."

Keith was sympathetic to his brother's plight. He knew that Aaron was struggling with his emotions as well as his pride. "Aaron, Kaia made a mistake, man. I said that then and I'll tell you the same thing now. She had a lot of responsibility and a lot of pressure on her. She's human."

"Yeah, but Eric was your friend. By getting involved with him, she disrespected me. And I just can't help feeling like a sucka for even wanting to be with her now. Do you understand what I'm saying?"

Keith did understand. "Yeah, I feel what you're saying. But that sounds like pride to me. And that can be a dangerous thing. Don't get so blinded by your pride that you let true love slip away. That would be real foolish."

Aaron thought about the logic in Keith's statement. "What would you do?"

Keith had to think for a moment. He wanted to give Aaron a genuine response. Finally, he said, "If I was in your shoes, I would let her have her fun in Atlanta. Women need that type of shit every now and then. When she comes back, you should talk to her. See where her head is at as far as this dude is concerned. And if she still loves you and you still love her, I would give it another shot. If for no other reason than for Phoenix. At least try to be a family for her."

Aaron nodded in agreement and thought about what Keith was saying.

Keith smiled. "Plus you know that Kaia's the only one who *ever* got you open like this, so you might as well stick with her."

Aaron laughed and went to spend some time with his beautiful daughter.

Symphany plopped down on the bed in the hotel room. "Kaia, which dress should I wear to Club 112 tonight?" She was trying to decide between a cute black dress and a sexy black dress.

Kaia shrugged her shoulders. "I told you to wear pants like I am." Kaia checked herself out in the floor to ceiling mirrors in the bathroom. She looked amazing in a pair of black linen pants with an off-white sheer silk blouse. The blouse had a plunging neckline and it showed off Kaia's ample bust. "I am *working* this outfit!"

Talia laughed. "You sure are, Kaia. But wait till they see *me* walk up in there! They better have tight security because this outfit could cause a stampede." Talia wore a red dress with a split high enough to expose more than a little thigh. Since Talia worked out regularly, she had the legs of a dancer. She looked stunning.

The girls complimented one another and Symphany opted for the sexy black dress. She went into the bathroom to get dressed while Kaia and Talia applied their makeup in the bedroom mirror. They were headed to one of Atlanta's hottest clubs to celebrate all the latest developments in their lives.

After arriving in Atlanta the previous night, the ladies spent the evening in their lovely suite. The suite boasted a full kitchen, and the girls made dinner and holed up in their room reminiscing on old times. They discussed Symphany's decision to enroll in college to study law and Talia's upcoming college graduation. They also discussed Kaia's problems and Symphany and Talia had comforted her. They made her see that she had emerged victorious from her war with her mother. They told her that because she had finally spoken up, Janice no longer had any power over her. Now, she was feeling better and the ladies intended to paint the town red by driving into Buckhead to attend the hottest party.

Earlier in the day, while Kaia and Talia slept, Symphany had gone out to handle the business she'd come for. She didn't tell her friends the details, but she had come to Atlanta to purchase a house for her mother. Symphany had never disclosed to the girls how much she was actually worth. But after making her first $10,000 in the drug game, Symphany had invested her money in a stock portfolio that couldn't lose. The first year, her money had multiplied tenfold. And now, five years later, she had a large nest egg and wanted to use some of it to relocate her mother to Atlanta, which was where Symphany's mom was originally from. The thought of surprising her mother on her birthday with a deed to her new house made Symphany smile. Now that it was done, Symphany couldn't wait to go out and let her hair down.

Symphany emerged from the bathroom looking fierce! Her hair fell in a perfect wrap ending at her chin. She wore a strapless black minidress and completed the look with slinky black Ferragamo stilettos. She walked over to the mirror and began to apply her makeup as well.

Talia hollered. "Wow, girl, you look good! Don't hurt nobody out there tonight!"

Kaia smiled. Symphany looked like a model. Kaia wondered what Keith would say if he could see her now. "So what's up with you and Keith?" she asked.

Symphany laughed and grabbed her coat and her purse. "Let's get going. I'll tell you all about the plans I have for his sexy ass on the way to the party."

Before they knew it, the weekend was over and the ladies were loading their luggage onto the plane at seven o'clock on Sunday morning. They settled into their seats for the two-hour flight. Symphany and Talia were seated side by side. They took their meal trays down and began a game of "Pitty-Pat". Kaia had a window seat next to an old white lady with bright red hair. Hoping the woman wouldn't talk to her during the flight, Kaia leaned back in her seat and decided to utilize her time in the air to write. She had always enjoyed writing as a youngster. It had been a kind of self-therapy for her during her tumultuous years under Janice's roof. Since she gave birth to Phoenix, she hadn't found the time to write anymore. This seemed as good a time as any.

As Talia beat Symphany mercilessly at cards, Kaia found herself writing a letter. To herself.

Kaia,

I know it seems strange to write a letter to yourself. But it feels a little more rational than talking to yourself out loud. This weekend was a good one. You got a chance to chill with your girls and get your mind off of the drama in your life. You sure have had a lot of drama in your life, girl.

Now, you're going home to face the same things that were there when you left. You have to deal with the whole Aaron and Giselle situation. Don't get emotional about it. Remember what Talia said about love. She told you that you were lucky to have had a love like you had with Aaron. Most people go through life longing for a love like that. Many people settle for a substitute that barely resembles real love. You had the real thing. And you both made mistakes and messed that up. You're human. Don't regret anything. Just take the lesson for what it's worth and learn from it.

You learned a lot of things during this trip. You realized that you have two of the best friends in the world. And you realized that Giselle did what she did because she is a miserable person. Misery loves company. And by allowing her to see that she had hurt you, you gave her what she wanted. So now, the next step is to forgive yourself. Forgive yourself for the mistakes you made and for the things that you regret. Then, you should try to forgive everybody else. If you forgive Giselle, that doesn't mean that you have to be her friend. It just means that you no longer give her any power over you to hurt you anymore. I know you want to beat her ass. Don't do it. Let her be miserable by herself. She will get hers eventually.

Forgive Aaron. Maybe he shouldn't have cut you out of his life like he did. But he was hurt. And people do irrational things when they're hurt.

And last but not least, forgive Janice. You know that she probably never received affection from her own mother. So she probably didn't know how to give it to you – or Nubia and Asha. She funneled her hatred of Daddy into a hatred for you. That's her problem and she's the one who has to find peace within herself. You know that you are smart, pretty and a damn good mother. So don't let Janice – or anybody else – make you feel like shit.

The last thing I want you to know is that I love you. I don't care if it sounds conceited. I love you! All your life you've wanted love. Maybe that's because the only person who loved you unconditionally was murdered right before your eyes. And then you thought you needed love from Aaron.

*Now, you should see that all the love you ever needed is
the love of self.*

Don't forget that.

Love, Kaia

After landing at Newark Airport in New Jersey, the ladies filed off
the plane and claimed their luggage. They decided to get a cab to take
them back to Staten Island since Symphany and Kaia had both left their
cars at home. Talia fiddled with her garment bag and balanced her carry-
on bag on her shoulder. Kaia adjusted the handle on her rolling suitcase
and prepared to go outside to fight for a taxi. But then she noticed that
Symphany just didn't look good. She had her Louis Vuitton luggage at
her feet and she appeared to be trying to fight off a sneeze or to resist the
urge to vomit.

"Symphany, are you okay?"   Talia must have noticed that
Symphany looked ill as well, and she rushed to her friend's side.

Symphany was sweating profusely and her eyes watered.

"Symphany!" Kaia hoped to snap her friend out of whatever it
was she was going through.   But Symphany couldn't seem to bring
herself to respond.

Suddenly, as if overcome by an intense force, Symphany
collapsed on the floor of the airline terminal. She thrashed around on the
floor with no control over her movements – her eyes rolled in the back of
her head.

Kaia dropped to her knees and held her friend in her arms.
Symphany continued to convulse as Talia screamed for help.

"Somebody get an ambulance! Please help us!" Kaia tried not
to cry but Symphany wouldn't stop shaking. After about two minutes,
Symphany seemed to relax and Talia and Kaia were relieved to see a
team of paramedics headed swiftly in their direction.

But just as things began to calm down and Kaia and Talia's
nerves began to relax, Symphany had another seizure. Kaia couldn't
stop the tears from falling as she and Talia watched the paramedics go to
work on Symphany. They injected her with a syringe filled with some type
of medicine. A crowd had begun to form and they all watched breathlessly
as one of the EMTs ordered another to put Symphany in the "recovery

position". They laid her on her side and brought one knee up toward her chest. The female paramedic was quietly reassuring Symphony as the last convulsion came to an end.

As they strapped her to a gurney, the female paramedic explained to Kaia that Symphony had experienced something called status epilepticus – which was a prolonged epileptic seizure. They had to get her to a hospital immediately since Symphony had not regained consciousness. She asked Kaia if this had been Symphony's first seizure. Kaia and Talia looked to one another for an answer. Neither of them knew. They noticed that Symphony had sustained a cut to her head when she fell to the floor. The paramedics applied pressure to the wound and then whisked her off. Kaia and Talia raced after them, dragging their luggage behind them. They managed to overhear the EMTs talking about a lack of normal respiratory movements and a lack of oxygen.

Eventually, all the noise around Kaia seemed to mute. She could see a lot of people's mouths moving, but she heard no sound. She could tell that the paramedics were barking orders at one another. But she heard nothing. She knew that her boots must have been clicking against the floor as she trotted behind the paramedics. But she couldn't hear it. Nothing was audible to Kaia except her own thoughts.

'Symphony, please don't die.'

University Hospital housed a Comprehensive Epilepsy Center. Symphony was taken there by ambulance and whisked into one of the rooms. As they waited for word from the doctor, Kaia and Talia contacted Symphony's mother and explained what had happened. She was on her way before she ever hung up the phone. Kaia had also called Aaron and explained the situation. She felt guilty for missing her daughter while her friend was fighting for her life just doors away. Aaron had assured her that he had Phoenix under control and, to Kaia's surprise, he told her that he was on his way to be with her. Kaia didn't argue.

Talia's face was streaked with tears as she paced the floor. She summoned one of the paramedics as they emerged from the room Symphony was in. "What's going on in there?" she asked, urgency in her voice.

The lady seemed to understand Talia's anguish and she

reassuringly put her arm around Talia's shoulder and they sat down. Kaia joined them to hear the prognosis.

The paramedic said, "Your friend had an epileptic seizure and she has not regained consciousness. We have no way of knowing if this was her first seizure or if there's a history of this in her family. But at this point, they're running a lot of tests and trying to get her stabilized."

Kaia felt faint. "Is she going to make it?" she asked.

The paramedic shrugged. "It's too soon to tell."

Talia still had questions. "What causes epilepsy?'

"Epilepsy is a neurological condition. It starts with abnormal surges of electrical activity in the brain and that is what causes the seizure. Your friend had more than one seizure today which is not too common. Usually there is one and that's it. But while she was having the seizures, her respiratory system began to dysfunction and that can lead to brain damage. Hopefully, we got her here in time to avoid that. We did inject her with Diazepam at the airport. That should help."

"Damn. What if she knew all along that she had this disease, Kaia?" Talia was crying again. "Why didn't she tell us?"

Kaia tried to sound optimistic. "Ma'am, if she did know, how would a person treat epilepsy."

"Most people choose medication because it can prevent seizures in most people. She would have to take anti-epileptic medications. She could also opt for surgery or there is an option that involves a specific diet called the Ketogenic diet."

Talia snapped to attention. "That's it! She told me on the plane that she was on some keto-something diet. I couldn't understand why, since she looks so great already. But all she said was that she hadn't been sticking to her diet."

Kaia couldn't believe her ears. Symphany had known about this condition and kept it to herself. Kaia's emotions ranged from anger to fear.

"Could we have done anything if we had known that she had this?" Kaia asked. She would die if she found out that she could have helped her friend.

The paramedic shook her head. "You did exactly the right thing. You didn't restrain her or put anything in her mouth. That's the biggest mistake. Other than that, all you can do is make sure the person doesn't hurt themselves during the seizure and put them in the recovery position once the seizure is over."

154

Kaia and Talia both felt some relief to know that they had done all they could. They thanked the paramedic and she promised to pray for Symphany. Kaia and Talia held hands and waited for what seemed like days.

After about an hour or so, Symphany's mother arrived and was greeted by her daughter's teary friends. They showed her to the nurse's station and left her to fill out a mountain of forms. When they arrived back in the waiting room, Aaron, Sean and Keith had arrived and they had Phoenix with them.

Kaia fought the urge to laugh when she saw her daughter's hair. Aaron had arranged Phoenix' hair in a big sloppy Afro puff on top of her head. Phoenix ran to her mother and Kaia hugged her like she never wanted to let go. Aaron walked over to Kaia and hugged her. He told her that Sean had insisted on coming with them due to the history he had with Symphany. Kaia understood and looked over at Keith who seemed to have tears in his eyes. He was being strong, but Kaia knew that both Sean and Keith cared deeply for Symphany. She smiled a little, knowing that Symphany would be gassed to know that the men who loved her had rushed to her bedside.

Talia explained to Aaron, Sean and Keith what had happened to Symphany. Keith immediately went to the nurse to request some information on the Ketogenic diet. When he returned, they all read the pamphlet together to learn more about the treatment method Symphany had chosen.

According to the pamphlet, the diet consisted of mostly fatty foods such as butter, cream and peanut butter. But it said that foods like bread, pasta, fruits and vegetables should be severely limited. Kaia thought back to their trip to Atlanta and recalled all the bread and pasta they had eaten. The pamphlet also said that the patient must measure their food carefully at each meal since even a slight departure from the diet could ruin its effectiveness.

Finally, Symphany's mother reentered the waiting room. The look on her face made Kaia's hair stand on end.

"Symphany is in a coma," Ms. James began. "They said she may not make it. You all should go in and see her right away." Keith held Ms. James in his arms as she cried. All these tears were confusing to Phoenix, who was too young to understand why everybody was crying.

Aaron took Phoenix in his arms and turned to Kaia. "I'm going to stay here with Phe-Phe. You and Talia should go and see your friend."

Kaia agreed and realized how glad she was that Aaron had come. She took Talia's hand and they headed for Symphany's room. Keith and Sean followed close behind with Mrs. James in tow.

But as they approached Symphany's room, Kaia suddenly wished all of this was a terrible nightmare. She could hear the machines before she even entered the room. But when she did walk in, the sight of her friend laying there with a tube down her throat and machines buzzing by her bedside made Kaia feel like this was déjà vu. This scene was eerily reminiscent of the debacle with Janice. For a moment, Kaia wished it were Janice lying before her rather than Symphany.

Kaia walked slowly to Symphany's bedside. She took her friend's hand and stroked it gently. "Symphany, can you hear me?" Kaia whispered in her ear. She got no response.

Kaia continued. "We're all here, girl. Your mom is here. Talia is here. Sean and Keith are here. Aaron and Phoenix are waiting right outside." Kaia cleared her throat and fought the tears waiting in the wings of her eyes. "Now all we need you to do is wake up. Please, Symphany. Please wake up. We all need you. You're the life of the party, Symphany. Please open your eyes."

Kaia didn't fight the tears anymore, and as Mrs. James joined her at Symphany's bedside, Kaia clung to her for support. Mrs. James stroked Kaia's back reassuringly despite the fact that she felt just as helpless as Kaia did. Kaia pulled herself together and stepped away from Symphany's bed for a moment. She watched as Talia spoke to Symphany, telling her that she loved her. To Kaia, all of this seemed too much like saying goodbye, and she was not ready to say goodbye to her friend.

But despite her refusal to accept it, Symphany slipped further and further away from them. One by one, they all exited the room as Mrs. James kept vigil at her daughter's bedside. Talia and Keith went to the cafeteria to get some coffee while Sean went outside to smoke a cigarette. Kaia sat beside Aaron in the waiting room where Phoenix was sleeping in his lap.

Seeing the drained expression on Kaia's face, Aaron felt that the news wouldn't be good. "How is she?" he asked warily.

Kaia shook her head. "Not good, Aaron. Not good at all."

Without thinking about it, Aaron reached for her hand. Kaia was visibly surprised by this gesture and Aaron decided this was a good time to share with Kaia what he'd been feeling lately.

"Kaia, while you were in Atlanta, I did a lot of thinking about us. I know that Symphany is in bad shape right now and maybe this ain't the best time but I just want to tell you that..."

It was then that the door to Symphany's room flew open and Mrs. James came running frantically calling for the doctor. Kaia and Aaron's hearts sank as they sprung from their seats and ran in her direction. Before they could reach her, doctors and nurses had flooded past her, running into Symphany's room. Before they closed the door behind them, Kaia could hear the monotone beeping of the respirator.

Aaron held onto Phoenix while Kaia rocked Symphany's mother in her arms. "She's going to be alright. She's going to be fine." Kaia kept repeating these words to Mrs. James as if by doing so she could will them into actuality.

But that would not be the case. One doctor emerged from Symphany's room with a look on his face that held nothing but sympathy and regret. Mrs. James began to holler immediately. He didn't even have to tell her. Kaia fell apart and Aaron didn't bother to hide the tears that streamed down his own face. Talia and Keith turned the corner and saw all the mayhem. Without being told they all knew. Symphany was dead.

Talia cried on Keith's shoulder as the doctor ushered Mrs. James into Symphany's room. Kaia was inconsolable and Aaron hugged her tightly to his muscular chest, hoping this would offer her some kind of strength. But they were all devastated. As Sean made his way back to the corridor, he saw the mourning and anarchy and crumpled into a bawling heap on the floor. He knew the prognosis without having to be told.

Symphany was gone.

Chapter Fourteen

Breaking the Chains

The next two days were almost unbearable for Kaia. Preparing for Symphany's funeral was not what she wanted to be doing. But Symphany's mother had made arrangements for her burial. As Kaia stood gazing absently out her bedroom window, she knew that Talia was on her way over to pick her up. Mrs. James had indicated to both of them that she wanted them to play an important role in Symphany's funeral. Today was the day to find out what exactly those roles were. Kaia felt a lump in her throat at the very thought of it.

Aaron had attempted to be of some comfort to Kaia. But his efforts to draw her out of the fog she was in were unsuccessful. Kaia was devastated by the loss of her friend. Even though Aaron kept Phoenix for a few days to allow Kaia space and time to grieve, she still hadn't smiled since Symphany collapsed at the airport.

On this day, as she went through the process of dragging herself out of bed and into the shower, Kaia felt drained. She was tired of all the traumatic situations in her life. Her soul was weary. But the funeral was to be her final chance to say goodbye to her friend and she wanted to help Symphany's mom out in any way that she could.

She lathered her body as her mind rewinded to happier days in her life. She recalled her father and how he used to sing to her and teach her the words to the oldies. She thought back to the days before Giselle's betrayal when they had all been like sisters. Their years in high school together had been some of the happiest years of Kaia's life. She reflected on the day Phoenix was born. Despite Aaron's absence that day, Kaia had experienced the joy of that moment with Symphany at her side. She thought back to how encouraging Symphany had been that day, and how Symphany had held her hand during Aaron's sentencing. Symphany had been Kaia's best friend, and she was gone. The reality of it hit Kaia hard and she collapsed in gut-wrenching sobs as the water from the shower continued to douse her.

Talia and Kaia arrived hours later at Symphany's mother's house. Ms. James opened the door looking drawn and empty. They hugged her and she escorted them into her humble home, where Sean was seated on the living room sofa. Kaia and Talia were both surprised to see him there.

"Hey, Sean." Kaia offered weakly. Kaia had never been too fond of Sean, but Symphany had cared for him. That would be their common bond in the days to come – their love for Symphany.

Sean greeted the girls as they took seats in the living room. Ms. James had apparently been thumbing through old photos of Symphany and her brother before Kaia and Talia had arrived. Talia picked one up and let out a hearty laugh. Ms. James smiled knowingly.

"If Symphany knew that I showed you that picture she would have a fit," Ms. James said with a chuckle. "She tried to steal it from me every time she came over here to make sure that no one else would see it."

Talia showed Kaia the photo of Symphany as a toddler standing in a tub of sudsy water, naked as a jay bird. The smile she wore was typical of Symphany. It lit up the room. Kaia smiled as Talia and Ms. James continued to reminisce about the old pictures. Sean held up one of Symphany wearing a flowing white dress, which resembled a non-traditional wedding gown. Her long hair fell at her shoulders and the look on her face was calm and serene, the smile she wore was glorious.

"When did she take this picture?" Sean asked.

Ms. James took the picture in her hands and a tear fell from her eyes. "That was at my niece's wedding a few years ago. Symphany was the maid of honor and everyone kept mistaking her for the bride." Ms. James beamed at the memory. "She looked so pretty that day, and she never even bragged about the fact that she paid for the wedding."

Talia was surprised. Symphany had never mentioned paying for hercousin's wedding. "She did?"

Ms. James nodded. "Symphany was a very generous person." As if a thought had suddenly occurred to her, Ms. James looked at each of her daughter's friends for a long moment. Then she spoke.

"I knew that my daughter was doing something illegal." The surprise on Kaia's face was evident. Ms. James continued. "No one can make the kind of money she made without doing something they ain't supposed to be doing. She would tell me that she hit the number or some other bogus story but a mother always knows. I sat her down one day and told her that she was walking on a dangerous path and that she needed to step back and decide what she wanted to do with her life before it was too late. Symphany cried in my arms that day. She was ashamed of how she made her money. But I told her that God forgives even the ugliest sin. From that day on, she promised to stop dealing with drugs." Kaia and Talia exchanged knowing glances, both remembering their gathering at what Symphany had called her 'retirement party'. Ms. James continued.

"Life is short. Before you know it, it can pass you by. Be happy while you're living because time waits for no one." Taking a deep breath, Ms. James continued. "I saw a change in Symphany over the last few months of her life, and today, Sean helped me to see why that change took place." Sean wiped his eyes and nodded in agreement.

"Sean said that while they were in Virginia last summer, Symphany had her first seizure," Ms. James said.

Talia gasped and Kaia furrowed her brow.

"I was shocked to find this out, too," Ms. James said. "She recovered, obviously, and she started using the diet they suggested to fight the epilepsy."

"She didn't want to take medication every day of her life," Sean explained.

Ms. James managed a smile. "But I believe that seizure changed her life. Symphany started appreciating each day. She started taking advantage of every moment. And when she left that damn drug game alone, she was a happier person than I've ever seen her be. That's what each one of you should learn from her death. Tomorrow is not promised. Live life to the fullest."

Fighting back tears, Ms. James turned to Kaia and took a deep breath. "Symphany loved all of you girls," she said. "But you were like a sister to her, Kaia. You were her best friend. For that reason, I'd like for you to deliver her eulogy."

Kaia's mouth fell open in shock. Shaking her head she said, "Ms. James I wouldn't know what to say..."

"Say what's in your heart. You knew Symphany almost as well as I did. You girls grew up together. I think she would want you to do it."

Talia agreed. "Kaia, you write so well. You always wrote the best papers in high school. Plus, I think Ms. James is right. Symphany would want this."

Kaia's eyes welled up with tears and she nodded. "Okay. I'll do it."

Ms. James patted Kaia's hand reassuringly. "Thank you," she said. She looked at Talia and winked. Kaia would never know that Talia had suggested to Ms. James that Kaia be asked to read the eulogy. Despite her own grief, Talia had noticed how traumatized Symphany's death had left Kaia. She figured that writing the eulogy would help Kaia work through the pain. Talia said a silent prayer that it would be a comfort for all of them.

Sean cleared his throat and spoke. "I miss her so much."

Ms. James nodded in agreement. "We all do, baby. We all do."

They sat and reminisced for a little while longer. Soon, women from Ms. James' church arrived with casseroles, hams and macaroni and cheese. Before they realized it, the kitchen was full of food. Everyone comforted Ms. James and prayed with her. Kaia and Talia were soon overwhelmed with all the grieving and rose to leave.

As they gathered their coats, Ms. James managed to pull Kaia to the side. "Kaia," she said. "Symphany confided in me that you have a lot of problems with your mother. In fact, she told me that seeing the pain your mother caused you made her appreciate me even more."

Kaia hung her head as the pain of this truth seared through her. She nodded and a tear fell from her eye.

Ms. James continued. "I never realized how much of Symphany's childhood I missed until it was too late. I thought that working to get enough money to give them whatever they wanted was what good mothers do. But I think I may have taught them that money is all that matters. I managed to fix my mistake before it was too late. I think that someday, your mother will realize what a great daughter she has. I think she will come around eventually.

Kaia shook her head. "I doubt it."

Ms. James took Kaia's chin in her hand and tilted her face so that Kaia's eyes met her own. "Well, now that my daughter is gone, it looks like the two of us are orphans. If you ever need a mom, you call me. I mean that. Anything you need, I'm just a phone call away."

Kaia smiled through her tears. She felt a twinge of joy in the midst of her despair. "Thank you, Ms. James." Kaia hugged her tightly and rested her head on her shoulder. Ms. James returned the embrace and said, "Call me Monique."

At that moment, Kaia realized that she had a mom at last.

After leaving Symphany's mom's house, Kaia found herself inundated with thoughts of her biological family. Without thinking about it, she found herself driving in the direction of Asha's house.

She parked the car and walked steadfastly toward the door. She rang the bell and waited. Asha appeared in the doorway and greeted Kaia with a smile. "Come in."

Kaia removed her coat and sat on Asha's sofa. Asha sat beside her and for a moment, the mood was awkward.

Finally, Kaia broke the ice. "How is she?"

Asha shrugged. "She's going to make it. She has to change the way she eats and take medication. But she'll make it."

Kaia nodded and tried to battle the disappointment she felt. "I'm glad," she lied.

Asha took a deep breath.   "Janice admitted that she killed Daddy."

Kaia couldn't hide her surprise as Asha continued.

"She told Nubia and I that Daddy's drinking was out of control for a long time. Their marriage was definitely rocky because of it. You probably don't remember this since you were so little when it happened, but she kicked him out of the house a few times when they fought. I guess Nubia and I were just glad to have some peace and quiet so we never complained about it. But you were a toddler then and a daddy's girl. You would cry and cry for him to come back. We all tried to console you but all you wanted was Daddy. Little did we know that Janice felt that you're crying for Daddy meant that you didn't like her. She felt like you preferred him over her, and she resented you for that. Soon, everytime she looked at you, she saw Daddy."

Kaia couldn't believe her ears. "She told you that?"

Asha nodded. "She told us that on the day Daddy died she was arguing with him and you ran to his defense."

Kaia shook her head. "That's a lie. I told them *both* to stop yelling. I was telling them to stop it and..."

"And Janice snapped." Asha explained. "She snapped, and she slapped you. She said that when Daddy defended you it enraged her even more and she went for the knife." Asha paused as if she were still in shock. Shaking her head in amazement she continued. "I think that after he died, she felt like she had you right where she wanted you. She had all the power over you since Daddy couldn't defend you anymore and she abused that power. I think she felt that she was somehow hurting Daddy by hurting you."

Kaia was disgusted. "She hurt Daddy enough when she killed him."

Asha nodded in agreement. She looked Kaia in the eye. "You shocked her when you brought this up. She thought you were too young to remember what happened. She said you never mentioned that day and she thought it was forgotten."

Kaia let out a sarcastic laugh. "I wish I could forget it. I'll never forget the look in her eyes while she stabbed him to death - right in front of me. She killed the one person who showed me love."

Asha knew that last comment was meant for her. "Kaia, I'm sorry," she said. "I'm sorry for what Janice did and I'm sorry for the childhood you had. I should have been there for you. But, honestly, I never understood why Janice was so hard on you. She's our mother and I guess I was just happy that it wasn't me she hated. That was selfish and stupid and I am really sorry. We left you alone to weather all your storms and that's not how family is supposed to be."

Kaia let the tears fall and she and Asha embraced. It felt good to hug her sister. She wished Symphany were alive so that she could tell her about it.

Kaia rose to leave, telling Asha that she would call her. She explained that Symphany's funeral was the next day and, to her surprise, Asha offered to baby-sit Phoenix. Kaia smiled at the thought of Phoenix getting to know her aunt and she agreed.

"I just found out that I can never have any children." Asha's expression turned sad as she said this and Kaia felt sorry for her.

Asha continued. "I wish we had the kind of mother I could tell something like this to. But at least now I can talk to my sister."

Kaia smiled. "Yes you can." She turned to leave and then stopped in her tracks. "What's up with Nubia?" she asked.

Asha rolled her eyes. "What you said to Nubia was the absolute truth. She is destined to repeat Janice's mistakes unless she opens her eyes. She still feels that Janice can do no wrong. I think she'll come around eventually, though."

Kaia shook her head and left, promising to bring Phoenix by in the morning. As she pulled away from the curb, she smiled at her reflection in the rearview mirror. Despite the fact that she knew Janice would never be the kind of mother she needed, Kaia felt good. She had closed the stormiest chapter of her life. And that felt like flying.

Chapter Fifteen

Fly

Kaia parked her car on Wright Street in Stapleton and stared at the hearse in front of First Central Baptist Church. Knowing that today was the time to say goodbye to her best friend hurt like hell, and Kaia laid her head on the steering wheel and cried. Her sobs echoed off the car's interior and Kaia jumped when she heard a knock on the window. She looked up to see Aaron, dressed to kill in a Black suit standing on the driver's side. Kaia rolled down the window, embarrassed that he had seen her falling apart.

Aaron smiled warmly at Kaia. "You look like you could use a friend right now. Why don't you do me the honor of escorting you inside."

Kaia smiled weakly and stepped out of the car. Aaron took her hand and they walked together to the church.

Once inside, the smell of flowers overwhelmed Kaia. Floral arrangements surrounded Symphany's coffin. The styles of the flower arrangements ranged from simple to elaborate and Kaia smiled at one that resembled an angel. For that was just how Symphany looked lying in the silk-lined ivory casket. She wore the same dress that she'd worn in the picture Ms. James had shown Kaia and Talia. Kaia smiled, knowing that this was how everyone would remember her - looking beautiful, glorious and at peace.

Aaron led her to a pew where Keith was already seated, looking just as distinguished as his brother in a pinstriped suit. Talia soon joined them and soon the church was becoming packed.

A young woman wearing a short black dress and heels sauntered up the aisle and sat two pews in front of them. To Kaia and Talia's amazement, it was Giselle.

"Can you believe she had the nerve to show up here?" Talia whispered to Kaia.

Kaia shook her head. "Nothing surprises me about Giselle anymore."

As if on cue, Aaron squeezed Kaia's hand. She looked at him with pain in her eyes. The very sight of Giselle reminded Kaia that Aaron had slept with her. But something in Aaron's eyes told Kaia that there was more to the story. Aaron leaned in towards Kaia and whispered,

"Don't let her upset you. Giselle is just miserable right now."

Kaia nodded and made a mental note to ask him what he meant after the service. As the church filled to capacity, Rev. Rice directed the ushers to begin seating people in the church's balcony. Kaia sat in awe thinking, *'Symphany touched all these lives. All these people must have loved her as much as I did.'*

Soon, the family's processional began, led by Symphany's mother. Aaron noticed that Symphany's brother sat shackled in the front pew between two white men who were obviously policemen. Aaron guessed that her brother had been allowed to attend Symphany's funeral under heavy guard. Knowing how horrible prison was, Aaron sympathized with him.

Once Symphany's family was seated, Rev. Rice took to the altar and addressed the congregation. He introduced one of the church members, a stout woman who sang the most beautiful rendition of "Precious Lord" Kaia had ever heard. The tears began to flow from eyes throughout the church as Rev. Rice began his sermon.

It seemed to Kaia and Talia that Ms. James was psychic. The pastor was reiterating everything she had told them in her living room. Live life to the fullest. Tomorrow is not promised. Don't sweat the small stuff. He reminded everyone not to let a day go by without telling the ones you love how you feel.

When Aaron heard this, he squeezed Kaia's hand. She looked at him and saw his eyes heavy with tears. But before he could manage to utter a word, Rev. Rice called her name to deliver the eulogy.

Kaia stood on shaky legs and steadied herself. She made her way down the aisle and stood at the podium beside Symphany's casket. The sight of her best friend lying cold and lifeless caused Kaia to break down. She cried softly, trying to gather the strength to read the eulogy. As she struggled to get her emotions under control, Talia joined her at the podium offering her friend silent support. Kaia gripped her hand and faced the congregation. Clearing her throat, she began:

Symphany Amber James entered this world at 7:32 on the morning of July 10th, 1974. She was a small baby weighing only 6lbs. But according to her mother, what she lacked in size she made up for in personality. She was a happy baby with a contagious smile. That smile would never change, and it would prove to be infectious to everyone who knew her. Symphany was one of a kind.

I could stand here and tell you that she had one brother, a mother who adored her and scores of cousins, aunts and uncles. But you can read all of that for yourself. It's in the programs you received this morning. Instead, I want to talk about the person that Symphany James was and what she meant to me.

Kaia paused, fighting the tears as the congregation erupted in a chorus of encouragement. She looked at Ms. James, who sat in the front pew with tears in her eyes. She met Kaia's gaze and smiled reassuringly.

"Take your time, baby," someone called out.

Kaia continued.

I met Symphany at a time in my life when things weren't going well for me. I grew up in a household filled with silence. But when I met Symphany, she brought laughter into my life. She became my escape from my reality. I remember telling her that I felt like an outcast in my own family and that I always wished I had a better relationship with my sisters. Instead of brushing me off, she listened. She could have told me that she couldn't identify with my pain, since she had the sweetest mother on Earth. But she didn't do either of these things. Instead, she put her around my shoulder and said, "I'll be your sister." And from that day on she was.

Symphany taught me that family isn't always the people who share your bloodline. Sometimes, relatives can be worse than enemies and your friends take on the role of family. Symphany was one of those friends. She listened when I talked. She cried when I cried. She made me laugh when I was sad. She shared my triumphs and my failures. She held my hand as I gave birth to my daughter. She showed me a light at the end of the tunnel, when I was just about to give up and succumb to the darkness. In many ways, Symphany saved my life.

She was the kind of person who would do something for you and never remind you about it. She did it from her heart. She gave selflessly and she expected no more than your love in return. Symphany James was my hero. She was my friend, my family and my teacher. She taught me to live as if each day were my last. She taught me to dance like nobody's watching. She taught me not to feel sorry for myself and never to give up. She taught me that survival is the best revenge.

The night before she died, Symphany, Talia and I partied in Atlanta. She looked so beautiful and she danced the night away. She stayed on the dance floor until the last song was played. And she was happy. That's how I will always remember her. Dancing and laughing and just being happy. I will never forget the love that she showed me and the times that we had together. Symphany James saved my life.

She touched everyone in this room in some way. If you knew her, you were blessed. And today is a kind of celebration. An angel has returned to Heaven. And I know we'll all see her again someday.

Kaia returned to her seat accompanied by Talia as the congregation voiced their agreement. Talia squeezed Kaia's hand and whispered in her ear. "That was beautiful, Kaia. I know Symphany heard every word you said."

Another soloist sang "His Eye is on the Sparrow" as the congregation prepared for the final viewing of the body. Aaron took Kaia's hand in his and led her to the front of the church. Symphany's mother gazed down at her daughter one last time, then bent and kissed her face. She cried softly as relatives escorted her from the church. As Kaia and Aaron approached the casket, her heart raced. She looked at Aaron for support and he wrapped his arm around her slim waist.

She stood at the casket and looked at Symphany. She looked so pretty laying there. Kaia thought she looked at peace. She leaned close to Symphany's body and whispered, "I love you, Symphany. I will never forget you." She reached for Symphany's hand and held it. It was so cold and the realization that this was the last time she could ever hold Symphany's hand hit Kaia like a ton of bricks. She sobbed into Aaron's shoulder as he ushered her from the church.

Once outside, Kaia and Aaron watched the pall bearers load Symphany's car into the hearse.

"Kaia, I don't think you're in any condition to drive," Aaron said, gently.

Keith and Talia joined them and Keith interjected, "Neither one of them should be driving." Kaia turned to see that Talia was sobbing on Keith's shoulder. Kaia assumed that she, too, had been overwhelmed by her final farewell to Symphany.

"I'll drive Kaia's car and Talia can ride with you," Aaron suggested.

Keith agreed and escorted Talia to his car. Aaron opened the passenger side of Kaia's car and helped her in. He got in the driver's seat, started the ignition and turned to Kaia.

"Kaia, I love you, baby."

Kaia thought she had heard wrong and she looked at Aaron quizzically. Aaron took both of her hands in his and repeated himself.

"I love you, Kaia. I know we made mistakes and we hurt each other but I still love you. I hate to see you in so much pain and if there's anything I can do to help you, I'm here."

Aaron released her hands and put the car in drive. Kaia sat dumbfounded. She had wanted to hear those words for so long yet there were still so many unanswered questions.

"What about Giselle?" she asked.

Aaron took his eyes off the road long enough to look at Kaia with a puzzled expression on his face. "What about her?" he asked.

Kaia rolled her eyes. "Aaron, don't act stupid. What about your relationship with her?"

Aaron laughed out loud and looked at Kaia like she had lost her mind. "Relationship? I've never had a *relationship* with that girl. She told me about you and Eric and I never got in touch with her after that."

Kaia was confused. "But you spent your first night home with her, Aaron. That had to mean something."

Now Aaron was confused. "What?? My first night home was when I came and took Phoenix home with me. What made you think I slept with Giselle?" Aaron asked, incredulously.

Kaia thought back to the phone call she'd gotten from Giselle at work. She realized for the first time that Giselle had been lying. Kaia sat back in her seat and told Aaron the details of that phone call. Aaron was mystified.

"That girl has issues, Kaia. She ran into me and Keith at Perkins the morning I came home and I brushed her off. She must have called you after we left." Aaron shook his head as the truth began to sink in.

Kaia was dazed. "Aaron, then whey did she show up at your house like she's been coming there forever?" she asked. "She didn't call first. She just showed up." As much as Kaia wanted to believe Aaron, it was too much for her to accept that Giselle could be so cruel.

Aaron turned left, following the other cars in the funeral processional. "Baby, she just came by. I didn't know she was coming and I didn't invite her." Aaron shook his head. "Women can be very conniving, Kaia. I sat her down after you left and told her that whatever she thought about me and her was not going to happen. Kaia, there was never anything going on between me and her."

Kaia wasn't sure whether to laugh or cry. She was thrilled that Aaron hadn't slept with Giselle. But it hurt to know that Giselle had tried so hard to steal her man. Plus, Kaia felt guilty about being with Eric. "Why not, Aaron?" Kaia asked with her head hung low. "I cheated on you so you could have done what you wanted with Giselle to pay me back."

Aaron gently pressed the brake pedal as the processional turned into the cemetery. "Kaia," he said. "You being with Eric really fucked me up for a minute. But that don't change how I feel about you. When you gave birth to Phoenix, I should have been the one holding your hand. If I had made better decisions, you never would have turned to Eric in the first place. I still hate the thought of you being with him. But I still love you."

Kaia smiled and took Aaron's hand in hers. "I love you, too, Aaron. And I'm sorry."

Aaron smiled back and leaned across the seat to kiss Kaia. He kissed her softly three times and then sat back in the driver's seat. "So what about Eric?" he asked. "When are you going to end everything with him?"

Kaia was confused again. "Let me guess," she said. "Giselle has you thinking that I'm still seeing Eric?"

Aaron nodded. Kaia shook her head. "Aaron, I stopped seeing him as soon as you found out about us. Eric has been history for a long time."

Aaron laughed. Now it was his turn to be relieved. "Damn, that girl made us waste a lot of time.

Kaia agreed. "Let's not waste anymore." They exited the car and followed the droves of people walking towards Symphany's final resting-place.

After Symphany's remains were interred, Ms. James took Kaia's hand and pulled her off to the side. She didn't bother to wipe the tears that streamed down her face as she summoned Talia to join them. "Kaia, thank you for those beautiful words this morning," she began. "I want both of you to come by Symphany's place tonight. We're having our family gathering over there since Symphany put so much into decorating the place. I think she would want us to show it off." Ms. James choked back a sob and continued. "Symphany left something for you girls. I'll give it to you when you come by tonight."

Kaia and Talia returned to where Keith and Aaron stood. Talia and Kaia fought back tears as each of them wondered what Symphany could have possibly left behind for them. Talia finally spoke. "Kaia, why would she leave us something? Do you think she knew she was going to die?"

Kaia shook her head. "I don't know, Talia. I don't know."

Talia asked Keith if he would mind dropping her off at home and he agreed. Kaia hugged Talia, realizing that she was the only friend she had left. "I love you, girl. I'll see you tonight."

Aaron unlocked the car door, but Kaia stopped him. "Take a walk with me," she said.

Aaron knew Kaia was under a lot of pressure but this request was quite strange. "Here?" he asked, looking around at all the tombstones.

Kaia nodded. "I want to show you something."

Aaron followed Kaia closely as she led the way up a steep incline. She stopped in front of a grave with a simple tombstone. Aaron read the inscription.

Maurice Lawrence Wesley
January 3rd, 1945 to May 28th, 1978

Aaron turned to Kaia with a perplexed look on his face. "Is this your dad, baby?"

Kaia nodded, and choking back tears took Aaron's hand. "I haven't come to visit his grave since the day he was buried. Janice never brought us here to visit his grave and when I got old enough to come on my own I never did." Kaia paused.

She collected herself and turned to Aaron. "I want to introduce you to him the way you introduced me to your mother once upon a time."

Aaron smiled. He was moved by the memory of introducing Kaia to his mother so many years ago.

"That's sweet. You remember that, Kaia?"   Aaron asked.

Kaia nodded. "I remember everything about us." She turned to the tombstone and said. "Daddy, this is Aaron. I love him very much. And I wish you could be here to get to know him. You would love him. He takes good care of me and Phoenix." Kaia wiped the tears that fell from her eyes. She turned to Aaron and held him around his waist. "I miss him," she said.

Aaron held her as if he'd never let go.   "I know you do, sweetheart. I know you do." Aaron held Kaia close to him as she cried for the father she lost as a child and the best friend she lost as a woman.

Kaia and Aaron arrived at Symphany's house at 6:00 that evening. They had picked Phoenix up from Asha's place and she was now with her Uncle Keith for the night. Phoenix had been thrilled to see her parents together and Kaia was just as happy. It seemed they would finally be a family after all.

As they entered Symphany's home, Kaia could hear lots of people conversing and mingling. To her surprise, she also heard laughter coming from the living room. As she and Aaron entered, Kaia saw that Talia had gotten there first and was sitting on the sofa next to Ms. James. Everyone was smiling and laughing at home movies Ms. James was showing of Symphany and her brother growing up. Kaia smiled, too, at the sight of a seven year old Symphany falling down as she tried to learn to ride a bike. Kaia noted that each time she fell, Symphany got up, dusted herself off and got back on the bike. In Kaia's opinion, Symphany had always lived her life that way. She never gave up.

Ms. James invited Kaia and Aaron to help themselves to the food in the kitchen. There were hams, a turkey, stuffing, macaroni and cheese, potato salad, collard greens and more courtesy of all the women in the church and in the James family. Aaron picked up a plate and dug right in. Kaia smiled and cracked a joke on Aaron about the size of his appetite. "They don't feed you like this up north," he explained. "I miss real soul food like crazy!"

Kaia helped him pile some more potato salad onto his already full plate. As the two of them reentered the living room, Kaia met Talia's gaze. Talia looked steamed. Kaia scanned the room for an idea of what was making Talia so angry and it wasn't long before her sight fell on the one person she least expected to see. Giselle stood near the wall unit talking to Sean.

Talia was at Kaia's side before she knew it. "Can you believe that bitch came over here?" Talia demanded.

Kaia shook her head.

"Why is she doing this?" Talia asked, rhetorically. "Symphany wasn't even speaking to her anymore."

Kaia decided to put an end to the guessing games. She stalked across the room in Giselle's direction as Aaron searched for someplace to put his plate down. He could tell by the look on Kaia's face that there was about to be a scene.

Giselle spotted Kaia making her way toward her and she stood her ground. Folding her arms across her chest, Giselle grinned menacingly at Kaia until the two women stood face to face.

"Hello, Kaia. I see you and Aaron are speaking again," Giselle said. "That's nice."

Kaia reminded herself that this was not the time or place to beat Giselle's behind. Instead, she said, "What are you doing here?"

Giselle shrugged. "Symphany was my friend, too, Kaia."

Talia balked. "Bitch, please! Symphany couldn't stand you. She wasn't speaking to you, and she damn sure wouldn't want you here. So leave."

Giselle pretended that Talia's words hadn't hurt her. She put her game face on and sighed. "Talia, you can't tell me to leave because this is not your house. Besides, I was invited."

Kaia and Talia laughed. "Who invited you here, Giselle?" Kaia asked. "Are you going to lie and say that it was Aaron the way you lied about him spending the night with you, showering with you and all the other bullshit you told me?"

Giselle stood her ground. "So, Aaron told you I was lying and you believed him?" Giselle shook her head. "You always were naïve."

Kaia could no longer resist the urge to punch Giselle in the face, but as if on cue, Ms. James joined the tension-filled group.

"Okay, you're all here," she said. Kaia looked at Symphany's mother inquisitively and Ms. James explained. "Symphany left something for all of you. Come with me."

Giselle, Kaia and Talia followed Ms. James into the master bedroom. Once inside, Giselle sat on the edge of the bed while Kaia took a seat beside Talia on the chaise lounge. Ms. James stood before them. In her hands, she held four envelopes.

Ms. James began. "Symphany had a will drawn up before she died. Apparently, she had a pretty sizeable estate and she left instructions on how she wanted her things divided."

She handed each of the girls an envelope with their name on it. Kaia received two – one had the name "Phoenix Grace Banks" written on it.   "Symphany stipulated that Phoenix' envelope should not be opened until her 18th birthday," Ms. James explained.

Kaia placed Phoenix' envelope in her purse and stroked the one with her own name on it. "Monique, did she leave you one of these?" Kaia asked.

Ms. James nodded. "Yes. Actually, she left an envelope for me, her brother and for you girls."

Talia's hands trembled nervously. "Can we open them?" she asked.

"Sure you can, baby." Ms. James seemed as curious to find out the contents of the envelopes as they were. Talia opened hers first. Kaia, Giselle and Ms. James looked on. Talia's envelope contained a letter in Symphany's fancy handwriting. She opened it and read aloud.

Talia,

If you are reading this letter, I am either hospitalized or worse. Don't hate me for not telling you about my illness. I never like it when people feel sorry for me. I want to enjoy life with you and the girls and to make the best of everyday. Please forgive me for being so proud.

I want you to know that you are a very genuine and sweet person. I always admired your intellect and your quiet confidence. Don't ever change.

I have left you a little cash to make sure that you never have to ask a nigga for shit. (smile) If you're still in

college, use this to pay your tuition and when you
graduate, you can open up your own accounting firm. Be
your own boss and don't answer to nobody. I love you,
girl. I believe in you. And I know that someday, you are
going to be an icon. Don't stop dreaming for a minute.
        And smile sometimes. It looks good on you!

Love, Symphany

Talia stared wide-eyed at the check in her hand. There were way
too many zeroes. She rubbed her eyes, thinking they were playing tricks
on her. "Fifty thousand dollars!"
        Kaia immediately tore open her own envelope.   She read
Symphany's elaborate script.

Kaia,

By now, you know about my epilepsy. Please
don't be mad at me for keeping this secret to myself. I
found out that I had it and I wanted to pretend it was a
nightmare. I know that might seem silly, but when you're
faced with death, sometimes the way you choose to deal
with it is not always the best way.
        Kaia, I love you like a sister. Out of all of us,
you've always been the one that had the hardest
upbringing, the roughest uphill battles. I hope that this
money helps you to finally be comfortable enough
financially. I know that you and Aaron will be together
someday. The choice is yours as far as whether or not
you want to tell him about this money. If I were you, I
would put it away for a rainy day. Women always have to
have a cushion to fall back on. But don't let me tell you
how to deal with your relationship. You were the one who
was lucky enough to find real love. Unfortunately, I was
luckier at hustling. (smile)
        I have also left an envelope for Phoenix. I wrote
her a letter telling her that since I can't be there when
she becomes a young lady, I will be her guardian angel
instead. Please her about me, Kaia. Tell her about

the fun we had and the mistakes we made. Let her know that you only get one shot at life. Tell her to spread her wings and fly while she still has time. The money I left for her should take care of college (unless she gets a scholarship to Yale, which I know she will). So make sure you use your money to spoil Phoenix as well as yourself.

Kaia, please look out for my mom. I didn't always realize how special she was. It took your ordeal with Janice to make me see how lucky I was . Since I'm her only daughter, I want you to step into that role now. Take care of her and she may turn out to be the mother you never had and always deserved.

Never give up, girl. You're stronger than all of us. I love you.

Symphany.

Kaia dried her eyes and stared at the check in her hands. Symphany had left her $50,000 as well. Kaia stood, speechless, and embraced Ms. James with outstretched arms. "I told you she would want us to be a family," Ms. James said with a smile. Kaia nodded, still to choked up for words.

Giselle tore her envelope open with savage ferocity. She looked for a check but found none. She turned the envelope upside down and shook it. She found nothing but a letter.

"Why don't you read the letter instead of looking for the money first!" Talia snapped. She silently prayed that Symphany hadn't left a damn thing for Giselle.

Giselle read her letter.

Giselle,

I know you are wondering where your share of the money is. Let me end the suspense. You're not getting any. *I wanted you to witness what real friendship is like. All the years that we spent together as friends never meant anything to you. It couldn't have. Otherwise you never would have betrayed Kaia like you did. Each one of us was in a position to snitch on you many times over the years. You were never faithful to anyone in your life. But we were real friends. And even though you were a scandalous bitch, we still remained true to you.*

Instead of giving you a portion of the money, I've given it to Phoenix. She will be raised to know what real love, loyalty and friendship is all about. You will never learn. I hope you've learned a lesson about stabbing friends in the back. I know that you're most upset about the money you missed out on. But what you should be upset about is the loss of something far greater than that: real friends. You may never have a chance to experience that again. But I hope you learn to reciprocate the love that people show to you before it's too late.

Peace,
Symphony

Ms. James fought the urge to laugh in Giselle's face. Kaia and Talia all but jumped for joy. Giselle stuffed the letter back into the envelope and placed it inside her purse. She finally made eye contact with Kaia. "I guess you're happy now, huh, Kaia?"

Kaia shrugged her shoulders. "I'm going to be happy no matter what you or anyone else does to try and prevent that," she answered.

Talia held the door open for Giselle. "I think I speak for Symphony when I say, please leave."

Giselle walked out the door, embarrassed and bitter. Kaia, Talia and Ms. James shared a group hug. Aaron entered the room and saw the huddle of crying women. He debated whether or not to leave them alone, but before he could turn away, Kaia spotted him "Hi, baby," she said with a smile. Aaron walked over to Kaia and hugged her.

"What just happened in here?" Aaron asked. "I just saw Giselle storm out the front door. She didn't say anything to anybody."

Talia laughed. "She just got a taste of her own medicine."

Kaia introduced Aaron to Ms. James, who hugged him like he was a son-in-law she'd been anxious to meet. Aaron hugged her back, wondering what all the commotion was about.

Ms. James stepped back, wiped her eyes and looked at Kaia and Talia. "Symphany really loved you girls."

Kaia nodded. "We loved her, too," Talia said.

"Ms. James," Kaia said. "Does our inheritance hurt you financially in any way?"

Ms. James chuckled. "No, honey," she said with a smile. "Symphany left me this house, plus a house in Atlanta. She also left me a big bank account and a damn good stock portfolio. I don't have to work another day if I choose not to."

Kaia was relieved. Talia couldn't hide her shock. "Symphany really should have been the one to study accounting. I don't think I could have amassed such a fortune in such a small amount of time."

Ms. James nodded. "She was a good business woman, and now you must be the one to get the accounting degree. Not just for you, but for Symphany as well."

Kaia, realizing that Aaron had no idea what they were talking about, excused herself and escorted Aaron outside. They stood in front of Symphany's house with the cool February air encircling them. Kaia held out the envelope she'd just received and watched as Aaron read the letter, then the check.

He stood with his mouth agape. "She left this for you?" he asked. Kaia nodded. "She left the same thing for Talia. Giselle would have also gotten an inheritance. But Symphany revised her will and gave Giselle's share to Phoenix."

Aaron laughed. "Damn, that's cold." He chuckled at Giselle's misfortune. "That explains why she rushed out of here like a bat out of hell."

Kaia laughed, too. "Symphany really got her this time. I'm so happy and so devastated at the same time." Kaia folded her arms across her chest to ward off the cold air. Aaron, understanding how conflicted Kaia must feel, tried to find the words to ease her pain.

"Baby girl, I think the inheritance was Symphany's way of making sure that you and Talia found reasons to celebrate her life rather than mourn her death."

"That's deep, Aaron." Kaia gave his theory some thought.

"She really gave you a lot. Not just in her will, but while she was alive. Symphany gave you a family when I wasn't around and she gave you friendship that wasn't phony. And now, she's given you financial independence. That's huge!" Aaron paused. "Kaia, in her letter Symphany advised you not to tell me about the money. Why did you decide not to listen to her?"

Kaia smiled. "You weren't always up front with me about how involved you were in the drug game. But you never held out on me as far as money was concerned. I appreciate that. The last time I took a friend's advice on how to behave in my relationship, it cost me both my relationship and the friendship. Symphany loved me and she was looking out for me when she wrote that. But I think I finally learned that sometimes I have to think for myself. I guess I had to grow up fast in order to be a mother, but there are still some areas that I've taken longer to mature in. Well, I get it now. And if you and I are going to try and overcome our past mistakes to make this work, we have to be honest with each other."

Aaron pulled Kaia into his arms and kissed her with a gentle passion that Kaia hadn't felt for far too long. He stared into her eyes and said, "I know that I was meant to be with you. At one time I wasn't so sure because I felt like you betrayed me. But I know now that I could never be happy with anybody else. Thank you for telling me about the money. But I don't want or need any of that. That's for you – a blessing from your best friend. But I can't tell you how much it means to me that you told me about it. I love you, sweetheart."

Kaia thought for a moment that all the pain and misfortune in her life had resulted in ultimate joy. Her mother would probably never change. Nubia would probably never speak to her again. Giselle was never her friend. And Symphany was gone forever. But Kaia realized that God had allowed her to survive all these things to show her the rainbow after the storm. She had a beautiful, healthy daughter. She now had a family - no matter how unorthodox – in the form of her 'sister' Talia and her 'mom' Ms. James. Aaron was in her arms once again and Phoenix would have a real family. Phoenix' fourth birthday was days away and for the first time, Aaron would celebrate it with them. Kaia looked up towards the gray sky and said a silent prayer of thanks for the way her life had improved. As she glanced over Aaron's shoulder, she saw a black butterfly fluttering among the bushes. Kaia decided that was what she felt like – a black butterfly that had finally learned to spread her wings and fly.

Epilogue

Kaia kneeled down beside Symphany's grave. She placed the bouquet of sunflowers next to the headstone, which read,

Symphany Amber James
July 10th, 1974 to February 9th, 1996
Beloved Daughter, Beloved Friend

Kaia said a prayer and began her conversation with her friend.

"Hey, girl. I came to see you today because I have some real good news. I know that you already know that yesterday was Phoenix' 8th birthday. She had a pajama party and all of her friends came. She got so many toys and Keith even took her shopping for clothes. You know how much she loves clothes." Kaia paused, wishing for the millionth time that Symphany were alive to hear her news. But somehow, Kaia believed in her heart that Symphany heard every one of the conversations she had with her during her monthly visits to Symphany's gravesite.

"But the good news," Kaia continued, "is that Aaron proposed to me. Right after Phoenix blew out the candles on her cake. It was beautiful, and Phoenix is thrilled." Kaia cried tears of joy as she recollected. "I know you're probably saying, 'it's about time!', but we wanted to be sure that we could make it work. I love him so much, Symphany. I just wish you were here to stand beside me at the altar."

"I need you, girl. I miss you and your crazy sense of humor. Your mom is doing fine. I called her to tell her about the engagement and she insisted on throwing us a party. You know how Mommy is when she gets an excuse to throw a party. I told her we're not going to have a big wedding, but she sold me on doing an African-inspired theme. I'm sure it will be lovely. I just wish you were here sharing all of this with me."

"My mother still hasn't stopped her foolishness. She and Nubia stopped speaking to Asha since Asha and I are so close now. Can you believe that? I don't let it get to me, anymore. It just goes to show that birds of a feather really do flock together. Asha and her husband separated. And get this, I hooked her up with Keith! Those two are so lovey-dovey they put Aaron and I to shame."

"I have another bombshell. Talia, the big time accountant, is pregnant. She met this guy from Brooklyn named Lance. He works for one of her clients - an advertising company – and they both said it was love at first sight. You know I'm going to throw the bouquet right in her face at my reception." Kaia laughed. "She says they're in no rush to get married but we'll see. Once the baby's born and she can fit into a slinky dress, she'll be planning a wedding in no time. By the way, it's a girl and she plans to name her Symphany. I knew you would get a kick out of that."

"And before I forget, Giselle just had her fifth child. That makes three kids with three different daddies! It's scandalous! She doesn't bother Aaron and I anymore and that's all that matters. I just hope she doesn't pass her trifling ways on to her children."

Kaia rose to her feet and dusted herself off. She arranged the flowers neatly and toyed with the 5-carat diamond on her left ring finger. "You know I'll be back to see you soon. I love you, Symphany. I'll take care of your mom and you be sure to take care of my dad. I'm on my way to visit with him now." Kaia glanced in the direction of Maurice's grave and smiled. It comforted her to think that somewhere in Heaven, Symphany and Kaia's dad were shooting the breeze.

"I hope you can hear me. I miss you, Symphany."

As Kaia turned to leave, another butterfly the color of midnight landed on the sunflowers she'd placed at Symphany's tombstone. Kaia smiled, knowing that this was a sign from her friend. Kaia knew in her heart that Symphany had been there all along, and would continue to be with her all of her life.

Kaia's smile rivaled the radiance of the sun. "Now I *know* you can hear me. See you soon, girl. See you soon."

TRIPLE CROWN PUBLICATIONS

ORDER FORM

Triple Crown Publications
P.O. Box 7212
Columbus, OH 43205

NAME _____

ADDRESS _____

_____

CITY _____

STATE _____

ZIP _____

BOOKS AVAILABLE

#QTY	TITLE	PRICE
	GANGSTA	$15.00
	Let That Be The Reason	$15.00
	A Hustler's Wife	$15.00
	The GAME	$15.00
	Black	$15.00
	Dollar Bill	$15.00

SHIPPING/HANDLING (Via U.S. Priority Mail) $ 3.50

TOTAL $_____

FORMS OF ACCEPTED PAYMENTS:
Postage Stamps, Institutional Checks & Money Orders